Taken to Evernor

Xiveri Mates Book 8

Elizabeth Stephens

Contents

Glossary	
Nalia	1
Herannathon	23
Herannathon	38
Nalia	54
Herannathon	66
Nalia	81
Nalia	92
Herannathon	103
Nalia	119
Herannathon	125
Nalia	137
Nalia	144
Herannathon	147
Nalia	168
Nalia	170
Herannathon	190
Nalia	197
Herannathon	223
Nalia	226
Herannathon	259
The Shekurr	267
Taken to Sky	287
Prologue – Ashmara	288
Jerrock	289
Jerrock	294
All Books by Elizabeth	303

Glossary

Asgid (*ass-gidd*)
Cross-quadrant species characterized by dark charcoal skin, two arms and two legs, often smaller in stature

Centare (*cent-are-ay*)
No in Meero, the most common trading language; primary language of the Niahhorru

Eck (*eck*)
Common Eshmiri curse

Egama (*egg-ahm-uh*)
Giant-like warrior species characterized by olive green skin and one large eye

Eshmiri (*esh-meer-ee*)
Second largest group of space pirates; known for their short, stocky builds, laughter-like language, and fighting pits on the asteroid Evernor

Evernor (*evv-err-norr*)
Eshmiri-controlled asteroid known for trading and gambling and its rotational gladiator tournament

Hiannru (*he-ann-roo*)
Spear-like spikes that protrude from a Niahhorru male's spine

Hypha (*high-fuh*)
Cross-quadrant species characterized by orange skin, large, black eyes, and four fins growing out the sides of their faces

Kor *(kohr)*
Trading city located in the grey zone between Quadrants 4 and 5; ruled by the Niahhorru species commonly referred to as space pirates; their leader is Rhorkanterannu

Krisxox *(chris - zawcks)*
Voraxia's chief battle strategist

Lemoran *(lehm-oh-rahn)*
Primary and native species of Lemora; known for their blocky, rocky builds and massive, dark grey horns

Mok bir *(mock brr)*
Table game played with batons in which players attempt to throw batons at each other and block incoming batons; gambling is a common function of the game, as is cheating

Mok biz *(mock bzz)*
A more popular version of mok bir played with tokens rather than batons

Niahhorru pirate *(knee-ya-hoo-roo)*
Planet-less species; they operate the trading post of Kor and patrol and control most of the Grey Zone; are known for their technological prowess; characterized by grey skin mostly covered in a thick exoskeleton of armored plates, hiannru tines that protrude from the backs of their heads and spines, and silvery skeins that drop to cover their more sensitive eyes

Ontte *(aunt-tay)*
Yes in Meero, the most common trading language; primary language of the Niahhorru

Oosa *(ooh-sah)*
Species of Quadrant Eight; ruled by Reoran; large blob-like figures that illuminate from within whenever speaking or expressing emotion; extremely difficult to kill

Rekkaru *(wreck-are-oo)*
Cross-quadrant species characterized by small bodies, two arms and two legs, with thin, translucent wings

Shrov *(shrohv)*
Common Meero curse

Sky *(sky)*
A constructed and roving planet known for its technological prowess as well as for producing the most feared and infamous of killers in the known Quadrants and beyond, Sky assassins

Sky Assassins *(sky assassins)*
Modified by Sky Architects to be the most efficient killers in the world, they are cyber and bio-genetically engineered from predatory species and advanced technology, often against their wills; once taken by the Sky and reprogrammed, assassins have no memoris of their past lives

Tokens *(tokens)*
Credits are the common form of currency exchanged between Quadrants; credits are carried in various devices referred to as tokens; most commonly, tokens are made from yamar and shaped like black boxes, though more sophisticated models look like discs and are made of yeeyar

Yamar *(yeam-are)*
Yamar is a precursor to yeeyar, is a static non-biological power source, and is the common communication/translation tool of the Eshmiri Reavers

Yeeyar *(yeeh-yare)*
Yeeyar is an advanced power-source used by the Niahhorru pirates of Kor; it is a biological organism that can be melded with other static metals and glasses to create spaceships, payment discs and Niahhorru communication tokens

To the smut book lovers,
the monster fudgers,
and the spicy book *movement*.

This one is, unapologetically, for you.

1

Nalia

The volume of the shrieking crowd gets louder, louder and louder still as I'm lowered into the arena. It's the third day this has happened, so I shouldn't be surprised by it. And maybe I'm not surprised so much as I'm tormented by it. Because through some aggressive miming with one of my giggling captors, I've managed to understand two things.

This is a tournament.

And I'm one of the prizes.

My eyes squeeze tight as the roar of the crowd drowns out my thoughts. I'm completely naked, burned to shit by the suns overhead, of which I can see at least three at any given time and as many as six when things are at their hottest. The crystalline pink cell I'm in remains cool even though it lets sun rays in and I notice my pasty ass get pinker and pinker by the day, and that's even with the additional translucent grey dome shimmering up above everything, fully encasing this arena.

An arena dominated by violent creatures, gladiators that are built for killing — and they do. The red sands are covered in red, white, grey, black, green and pink blood from so many different species.

Alien species.

The thought slams its weight into me sporadically and violently, a battering ram against which I have no defenses, and it catches me off guard every time. These are aliens. *I'm* an alien to them. This isn't Earth. Where am I?

Who gives a shit? Get it the fuck together. A voice I've heard only once, maybe twice, slides in between the wrinkles of my panic. I reach out to grab hold of it, but it flutters off just as quickly and instead, tears squeeze out between my eyelashes.

I hold my left hand against my forehead, trying to press through the pain of the headache that splits my skull right down the middle. The headaches have been severe for as long as my memory lasts — which isn't very long — since I woke up in a vat of blue liquid and was chained up next to two giants. I was terrified of the giants, but it turns out that they weren't the problem.

He was. The male with red skin half covered in metal — or made of it — and the bionic silver killing arm.

The crowd roars and I know without having to look down and see the gates rolling open that they're doing just that. I can feel the rumble vibrating through the air, vibrating me in my cage, and I tense, wondering who will walk out of the darkness through that rusted metal and face off in the arena below.

I'm a fucking idiot. I'd been aboard the ship with the giants and the red asshole and when it was boarded by even more aliens, I panicked and grabbed an escape pod and took it wherever. To Earth? Is that where I thought it'd take me? Ha. A fucking joke. Because instead of landing anywhere familiar, I landed *here*. At least the aliens that captured the red fucker had looked familiar, some of them anyway, and there had been women — females — with them. Here, *nothing* is familiar…

Well, except *him*.

The one that's insane.

Glimpses of him cut across random scraps of my shredded memories. *His silver eyes sear into me as he pulls me against his chest, cradling me while I sit huddled beside the familiar female aliens, the ones with faces shaped like mine, though their skin had been other colors. Red. Dark brown.*

I look down at my arms. My once white and freckled skin is now red — but not alien red, oh no, *burned* red. I frown at it while memories from that ship and from before push at the boundaries of my mind, but it's like a fist punching into rubber and that rubber sits at the front of my noggin, screaming *PAIN*. The headache cuts in again and I moan, fighting…*I'm a fighter, how'd I get so weepy and mopey?* Fighting…*I'm not going to die in this damn cage.* No, I'm not.

I didn't give up with the cyborg serial killer, I didn't give up when I crash landed on this planet, I'm not going to give up just because I'm a prize, likely to be won by this freaky freaking psychopath.

I open my eyes. The headache passes, fading into a dull throb. The fist releases and the rubber settles back into the expectant puddle that it was.

I watch the grey scaled alien with the glossy eyes and the spikes shooting out of the back of his head take a lap of the arena. The crowd loves him and my cage shakes all over again when the announcer says his name. I can't possibly hope to replicate the high-pitched squeals they make, but I know it's his name by their tone and inflection — after all, I've heard it a half dozen times now. Of all the battles I've seen fought here, his battles have tended to be the most...gratuitous. And because of that, he's showered with more prizes than any of the others. I know he's going to win me...and I'm going to survive it.

Whatever he has planned.

I glance up at the other six cages hovering just below the roof of the dome alongside me. Some of the creatures inside of them look worse off than I feel. Some of them are actively rooting for one champion or another. One of them looks bored as hell. I wave at the impossibly tall, waif-like orange creature. She lifts one arm in response, but it isn't orange like her other one. It's silver and sleek. It *should* remind me of that horrible time with the cyborg slasher, but it doesn't. It's the eyes. Her eyes look kind and curious, even from here. At least, when she looks at me. When she looks down, she looks...bored, maybe resigned to whatever fate — whatever victor — these sands have in store for her.

I follow her gaze unwillingly to the field below. *Grey. He's grey all over.* He's got four arms and right now one of them is pointing at me. He's always pointing at me, as if to remind the announcers of what he wants.

The dome shakes one more time and one of the announcers zips past on a rather decrepit-looking metal platform, just wide enough for him to stand, with a railing propped up by rusty pipes just tall enough for him to lean his bulky arms on. He's all chest with a tiny head and hips, rags dripping from every inch of his bulky brown body, but I don't care how he looks. All I care about is how much he's laughing. Jesus H. Christ. He's always fucking laughing. It grates.

My headache splinters and I curse under my breath until the roar of the crowd drowns out whatever the announcer giggled last. Whatever it was seemed to appease the four-armed silver-hued savage because he's moving across the red sands faster than he was. I don't like that. I don't like that at all... Because I know what comes next...

There's a collision and I clench my teeth, but I don't clap my hands over my ears or close my eyes. I figured out quickly that it's scarier imagining what's happening and only seeing the aftermath than it is to watch how it plays out. So, I keep my palms pressed to the pink crystal floor and watch the grey guy who's been chasing me across the universe tear the green beast apart.

The creature is huge — larger than he is — with mottled green skin and horns. It doesn't stop the grey guy from ripping off his arms. My grey killer rips his larger opponent to *pieces*. When he's finished, he's bathed in green and all four of his hands are fisted, held above his head in victory.

It's done. Thank fuck. I plop down onto my right hip and rub my face. I've got to get out of here. I've got to get somewhere normal. *Normal. Heh. What's that anyway?* I've got to make these fucking headaches go away. I need an Advil. *Advil.* Hm. That's a new one. And then the dome vibrates.

That's also a new one. And new in this place is never good. I glance down. The victor, despite having won, is rolling his shoulders back and positioning himself at one end of the arena. The stone seats rising up on all sides of him boast spectators in as many shades as there are colors in the universe. They're all shouting and screeching and waggling their stone and jellied limbs all around. They're foaming at their fanged mouths, puckering at the tentacles, as the rusted metal gate rolls open and two one-eyed *giants* strut into the arena to the sounds of insanity.

Okay well *fuck*. I thought the horned green guy was big, but he had nothing on these creatures. These fuckers are huge and are the same species that were stuck aboard that ship with me and the maniacal, mechanical monster. I feel momentarily bad for them until I register the bloodlust on their faces. These are not those giants. My throat locks up as I glance back at the grey guy. *He's going to lose.* I don't know why that premonition bothers me, but it does. It does a lot.

"He's half their size…" I roll up onto my knees and peer straight down through the smudged transparent floor. I'm sweating and it's disgusting to see the smudges my sweat leaves behind. I try to clear it with my hands, but that only makes it worse. "What the fuck is going on?" I mutter, but it's very clear what's going on. He fought once. He's going to have to fight again, this time *two* opponents, each twice his height and twice his breadth. "Jesus."

My fingers twitch, as if reaching for something, but I don't know what. A haze passes through my mind and I feel momentarily stunned by it, but it passes just as fast, breaking over the crest of another headache. The sound of crashing cuts through both and I start at the sight of the grey guy releasing a battle cry and launching into a sprint.

I tense, hold my breath, watch him skate across the packed sands, moving faster than he has a right to given his size and the fact that he's wearing armor. Or is it armor? Maybe, it's just his skin… The first giant meets the grey guy in the center of the arena while the other holds back. I wonder why until the victor slips under the first giant's arm, spinning onto one knee and back up, slashing his massive dark grey claws against the back of the first giant's knee.

The giant buckles, but the injury isn't enough to ground him. He spins, moving slowly compared to the victor but not so slowly that his fist doesn't connect with the victor's shoulder. And he's powerful. I can feel it from here, at least my arm feels something, a mirrored sensation, though that can't be right. I have no connection to the victor. He terrifies me. I should want him dead. But...

My gut clenches as the victor whips in a circle, spinning right into the other giant, who proceeds to kick him in the center of the chest. I hear the cracking sound, even through the protective bubble I'm in. I cover my mouth, tasting grease and sweat. The victor hits the arena wall and the fans above him dangle their spindly legs and their sharpened claws, trying to reach him. He's a celebrity here and this is the first time it looks like he might not make it... I don't know why my heart is beating so hard watching him struggle to rise, but I've chewed through my thumb nail and I'm working my way across the nails of the rest of my hand. They're all torn stumps already. There's nothing left.

I catch myself mumbling, "Get up, get up, get up..."

He looks up, like he's heard me, and our eyes meet for just a second. I freeze, absorbing the details of his face. His eyes are huge and glossy and stretch toward his hairline...well, where a hairline would be had he any hair. Instead of hair, two large ridges rise up and slip down the back of his head — they're a darker grey than the rest of his skin and look kinda like French braids.

They stop at the nape of his neck and, between them, huge, sharpened spikes stick out of the back of his head and rip all the way down his spine, ending at the top of his grey pants. Talons? Spines? Spears? I don't know what to call them. They're sharpened like swords, the tips blacker than their bases, and I wonder if that coloring is natural or if they've been stained by blood because, whatever they are, it's clear that they're weapons. He uses them as weapons now.

His gaze rips from mine and he leaps towards one of the giants advancing on him. He spins, catching the giant as it attempts to swat at him. The tines on his back open up the giant's hand. The giant recoils, blood spattering the sands, then attacks a second time. The victor kicks in the giant's knee while whirling and catching the second approaching giant in the jaw with his claws.

Fighting, tussling, pulling and punching continue until eventually, one of the giants makes a mistake and tosses the victor off of him and he lands directly against the other giant. The victor's spikes sink into the second giant's flesh and it releases a terrible, blood-curdling moan as it slips out of position and slinks to the side. It lands on one knee and, as the victor jerks forward, it finally collapses, clutching at the wounds scoring its chest.

I cringe as the victor turns to face the fallen giant and leaps onto its chest. It hits him in the side and again in the face, but it can't grab onto him. It's covered in too much blood already. And the victor is too quick. He ducks under the giant's next flailing strike and jams both hands into the giant's throat. My lashes flutter and I cringe through the sight of the victor pulling out the giant's tongue through the hole in his neck and tossing the organ up into the stands.

It lands amidst some pink fluffy creatures with blinking lights hanging from long illicum or antennae — possibly eyes since I don't see anything else that might be used for sight on their fluffy forms. They release piercing horn-like shrieks at varying intonations as the bloody green tongue lands among them. I don't know if it's horror though, or if it's glee.

My headache clenches my skull in a vise and I struggle through the sensation, surfacing from the pain in time to see the victor launching himself at the remaining giant. He tries to kick the giant in his offending leg and — *crack* — the sound ripples through the arena and the crowd emits a collective gasp. I clench my teeth, a pain in my right leg surfacing with enough force to steal my breath. I gasp, too.

His body sails across the length of the arena. He lands almost directly below me. He lies on his back, spikes sinking into the sand. He opens his eyes.

"Get up." I pound my fist on the bottom of my cage.

His lips curl and he smiles at me with teeth that shimmer an unusual color, I can't tell which. And then the victor, from all those feet below me, he…*winks* at me. *Winks.* Like a human would. It's the first expression I've understood here and I am so distracted by it, I don't notice the giant. The giant reaches for his good leg, but the victor brings it up and kicks the giant in the chin. The giant's head cocks back and dark green blood bursts from his bottom lip.

He releases a battle cry and slams his fist into the victor's stomach but the victor *catches* the fist — a fist the size of his own skull — against his chest and then, using both hands he turns the giant's fist on his wrist nearly to its breaking point. The giant roars and wrenches his arm back, incidentally yanking the victor up onto his feet. He swings with his other fist, but the victor manages to block the incoming blow with two of his four arms.

He braces his one good foot into the ground while the other leg hangs bent at a grotesque angle and wrenches up on the giant's fist. The giant pulls his free hand back in an attempt to hit him again, but he's just two seconds too slow. The victor brings his two free fists down on the giant's arm and this time, the crack is even louder than it was before.

The giant manages to break free on a spittle-laced scream. The victor lunges to attack — surely for the kill, this time — but he falls. I freeze, gut clenching, but the giant is making his way *away* from the victor, toward the end of the arena where his fallen friend lies. He…stands on his friend's bloodied back and rifles through the male's pockets. From them, he produces a single shiny object, flat like a disc and emitting a soft, pulsing light.

The announcer's platform whizzes through the air and the creature atop it takes the disc from the giant and examines it for quite some time. Then he says something to the crowd and they boo collectively before their boos return to screeches, stomps and cheers when the victor rises from the sands. The victor acknowledges the giant and the giant acknowledges him back with a mirrored head nod.

The giant then leaves through the metal door he came through, broken arm coddled to his chest. So many different objects, most of which I can't identify, are tossed down onto the sand. The victor lifts his upper arms and the cheering increases in volume, but he doesn't seem to be concerned with his fans or the prizes they're tossing into the arena alongside him. Instead, he's looking at me.

He keeps looking at me as the stands start to clear and a bevy of other creatures crawl from the woodwork — the ironwork — and start to clean up. Finally though, a flat piece of black material zips from the black tunnel behind the metal gates. It's the same swatch of black material that's come to collect the victor before. It looks sort of like a magic carpet, but it shimmers in the light like oil. He half sits, half collapses onto it and the carpet is immediately propelled into motion.

I watch him until he disappears through the arena's only door, following the same path the giant took. He does not look back at me again, which…feels strange. He always looks back. He always hovers by the door, waiting until my weird cube descends behind the arena stands into the pits where I've been kept these loooooong, hot and miserable days.

I find myself frowning as the darkness takes him away and more creatures emerge from it with wands and lit-up sticks and other electrical-looking implements that clean every surface, turning the green and black and grey blood-colored sands back to their usual burnt red.

Only after most of the spectators have cleared the rock and metal bench seats of the arena and filtered down into exits built into their base do the giggling announcers show back up to come for us prizes. But, as the other prizes are led off behind the arena stands, where we're usually separated into cells, one of the announcers comes and hovers directly in front of me. He smiles and waves at me giddily, but I just cross my arms over my chest and ball my hands into fists under my armpits. Then the asshole repeats the gesture and laughs wildly as he glares at me with a mirrored expression.

I'm still glaring at him as whatever connection holding up my cell breaks and my cell bobs in the air. I float behind the rusty red platform he rides as he begins to lead me away, but this time...he doesn't lead me towards the arena seats, towards the cells built directly into the ground. This time, he's leading me towards the rusty metal arena gates, through them, into the blackness beyond them.

Shit.

Don't be afraid. I look back over my shoulder, watching the other prizes as they're released from suspension. The orange female is looking at me with wide eyes, both of her palms pressed to the outside of her cell. She mouths something to me, but I have no idea what language she's speaking. I assume the words are encouraging nonetheless.

I snort at the thought. She could just be saying *good riddance.*

I press my hands to the glass, the moment feeling oddly final, as she's whisked off to the left and I'm carried into the darkness. It whooshes over me, an instant chill claiming my skin, making me feel clammy all over. I cringe, possibilities flitting through my mind. Is the tournament over? Am I being claimed as a prize *now?* If so, then why aren't the other prizes also being claimed now? It couldn't be that they're...they're not going to make me fight, are they? Shit. Do I even know how to fight? I look down at my grubby nails and my filthy hands, feeling…pitiful.

Enough.

I clench my grubby nails into my filthy palms and turn forward, take a steeling breath, and prepare myself for any eventuality as I'm brought down a long tunnel. I get the sense we pass underground when my ears pop, but things never get fully dark. The entire world is illuminated by these fascinating lights built directly into the walls around us. Orbs that shine in varying shades of white, yellow and orange float all up and down the cluttered halls. People — beings — make space for us to pass, but are otherwise unconcerned by our arrival as they bustle back and forth carrying various objects, *alien* objects, whose functions I can only guess at.

The hallway gets wider and wider and wider…my eyes…my mind…holy fuck. My fear slips off of my shoulders like a silk robe, displaced momentarily by a sheer and cutting *awe* as the space in front of me explodes open.

"Holy fuck."

I don't even know what I'm seeing. The space is *vast* — I mean it's an entire world. I thought the arena up top was the whole thing but beneath… Here? This? Holy… I'm speechless. The arena is a drop of water in the ocean, or rather, a leaf floating on its surface. The tip of a crazy hot iceberg. I feel immediately like throwing up as my headache comes back with a vengeance. I'm overwhelmed. I'm stunned. It's madness. *It's so fucking gorgeous.*

The cavernous space stretches beyond my sight and is littered in floating platforms of all manner of design and no manner of organization. Metal walkways descend into the bowels of this planet. Massive floating plateaus rise up from seemingly nothing, like they're rocks suspended on stilts. The rock whittles itself from a large platform to a narrow stem, like a flower in bloom.

I don't see what connects the platforms to the floor — I can't see any floor at all — just more platforms and walkways and structures zigzagging across this insane underworld, which is illuminated everywhere by floating orbs. It's *bright* down here, almost as bright as it is above, the rough-hewn red walls that make up the boundaries of this place radiating color and warmth.

Tents cover most of the visible structures and right now, we're heading to a particularly large one sitting alone on top of a rocky platform that's smaller than the rest. This rock shelf is actually connected to another rock shelf some hundred meters below it that itself looks like it is jutting out of the nearest wall.

Hovering over that rocky shelf now, an ominous feeling sinks into my stomach like a stone lobbed into clear water. I have a very strong suspicion of who or rather, *what* I'm going to find beyond the flaps of that massive tent and I'm breathing harder, suddenly very aware of my lack of clothing and my lack of weapon as we lurch to a jerky stop just before the closed tent flaps.

With a wave of the giggle monster's eleven-fingered hand, the front of my cage shimmers apart, fracturing like sugar in water. He gestures toward the flaps. They look like canvas, but hairier and they're only separated from me by six feet. It's only one foot down from my cage to the red, rocky floor. The air in here…I take a deep breath…it smells like metal and machines, like recycled air, a little like sweat, but mostly like rock. *It smells like the deserts of Arizona. I always liked it there.*

I shake my head, frazzled by the headache that chips away at my concentration, and glance at the giggling guy. He's just watching me expectantly with enormous black eyes and smiling at me with his tiny mouth, full of fangs.

"Who's in the tent?" I ask him, though I'm not sure why. I know already. I'm just stalling. Because I know who's in the tent…I just don't know what he wants from me.

He responds with another high trill.

"I can't understand you. Who is in the tent?"

The flaps that are his ears twitch. He laughs and points at the tent, mirroring the pointing gesture I'm making with my own arm, only he's nodding frantically, too. When I still don't move, his ears flap at the tips more quickly, almost vibrating, really. His smile also falls. Dang. So this is what these creatures look like when they're annoyed. He reaches up and ruffles the hair on top of his head, twirling the fur there so that it stands on end. It's brown. The same brown color as his skin and most of his clothing.

"I'm not getting out of this cage," I tell him, to which he replies feverishly and urgently and in an alien language I can't begin to make sense of.

I cut him off. "I'm *not* getting out." If I get out of this cage and make it down to that platform, there's nowhere for me to go. This platform stands alone, attached to nothing except for another rocky ledge some hundreds of feet below. The wide platform whittles down to an extremely skinny base and I'm not a rock climber — I don't think I am, anyway. There'd be no way for me to rappel down to the next ledge without rope and there's nothing on this platform but the tent. To get rope, I'd have to fight whoever's in there, first.

No, not whoever.

Just him.

"I'm not moving! Take me back to the cells." The irony. For days now — or has it been weeks? Time feels so inconsequential up there, down here, in this wild and rotten place — I've been wanting to get out of my tiny, one-room cell and out of this stupid pink glass cage. Now that I've got the chance though, and a big, fat, scary unknown before me, solitary confinement no longer seems like such a sorry state.

His black eyes widen and he starts to mutter under his breath. He produces a black box from his robes, opens it and starts to fiddle with gadgets inside. The glass cage lurches. I reach out like I'll grab onto something, but there isn't anything there except my greasy sweat, lubricating my exit.

"Quit it," I shout at him but the words get lodged in my throat when the cage tips all the way forward and the opening offers nothing to grab onto.

Legs tangling, I'm unable to get them beneath me and land hard on my side on the red rock below. It's a softish rock. I get the impression that I could scratch a hole into it with relative ease using my fingernails — a thought that inspires zero confidence whatsoever given how thin the neck of this mountain is. Even now, I feel it swaying slowly beneath me like a boat. *Less like a special ops CRRC. More like an amphib used by the Marines.* Huh.

"Ugh." I groan, sitting up to a chorus of laughter from the little jerk. "Fuck you, giggle man."

He shouts something back. It sounds like "eck" or maybe "ick." For whatever reason, it sounds like an insult and I can't believe the nerve of this guy.

"*Uch* to you, too, asshole!" I flip over onto my back and watch him gasp. It's so theatrical it's hard not to want to laugh.

He covers his mouth with one hand and with his other, reaches around to his butt...what...what the fuck is this guy doing? He says a word again and again and continues to prod at his butt, and then it clicks...*asshole*. That's what I called him.

I burst out laughing. My laughter is deep, moving from my throat to my chest to my abdomen, causing it to contract until it hurts. Laughter spills out of me like bile the morning after a bender until I feel like I actually might just throw up. The creature has started to laugh, too — or rather, his laughter has *resumed*. He's banging on the railing of his flying contraption, attracting attention, and soon, two other creatures of his same species fly up beside him and join in on this stupid moment, adding their own shrill trills. I'm not sure they even know why.

The glass cage I was in lifts farther away from the platform when I lamely try to reach for it. It seals itself back up and, as I continue laughing, does something truly incredible. It starts to shrink, getting smaller and smaller and smaller until it's small enough to fit into the palm of the creature's hand. He swipes it from the air and slips it in between the folds of his shirt and poof! Just like that. The only small semblance of safety I've known on this planet is gone, reduced to the size of a marble. The giggle creatures whizz away noisily and within just a few swift turns, are gone, disappeared beneath the wing of another glider — this one bright blue — a few dozen yards off.

I can't see thrusters or rockets or anything propelling any of these flying machines. It's like…magic. And I have no such magic. Which means that getting off of this red rock is going to happen through wit and wile alone. I take time standing up. Behind me, the tent sits in the center of the rocky red plateau, separated from the edge — and certain death — by about thirty feet. It gives me plenty of space to maneuver as I walk a slow circumference around the ledge, slowly taking stock of my options and finding absolutely none.

Zip. Zero. Zilch. Nada. Not one single path down presents itself. I even get so bold as to lie flat on my stomach and hang my head over the side. I stare at the underside of the surface and see that it's all craggy, but still not certain enough to attempt even if I had all my memories and all of them were of times training to be the universe's most preeminent rock climber.

My stomach grumbles and, with a groan, I shove back up onto hands and knees and take a deep, fortifying breath. The air in here feels light, somehow. I glance around, marveling at all of the species just going on their merry ways, climbing the metal and wooden paths up and down the rock walls. Sometimes, the paths disappear into the rock, but mostly they just follow the boundaries of the cave system which extends so far and so deep that I can't see the end. It just goes on and on and on.

Occasionally, floating metal islands or these rock formations appear and seem to house different buildings. Some are small enough to only house one single structure — like this one — while others are so massive they seem to hold whole coliseums of their own. Wait…I squint at a rock formation lower than this one way, way off in the distance…is that another coliseum?

"Jesus Christ," I mutter as I come back around to face the entrance of the tent. It's a tan color and looks like untreated hide. It's beautiful, marbled with a darker tan color. It stretches almost three of me high and is wide enough around it looks like it could house several rooms.

I swallow thickly and refuse to betray my fear, my tension, my anxiety. "I need to set the tone. I need to establish how it's gonna be between us." Because if I don't — if I act like someone cowed, that's exactly what I'll be.

"Okay." I take a step forward. "Buck up." I take a step back. "Nalia, just do it. *Do it.*" I storm forward, burst through the flaps of the tent and shout at the four-armed alien in front of me, "I am not a prize! I am a person and I demand to be treated with some fucking dignity!"

Only…I blink. And then I blink again several times rapidly.

The tent is empty and I'm shouting at the furniture. It's *nice* furniture. Much nicer than I expected. Also, it's oddly familiar. Dark woods that conjure up images of *living rooms* complete with chairs that have four legs and arms and pillows on the base made of carefully stitched fabrics. There are even rugs strewn across the floor covered in bold reds that look like blood and bright yellows that remind me of flowers…flowers I can't remember, but that form in my mind's eye with such crystal clarity that I'm sure I've seen them before.

In some other life.

Large trunks lounge with their mouths wide open, like eager chicks awaiting the return of their mothers.

They're filled with all manner of stones and rocks and metals and weapons and fabrics. I go to one that's piled high with fur and reach down, touch it…it's the softest pink and feels divine.

I shudder. The familiarity of it freaks me out and I jerk my hand back. Everything in here is so *familiar,* everything except for the nets. Massive wooden support beams prop up the tent. They're huge, heavier than what their purpose suggests, except for the nets strung between them. There's a basket net that's shaped like a chair hanging from one beam between two chests. I go to it and take a seat, collapsing back as it's way, way too big for me. I get all tangled up and start to panic as I struggle to extract myself.

"Oooph!" I grunt, collapsing onto the floor beneath it. It swings mockingly above me while I brush off my naked skin and stand up.

Continuing my tour, I move in front of a short table topped by a basin. It's gold and looks like it was roughly, yet intentionally hammered. I stroke the interior with my fingers and frown at the sight of my fingernails, all chipped and bitten down as they are. *I didn't used to bite my nails. I started only when the wars did, at least, when I started to understand them for what they were. The end of it all.*

I look up, jolted by the thought and the splinter of a headache that accompanies it, and expect to see a mirror, but there isn't one. I glance around, irrationally curious as to where I might find one. I haven't actually seen myself since I woke up. The ends of my hair look raggedy as they drape over my chest past my breasts and stomach to reach my hips. It's too long. Except… that's not right either. I always wanted long hair…*but you weren't allowed to have it. Your job prevented you...* My job? I cringe as another headache cuts in.

I walk through it, staggering slightly as the pain cuts deep. I reach out and catch myself on a short table. Beneath my hand, a blade rattles against the wooden tabletop. I grab the knife and turn it over in my hand while I wait for my vision to unblur and the room to settle around me. It takes longer than it did when I first woke up in that spaceship, that horrible place with the mutilated giants and the man with the silver arm and the vacant eyes. One had been black and red, composed of an eerie shifting matter, but the other brown eye had been even stranger...it had been so...tragic. It felt familiar to me. It had given me hope. And then he'd crushed it.

Never again.

I grip the knife with purpose, my hand trembling a bit at the memory of the male with the red and metal skin. He's not here. I push the memory back and continue around the room, happy with my weapon, now in search of either a rope or a mirror. I find neither. You know what else I don't find? A bed.

"Does someone sleep here?" I mutter, glancing around and listening carefully, but it's hard to hear over the chaotic sounds of the cave world beyond these walls. I step towards one wall at the back of the tent and press my ear up against it, only...the tent wall wavers. It isn't a wall at all. It's a curtain. I drag it back.

"Oh my shit." That didn't come out right, some combination of oh my and oh shit that got stuck behind my teeth. I snicker at the outburst as I move forward, hypnotized by the large tub. It's made out of...wood, maybe? Honestly, I can't even guess. It's beautiful though, a deep, dark brown, striated with variations of the same shade. And piping hot water ripples on the surface, releasing steam in lazy bursts.

"Oh my shit," I repeat as I dip my fingers into the water. It feels like water, smells like nothing. That means it's safe, right? I don't hesitate and latch onto my opportunity. Dropping my blade into the tub, I dunk one foot inside then the other, then sit down with a splash. "Oh my shit," I squeal.

And then a dark, deep voice rumbles, "Svrennu giar hitata tansuey eyu."

I look up. Standing just at the curtain where I stood moments before is a beast three feet taller than I am, covered in blood.

My bottom jaw drops. "Oh my shit…"

2
Herannathon

Well, well, well. I am pleased. Oh, I am so pleased. This moment — this right here — makes all of the blood and the death and the battles fought without salvation tokens worth it. I throw my hands in the air and ball them into a fist, pumping the two on the right and startling the shit out of the human.

"Whooooh!" I roar. "*Finally*. How many tournaments did it take me to get you into my tent? Too many. That's for shhhrov…sure."

I bite my tongue to stop myself from cursing in the presence of a female. I've read excerpts from the human handbook that I managed to get ahold of, courtesy of a mok biz game gone right, that it isn't right to curse in the presence of a human female. They're sensitive or some shhro…shi…something.

I'm grinning wildly at the female as she grips the edges of the tub, looking bewildered at the sight of me, like it wasn't explained to her by the Eshmiri why she was brought here and that she doesn't have to sleep in that shh…hole she was sleeping in before all alone, without easy access to the Below.

Of course, I saw a couple of the other prizes at the Gogo racetrack even earlier this lunar. Manila, who owns several of the Gogo tracks herself and commands the entire mok bir tournament, loves to bet and cause all kinds of trouble — likely the Sky in her that the Eshmiri weren't able to scrape out — but most prizes aren't from these parts, aren't willing prizes, and don't know their way around Evernor. They don't know that *anything* is an option and lying, cheating, stealing and sneaking out are not just tolerated, but expected.

I try not to let it bother me that the female I've chosen isn't as devious as a pirate female would be, and I remind myself that this *is* the same female who stole one of Ashmara's shooters and crash landed here in the first place. Centare, this female — *my* female — will only need a little convincing before she loses that worried look in her eyes.

"What is it? Am I not what you expected?" I snort. I lumber up to the tub, plant my two lower hands on either side of it, and quickly leap in beside her. Water splashes her face and she squeals and lifts up her right hand and… "What the shr…comets!" I shout.

The human stabs me right in the chest plate. She *stabs* me!

"The shrov was that for?" I glance down at the handle of a knife jutting out of the thick plates that cover my chest. She applied force behind the blow and I'm tired from the earlier battle. It's buried deep — almost deep enough to reach more sensitive flesh.

I yank the knife out and toss it against the wall. "I just got out of the merillian tub! I have no desire to go back to it!" The knife plugs into the wego siding of the tent cleanly and dangles there for a moment before slipping out, dragging a small hole in the exterior of our tent through which I can catch mere shards of glimpses of the chaos that is Evernor.

The human female jolts as it hits the ground. Her teeth are pressed together fiercely against the underside of her red lips. Her skin is all flushed red — flaring like a Voraxian's colors might, a clear sign of her anger — but anger at what? That she didn't kill me? After all the sh… stuff I've done to get to her?

"Are you mad? Do you even know how many battles I've fought — how many I've killed — to be able to get you out of the prize stables? Did you not see the beating I took in the arena this solar?" Beating is too mild a word for it, but I'm too proud to offer her any others.

I jut one of my hands forward and point at her nose. She slaps it away and lunges up and out of the tub, spraying me with water. She makes her way over to the side of the tent and snatches the knife off of the floor where it fell and, by shrov, the lunatic female returns to me, jumping back into the tub on top of my chest, knees knocking against my ribs and forcing the breath from my lungs.

I catch her against my chest, my tines pressing against the back of the tub and squishing into the horaci exterior, expressly made to accommodate my hiannru by allowing them to press through without allowing the water to leak. She's got the knife against my chest again, where I assume she thinks I've got vital organs, though they aren't there, that's for sh…sure.

"Are you trying to actually kill me? Because you are awful at it." I mold my hand around hers on the knife and reposition it against the center of my torso. "Here. That's where my heart is, beneath layers of muscle and heavy plates and bone. Don't tell me yours is here? Underneath your chest mound — the humans call this *breast*, don't they?" I cup her breast in my lower left hand, and shrieking *shrov*. "*Fuck!*" Deena likes saying this word. I have grown fond of it. "Your chest breast is marvelous!" *Oh centare.*

My cock is about to come unsheathed, the thick plate that juts just a little ways from my body prepared to peel back, and when it does — when my cock extends from my body fully and hits air — I know it'll be painful. I need…need to get it together. Centare, I need *relief.*

I release her chest mound, but not fast enough. She doesn't like the way I'm touching her because her color gets even more red and her knife slashes with more accuracy. She cuts it across my cheek. There is a plate there, but it is thinner. I don't worry about that now, though.

"Shrov shrov shrov," I hiss. If my cock comes free of its outer shell, we will have a problem. *I will need release.* I don't have a synthetic currently in my hands — it's somewhere out there in one of the chests — but I have a *very* soft female in my grip and she has no defenses and I would be honored to perform a shekurr all of my own upon her, but…she's trying to kill me.

She lunges at me again and I run away from her frantically. The sight of her breasts bobbing up and down in the air as she charges is a problem. "Stop that!" I shout over my shoulder as I swerve between chaotically organized pieces of furniture I procured in advance of her arrival.

I push a chair over to block her path, immediately annoyed when she steps over it and crushes the pillow. "That's catacat silk! Don't you know? It's for you!" I drop down next to one of the open chests. There's fabric on the top and I immediately know it's the wrong one. I pass to the next, and then to the final one, finding this one filled with all manner of odd items I've gathered, not for her, but for me, down in the Below.

A synthetic — a few different models to choose from. Weapons. Bits and pieces of yamar and yeeyar I've been attempting to cobble together to form an off-world communicator — without success. A Voraxian holoscreen whose only contents are a partially completed and almost incomprehensibly translated guide to human females and courtship. A few blocks of pure kintarr that have more value than any of my other winnings — any except for *her*. The human that nearly all of the other gladiators have come to claim and take home to their sectors.

The human species is too new, too guarded by Niahhorru and Voraxians alike, known to be breedable and coveted for their softness. They have skin like an oroshi and colors that shift like a Voraxian's, flowing, coiled and colored hair like Quadrant One princes and princesses… They are coveted, humans. But let the other gladiators covet all they like. This one's *mine. She's been mine from before the beginning.*

My fists stiffen around the orange standard synthetic as the memory of seeing her for the very first time clouds my vision. She'd been one of so many humans suspended in blue tanks, but my gaze had still stalled on her. I don't know why. All I knew then was the same thing I know now — why doesn't matter.

I glance over my shoulder and see her continue to amble after me, though she's moving slower than she was before. She's got her hand pressed to the center of her forehead and she's wavering in between two chests, her hand outstretched as she holds onto one of my large net seats. It dangles from the rafters, offering little in the way of support.

"Good, little human. Stay there," I grit as my gaze loses it's battle with my mind not to drop to her breasts. So *shroving* soft… I start to heat from within and my plates begin twitching in response, flapping almost imperceptibly, making it possible for my body to release heat — and that's no shroving good with her wielding that knife like she is. She skewers me underneath one of my plates, she could do more damage than those shroving egama.

"Calm yourself, female. Cover your chest breasts and everything will be fine!"

But she doesn't. She just shakes her head quickly, as if shaking off a thought, and approaches me from behind. Her arms are down at her sides, her feet braced apart in a warrior's stance that looks so natural it gives me momentary pause. And then my gaze snaps to a single droplet of water running down her stomach.

I follow the trail it makes over her abdomen, which is flat and ribbed. She doesn't have the plushness that Deena does, Rhorkanterannu's mate, but she holds such an allure to me that it doesn't matter at all. I'm enraptured by the wild and glittering strands of her hair. *It grows between her thighs, like a barrier to keep my gaze from feasting on what it wants.*

If she isn't going to cover herself to help me from losing my mind, then perhaps she isn't here to stab me, after all. Maybe, when the handbook said that females don't practice a hunt to find their mates, I read it wrong.

Hope and desire war in my rib cage, stoking the flames. "Spread your legs," I command, filling my voice with authority, but she doesn't do that either. Instead, she lunges.

I hold up one hand to ward her away while my other three hands fumble with the damn synthetic. I grab hold of it just in time, because my cock can't shroving take it. I just manage to jam the synthetic over my cock, holding her with my upper two hands while my lower two stabilize the machine, just as my cock barrels out of its plate and hardens fully.

I bellow out a moan and hold the female to my chest as the first of the seed starts to leak out of me. This isn't a release — not yet — but I'm still surprised and a little terrified by the force of it.

It's been a long time since I participated in a shekurr — *too* long — and I haven't had the desire to partake in any of the pleasure houses. Most Niahhorru wouldn't. It's an honored thing, to enter a female. Most of the time, I'd do so alongside my brothers — five, ten, sixteen at a time. But Rhorkanterannu has shown us that it can be another way. What would it be like to have a female all to myself? To call her mate, or even...*Xiveri*...

Shrov. It's thinking like that that got me into this mess in the first place.

"Shrov...augh..." My eyes roll back, my shoulders roll back. On my knees, I tilt my chin up and peer at her through slitted eyes. My skein half closed, I watch her expression morph from fear to anger to shock, which is where it settles. Pink lights up her entire face — not red, but pink. Hmm. I don't know what to make of that. Her gaze passes down my face to my throat and to my chest. She leans back and looks between us, the knife dangling limply in her hand as her gaze rakes over my lap, settling hard on the synthetic in my hand. *Does she wish it were her?* The thought alone makes jets of seed spill out of me.

I moan.

"Fuck," she says, jerking again in my grasp.

I chuckle, thinking of the book and how it said not to curse in front of females. And here she is, legs spread around my hips, thighs balancing on my lower arms while my upper arms circle her back. I follow her gaze down and see my two hands clasped beneath her ass around the synthetic. A massive thing, it's nearly the length of her entire arm, as thick around as her thigh. It applies pressure and squeezes my cock gently. I adjust the settings along the back, fingering them to dial down as I attempt to retract myself from the stress of this.

She looks surprised — for now — but I'm not up for testing her, and I *really* do not want her to stab me while I'm coming to the sight of her.

"Are you j-jacking off?" she stutters. Though the sound of her voice is warped through the translation token in my ear, several things are clear. Her sweetness may just be an illusion. She's mouthy and it makes me grin.

"You know…I don't…" My hips thrust up on each word as I empty seed into the machine, wishing it were her body. "…have to use…the synthetic…aughhhh." I moan, rolling forward and collapsing onto my hands and knees. I lower her to her back on the red carpet, her equally red hair splashing out across it like blood from an artery. *Shrov, she's lovely.* And what's even lovelier? Her thighs spread apart, their pale insides gleaming up at me, the patch of her red lower fur parting to give me a full view of her pink slit.

I want to touch, but something tells me not to try, so I keep shroving the synthetic, working my hips harder into it, keeping it positioned between her parted legs. "Are you happy? That this is what you've turned me into? A mindless rutting beast worried about being stabbed in his own tent?" I'm grinning ravenously at the idea. "Wonderful. Just wonderful." I try to imbue some sarcasm in my tone, but it's not very effective. I'm exorbitantly pleased.

I moan like a beast as a release, greater than the last, swells up my spine, causing my ass and thighs to stiffen. *"Fuck,"* I moan, repeating the word in her tongue. I look into her eyes, watch them widen so that so much white appears on all sides of their brown and black insides. She's staring back at me without blinking and, as I start to reach a numbing climax, she makes this little noise, something caught between a gasp and a plea. That sound.

"Oagh," I grunt and she…she *touches* me. She reaches a delicate, five-fingered hand up and cups the back of my right upper arm.

Her touch — even against my much harder plate — it sends my nerves *scattering*. I grab her neck with my upper right hand. I don't squeeze, I simply lay my palm across the front of her throat. And she…doesn't try to stab or claw me again. Instead, her eyes, which blink up and down…flutter closed.

"Oph…hhhhh…" My moan comes out on a threadbare breath and I sink further against her soft body, closing the distance between us, but not enough — not enough for me to be able to press my chest plates to her chest breasts and chafe the shrov out of them, marking her as my own.

"Female," I groan, wishing I had a name to call her by. My other upper hand shoves into her hair, catching it near the root before flattening it to the floor. I can feel her resist momentarily, as if only to see if she can…she can't. "You can't move," I whisper, "You're mine."

"Uoah," she whimpers and the explosion rolls over me like a slow landslide. I pike my hips and haul up on the synthetic and empty my seed into it until my body fills with fire and my plates all lift out away from my body and my lungs seize. Even with my plates all lifted and my underskin so exposed, she still doesn't kill me. Instead, she seems to be having an unfamiliar, alien reaction all her own. Her eyes are glossy and filled with desire. I remove one hand from the synthetic and grip her inner upper thigh.

"Soft," I moan.

She starts to breathe harder. I can feel each of her inhalations beneath my roughened palm. "Female…"

I heave out a breath as I finally finish, desiccating my interior sac and finally releasing her hair and her neck. She swallows several times. I stroke the length of her neck, touching her more openly than I probably should. Bracing myself on all sixes, I try to marshal my heavy breath. It takes time for my swollen cock to shrivel back down into its husk. It takes equally long before I'm comfortable and able to pull the synthetic off and set it back in the trunk.

She doesn't move. She continues to lie on the floor as I return to cover her. "It self-cleans," I explain.

Undoubtedly, she's unfamiliar with synthetics. From what I've heard, the males of her species don't ejaculate in the same way we pirates do and their cocks are better built for oxygenated air. I wonder if she prefers them and frown. She better shroving not.

I frown. "Why aren't you speaking to me?" I scoff, "I read your human manual written by the advisor Svera — there are copies circulating wildly in the underground markets. Everyone is fascinated by the advent of this new species, since one of you has become queen of Voraxia. I learned that some of you follow something called *ree-lee-groin*. That you all are very afraid of sex. Is this the problem? Did I scare you with my co…"

I start to withdraw from her, feeling…better…much, much better, but before I can go anywhere, she reaches down the length of her body and grabs my wrist, the one belonging to the hand that had pressed against her upper thigh. She pulls it back there, puts it back to where it was, and then…she moves it higher.

"Oh female…" I growl. "Did it please you to watch me chase my own release?"

She doesn't answer, but pulls harder on my wrist, forcing my hand up higher and higher, until it fully covers her slit. She releases a high-pitched moan and I almost lose what sense I have. My depleted cock is the only thing that keeps me from shoving inside of her — that, and the fact that I don't have a name to give her. I long stopped caring that she'd been about to kill me moments ago.

"Let me help you…" I hiss as I prowl down her body, fully intent on licking her clean, allowing her to find release after release…but my palm presses down, fully covering her slit. I apply just the slightest pressure, using her pubic bone as a brace as I move down to reposition myself between her thighs, ready to settle in for the full lunar if that's what it takes — I've got no idea how long it takes to make a human female achieve her release, but I'm willing to wait however many eons it takes to find out — but before I get anywhere near her thighs with my tongue and lips, her back arches and her hips lift and she grabs my upper wrists and closes her eyes and *grinds* on my hand.

Her too soft skin drags against the plates just below my fingers and I jerk, worried that I'll tear skin that soft. "*Centare*, please…"

She begs me in her own tongue. "Don't stop. Harder…more…"

I rub my palm against her full mound, finding a circular, swirling pattern that makes her moans climb higher. My cock stirs, even as depleted as it is, wanting release…but I'm not sure. She is *so* responsive, it frightens me. It overwhelms me. She's an adversary that may be my undoing, because she's fighting a battle I've never fought before and she's besting me at it in my own arena.

I'm panting, the breath tearing in and out of my lungs. "Ontte, let me see how you melt for me."

Her head whips to the side, her hips are jerking against my hand feverishly, her mouth opens and I quickly, in a moment of insanity, retract the claws of my right lower hand and shove one finger inside of her slit. I breach her entrance, finding a delirious sort of wetness that fully and completely baffles me. There's no structure here, nothing, it's just…hot and wet and any male's fantasy, no matter the species. An Oroshi tentacle…an Egama knot…a Voraxian tail…a Lemoran's two cocks… No *wonder* the Lemoran paid the price he did for a human. With a softness such as this, she could take anything…*me*. All the way up to the plates. *Shrov.* She could be the queen of her own shekurr.

"Let me *feel* how you melt for me, female."

She moans and, before I know what's happening, her body has tightened, muscles standing out in relief against her arms and stomach and neck. Her thighs spread wide enough to make me worry for them, and then begin to quiver. She pulses her pelvis against my palm and I apply counterforce, no longer so worried about tearing her with the increase in wetness. She doesn't just melt for me, she *rains*.

Her body secretes fluid all over my hand and there's so shroving much of it. Her liquid squirts out from around my palm and I feel regret that borders on grief that I wasn't able to drink from her…but I'm not going to replace my hand with my mouth now. I won't risk it. Not when she looks so shroving blissed out. Her lips are parted, mouth forming a perfect O that I'd love to sink my cock into — who knows, maybe while my tongue is shoved deep inside of her.

She comes down on a heavy, shaky breath and, when she pulls back on my wrist, I carefully peel my palm from her body, but I don't extract my finger — not until her inner walls stop contracting. It's a stupefying, seductive sensation. *More.* It's all I can think.

But as I watch the stars clear from her eyes, I'm not sure she's thinking the same thing. She's blinking brightly, looking around and looking a little lost. I smirk, "That was quick. Is it always so quick with human females?"

I withdraw my finger from her body and her eyelids flutter, and then flutter again when I lick her juices off of my palm. She slowly curls her legs up to her body and slides out from under mine. My predatory instincts all bark at me to grab her, but I don't. I just smear her wetness over my chest plates and sit back onto my heels. I watch her bump up against the trunk and jerk, making her look like that lost female, again.

I frown. "You can't still be speechless. Not after this..."

She shakes her head, but it doesn't look like she has registered my question. And it makes me wonder something scandalous and shroving outrageous. I ask, "Can you not understand me?"

She speaks almost the same moment I do. "Do you *still* not realize that I can't understand you?"

I bark out a laugh and rise fully. I fought a hard day. Against Egama giants. Against my own cock and the sight of her chest breasts. Against every instinct in my body aching for me to *claim*. I'm exhausted. But this? This makes me feel light as air. This is shroving hilarious. "Shroving Eshmiri." I shake my head, trying to go through a list of beings I'll pummel for this. "They were supposed to give you a shroving translator."

She tucks her knees beneath her chin and winces back when I reach down to her, but I don't let her hesitation dissuade me. She glances at my palm. Some of the anger color in her face seems to dissipate. She's turning her odd peachy white color again. Never seen another color like it. I've seen planets with creatures of all colors of a prism and even humans in all shades of brown that can be believed, but across all the stars and all the cosmos I've seen so far, her particular clash of colors — the white skin with the orange hair — is entirely unique.

"My little sword fighter, let us fetch you a translator."

She slides her palm against mine and lets me pull her to her feet.

She honors me.

3

Herannathon

I don't know how to dress a human, but I suppose this will have to do. I step back from her and frown, wondering why everything looks a bit *off*. Her tunic drapes to her knees and is so low her chest breasts are nearly visible through the gaping neckline. She keeps holding it together, like she's afraid to let her mounds spill free. It must be a thing of honor, to keep them covered. Or maybe, it's a safety issue.

Perhaps, if human females are left to wander with their chests exposed, their human males fall into savage ruts and — by stars — if they have no access to synthetics, then perhaps they simply perish! What a sorry state for the males of their species. I shake my head, then I remember that they are not pained by oxygenated air, as we are. And if their females aren't pleased to be rutted at any given time, then the males would see the chest mounds and…what? Force the females? I laugh aloud. What a silly idea.

Centare, it must be for another reason that she covers such perfect things. I, for one, am certain that if I had such powerful mounds, capable of debilitating a male, I would wield them often in battle. I could've taken down that Egama giant without ever cutting his skin.

My right hands flex, not having liked the experience or, at present, reliving it. I did it for her and I'm pleased with the result, especially knowing now that she was denied access to the Below and access to a translator and likely has lived in fear these past solars since we landed and were separated.

But…I still wish that the Egama had not one, but two salvation tokens. I wouldn't have needed to kill him, then. I cringe, thinking of the first fighter I killed in that arena and *how* I killed him. The shroving Eshmiri wanted a spectacle as the condition of my female's release. A spectacle and a second battle. I delivered both, even though both battles took pieces out of me that I will never recover, no matter how much merillian they provide to heal me.

I straighten and roll my upper shoulders back. It's in the past. Here, this female is my future. I withdraw my lower hand from my pocket where it had been clutching a heavy bolt made out of a metal not from this time and refocus on the present, on the future, on the female standing just out of my reach looking at me like she's not sure about me.

Good girl.

She shouldn't be.

"Let's go," I tell her, gesturing to the yeeyar flat craft. It isn't my favorite mode of transportation, but it is at least yeeyar-powered and sophisticated enough to be commanded by the token I wear in my ear.

I step up onto the yeeyar glider and offer her a hand. "Come. Translator." I point to the token in my ear, and then to my lips.

She tilts her head to the side and she must understand me because she says, "You'll get me one of those?"

I nod. It's a lie. I can get her a translator, but not one of this calibre and I can't give her mine. *This* Niahhorru token speaks directly to the mothership, to Rhorkanterannu himself — well, it would with a communications disruptor, but I'm still on the hunt for one of those. Along with the key that Manila holds, it's the last item I've got to get my hands on now that the human female is in my possession and I don't plan on letting her go.

"Ontte." I nod a second time. She takes a tenuous step forward. I wonder if she can read my lie and decide to mask it with a smile. That causes her to stop. "What?"

She pauses, waiting in her rags, a skeptical expression on her face. Then, all at once, her anger color returns, turning her face a bright and blotchy red. "Ugh. Fine." She strides forward with a soft shake of her head and steps up onto the yeeyar beside me.

She's found her knife again and keeps it fitted snuggly between us and I can't help but laugh. "Good," I tell her. "Keep that with you. You'll need it."

We take off. She screams. Her arms windmill back, the knife quickly lost to the Below as we launch over the edge of the platform. I laugh and grab the front of her tunic, hauling her up against my chest and tucking her beneath my body as I drop into a crouch.

The yeeyar glider responds to the commands I give it via the yeeyar token in my ear. Two handholds appear in front of us and she latches on with a white-knuckled grip. I mold my lower hands over hers. She flinches, but must recognize that she doesn't have much of a choice, so she settles into the position, me bent over her, her hidden beneath the shadow of my much larger body.

I lean down and press my nose to the side of her face, basking in the rough texture of her hair. She smells good. She smells like some type of wood from the forests of a faraway galaxy. I grin and inhale deeply as the chaos of Evernors flits past us in its own mad delight, bringing so many different galaxies together in this one subterranean universe.

"You haven't seen Kor yet. Evernor is only a pale shadow of the delights we pirates have to offer," I tell her, watching her expressions become increasingly hilarious as she tries to take it all in. She blinks over and over and mouths words that she never speaks. "I'll slow down to give you a better look when we get near the reaver markets." I gesture at my eyes. She shakes her head. I grunt, "Shroving translator."

As she pulls back, I can't exactly *help* glancing down the front of her tunic at her chest breasts and am rewarded by the side of her head crashing into my nose. I don't manage to fully evade the blow and pain radiates through the front of my face as I rear back.

"What was that for?"

"Stop looking at my tits!" she shouts, proving my theory about the dangerous and delectable nature of chest breasts, or rather, tits.

"Tits?" Oh, tits. I like this word. It's short and dirty and quick. "Your *tits* are lovely. Next time I have you on your back, you'll hold yourself together for longer than a few seconds and let me suckle them. Then, you'll let me lick your pussy clean of all its many glorious fluids." I can still scent them on my own hand now, sure that the rich musk will be embedded there forever.

I reach around her body — to stabilize her, of course — but she gives my leg a kick and tries to swat at me with her hand. The motion makes her slip. I catch her wrist and return her fingers to the holds, careful as I navigate our yeeyar flat craft out of the corner of my eye and with the little attention I've got for anything but her.

Maneuvering between and below and above other crafts moving in every direction, several creatures aboard passing flyers offer me greetings. One Lemoran tips his horns in my direction. I grin back wildly. "Looking forward to killing you tomorrow!" I shout up at him, knowing he isn't competing in the games.

He laughs, "Not in this tournament, but I *will* have your prize."

That bothers me for reasons I don't like. His pink glittering craft is made out of a rare crystal mined on his home world. It is worth more than mine. She doesn't know that, but she still regards it with fascination I don't like, making me want to break the thing into a million fractured shards. "I'll take your kintarr along with your horns. Think I'll use them for hibi ale."

He laughs even harder and veers nearer to me. His striated, colored gaze drops once again to the female. No matter how I try to block the sight of her with my body, he still finds a way to see her and she, him. She's glaring daggers in his direction, a fact that makes his amiable expression twist up and causes me to snort.

"Haven't you heard? Clan Raingar's found itself a human miriga."

That would have shocked the shit out of me if I hadn't seen it with my own eyes. I grin. "A hybrid."

"Nob — really?"

I nod in confirmation.

"And the other half?"

"Drakesh." I glance down at his kintarr vessel. "Consider it a gift." He knows what I mean. Nothing comes for free in Evernor. Not even information like this. "And there are many more humans, pure-blooded just like this one."

"I've heard of the human planet in Voraxia…"

"Centare, there's another. One run by *us*."

He swerves even nearer and narrows his eyes as he looks at the human safely secured between my thighs. "What do you want for an invitation?"

"They're not for sale."

"Pagh!" He shouts after me, shaking a fist. "You know we don't barter in flesh. I just want to meet one of them…"

"We haven't opened the ports there for trading yet, but I will certainly let you and your token purse know when we do."

Ah, the art of the deal. Joy buzzes through me as I drop this first morsel, just to let it marinate. He's calling after me still as I zip off, diving down and away from the Lemoran before he has a chance to attempt another proposition. I have other, more urgent things to attend to now.

My female and I drop off on the edge of a market square and she stumbles slightly as her feet hit the smooth red rock. She watches with suspicion as the yeeyar flat craft shrinks in on itself until it's smaller than a knuckle and fits easily into my pocket, clattering against the bolt that already occupies it. *That always occupies it.*

I clear my throat. "Welcome to the reaver markets."

Conical black stalls stud the surface of this large plateau unevenly, in no discernable order, but I've been to this market many times and know my way around by now. I head straight to the only vendor I trust for this — not even one of my own, because there *is* another Niahhorru pirate stall somewhere in this mess — to the defective Sky, the only one ever liberated.

"Manila, heelee," I call, opening up my arms at the sight of the Hypha hybrid. "So surprising to see you outside of the Gogo racetracks."

"You know the Gogos require a rest day," she pouts, looking particularly put out about it. "And besides, the mok bir tournament is about to begin." Her eyes gloss over with excitement while her stalyx-enhanced hand begins drumming out a beat on the arm of her chair. She doesn't bother getting up at the sight of me, but the moment she spies my prize, her eyes brighten, she slides off of her lumpy wood and metal stool and offers the human a smile that makes me instantly nervous.

It looks *genuine*.

"My stars. You finally made it Below. I was worried you didn't know how." She comes to stand directly in front of my female and I get the sense that my female is much like a Lemoran or a Voraxian in the way that she views private space because she leans slightly away from the former assassin. Luckily for Manila and unluckily for my prize, Manila takes no notice. She envelopes the female in a traditional Hyphan embrace, clasping both of her forearms and pressing her forehead to my prize's, again making me nervous as it's a strangely intimate gesture.

"Uhermm…" my prize mumbles. It's not the first time she's made the annoying sound. It makes her sound weak, that sound. Very unpiratelike. And I know she's got some pirate in there somewhere. For a moment, I saw it smeared across the now damp carpet, back in my tent. I just have to help her find it. And I have so many ideas as to how…

"She *doesn't* know how. Eshmiri shroving bastards didn't give her a translator."

"I see." Manila grins. "So you've come to me. Why you think I'd have a translator for her is…"

"Manila," I bark, annoyed. I play this game with her every time and right now, I'm losing patience for it. But…it's Manila. Play the game, I must. I grin and unfurl all of my arms where they'd been clenched. The fingers of my bottom arms all crack as I step up to the females. "I want to be able to speak to my prize. What do I need to do to make that happen? Hm?"

I loop my arm around my prize's back and entirely ignore the way she leans even *farther* away from me than she leaned away from Manila. Then she shoves off my arm entirely and steps away from us. She backs up straight into a Rekkaru carrying a large tray, held up by straps around his neck. He grumbles at her, annoyed, but quickly smiles when he sees me and flies forward to offer me some of his mirachoi powder.

I nod and smile and exchange polite banter until he eventually realizes I'm not buying any of that toxic shroving powder — a poor man's muuir and I'd be caught armless before touching that addictive substance — and flutters off in a torrent of softly murmured curses.

"Cheap as ever, just like a pirate." Manila sighs, "I have no desire to trade with you."

"Aw, heelee, don't be this way. You know you love to trade with pirates. The last time we met on the pleasure planet, Dreyth? Don't tell me you didn't enjoy the shekurr you ordered from my brothers and me."

She smiles, gaze becoming distant. She paid an exorbitant price to have her own shekurr — an honored act among us Niahhorru, though we'd been more than happy to sate her needs at the price she offered us. We're shroving pirates. There is always a price. I remind myself of that as I take another step forward, coming between her and my prize.

I take her right hand and curl my fingers around the stalyx. I lean down very close to her cheek and breathe softly against her neck. "Do you not remember our time together during the shekurr? The way you shook for me?"

Her breath quickens and her smile curls. Her black hair lifts from the back of her neck — an odd relic of her time with the Sky. I've never seen another female's hair behave so...so *autonomously*. Her hair slides over my cheek and then cradles my chin. All at once, it flicks back and attacks, whipping my neck, drawing blood even through the thin plate.

"Your brothers were more memorable." Her smile falls and she bats me out of the way, successfully shoving me off balance.

Her stalyx arm is strong. She'd make a fair competitor in the games, but Manila would never. Since being liberated from the Sky, she doesn't like to get her hands dirty. It's why I like her. Genuinely. She doesn't kill. It brings her no pleasure. Something that can't be said for many of Evernor's beasts.

She returns to her vendor's tent, a large, conical grey tent illuminated by floating torches, and billows through the flaps. I don't follow — can't. She has Eshmiri shields protecting her stall, though you wouldn't know by looking at it. It's high tech. All her gadgets are.

"I don't have much," I hear her shout from beyond the blackened threshold. She has a few yamar-powered bots buzzing around the flaps. They hover near me when I get closer and I know they're blaster-capable and fully operational. "I barely have enough for my friends and you certainly are not that," she huffs, reappearing.

"You know we're friends. The closest, Manila." I grin to show all of my teeth.

"Hm. And so far your *friendship* has gotten me very little. What will giving up my very last yamar translator to your prize give me? I recall your last few favors for salvation discs costing you more than you could afford."

"Oh heelee, you must be able to do better than yamar," I start, but Manila's gaze is distracted and glittering in delight.

That can't be good.

I turn to see my prize examining objects from a tray carried by a different Rekkaru. I groan. Clearly, the first one called his friends to tell them I'm here because they're swarming now. There must be fifteen — twenty — Rekkaru carrying trays gathered just a few paces back. Most of what they carry is food. Some of it may even be edible.

The Rekkaru nearest to her is carrying a tray covered in baked Rekkaru delicacies, most of which I can't stomach, but my prize seems to be considering them. She reaches for one and the Rekkaru holds out his token — an ancient yamar relic shaped like a box, but it still works well enough to collect the tokens he expects her to transfer to him. She doesn't. Instead, she reaches for his token itself.

"Oof!" I shout, surging to intercept before he calls her a thief. Evernor loves thieves — loves to torture them.

The Rekkaru swats the back of her hand and she gasps loudly. I move to step between the two of them, but before I can sputter the honest explanation that she wasn't given a shroving translator, she picks up the baked knot she'd been reaching for and throws it at the Rekkaru's charcoal-colored head, leaving a white imprint there from the powder it's been rolled in.

The Rekkaru gasps in imitation of my prize. "You… you…" he stammers.

"I don't understand you!" my prize shouts. She grabs another roll from the tray and turns, throws her arms out and shouts at everyone, "I don't understand any of you!" She throws the knot and it clonks another Rekkaru in her chest. The Rekkaru makes a high-pitched trilling sound and glances down at her shirt, stained now in pink.

"You savage alien," the Rekkaru shouts back, "This is not how things are done here!" She grabs a roll from her own tray and throws it at my prize who, in a move that surprises me, snatches the roll from the air and tosses it back to hit the female in the forehead.

"She's got a good arm," Manila says, having come to my side. She stops a passing Rekkaru and offers him a dozen credits for the food items on his tray. She passes me one and takes one herself.

"Is this really happening?" one of the Rekkaru shouts as my prize lunges for her tray and snatches up three more rolls, dispersing them through the air. She hits her mark every time.

My female is clonked in the head by an incoming stuffed Eshmiri bread — this one having been lobbed by a Hypha vendor at the tent across the aisle. I fire back in retaliation and the bread in my hand is stale and hits so hard that the Hypha staggers back, falling over the stool behind him in a pile of fabric and curses.

Manila laughs, but it's my prize who, turning back to look at me, shouts, "Food fight!"

I have never heard of a fight with food, but it's clear this is a tradition among her people because she dives vociferously for the Rekkaru holding the tray of breads nearest to her and, as he falls, proceeds to shove his face in powdery things. Food of all kinds hurtles towards her in reply and I'm grinning wildly as I food-fight my way forward, wielding a geeran drumstick as a weapon rather than a blade. It feels…good, this kind of fight. If only the tournaments were fought in this way.

I reach my prize in the midst of the chaos and lift the tray from the ground where the Rekkaru abandoned it. I use it as a shield and grab my prize by the arm, intending to bring her out of the fray and behind the safety of the overturned table Manila is using as a fortress.

Instead, my prize shrugs out of my grip and runs after a fleeing Rekkaru waving a fistful of crumbed bread in her hands above her head. She's splattered by seventeen different kinds of sauce and glaze and powder as she sprints. And yet, it doesn't deter her. Nor does it seem that she's the only one under fire. Order doesn't exist in the Grey Zone. In reaver or pirate territory, rivalries are lit fuses attached to explosives, and everyone is one spark away from revelry or warfare at any given moment.

I can feel something soft attach itself to my hiannru tines. I spin and hurtle the bun in my hand towards the Voraxian-Lemoran hybrid in the crowd. He catches it, takes a bite and tosses it towards Manila, who squeals in delight. She calls her bots to her and reprograms them with simple commands so that when they rise again to flank her, they shoot bread instead of blasts.

They fire at regular intervals, fast and at everyone. Soon, the dozens that had been attacking each other have retrained their attention on her. Buns and breads fly. Manila squeals, lifts a tray and laughs long and loud.

I use the opportunity to my advantage and sprint off down the aisle. Shrov! The female is quick and she's causing destruction everywhere that she goes. Vendors and buyers are either standing in cryosleep, stunned, or they're rushing around arming themselves with whatever foods happen to be at hand. One vendor has a vat of Niahhorru pudding that I ordinarily would spend many credits on strapped to his chest. His ladle goes in, comes out, and white pudding flies through the air. I sprint past him, but I'm not quick enough. Pudding slaps me across the side of the face and I release a sound somewhere between a laugh and a snarl.

I round the next bend, the end of the market in sight. My heart leaps into my throat at the sight of the Eshmiri patrol approaching from the sky. She doesn't seem to see them and is still sprinting after the Rekkaru who, in his own defense, is tossing whatever objects he passes over his shoulder. He's sprinting right to the edge of the market and, at the final moment, he leaps.

My prize must be confused about her own species because she doesn't immediately come to a stop. She looks like she'll try to take flight just as he has. But humans don't have wings. At least, I don't think they do. Perhaps, she'll produce them from…centare. Centare, centare, centare.

She's going down.

I speed up as blobs of food hit me in the chest and hiannru and face and thighs. My prize screeches as she absorbs the fact that she's just come upon the end of the market and her only exit is a freefall. She's unable to stop herself. Her arms windmill. She starts to slide and slip right over the precipice. I'm almost on her and leap…

I snatch her wrist in one hand as I go over the edge, hurtling down into the below of the Below. Two of my hands on the ledge above us force us to a jerky and dangerous stop. The muscles in my armpits burn and I curse.

My prize looks up at me. She doesn't scream. She smiles very tenuously and I am pleased. I grin in reply and feel heat ravage my body. I pull her up with one arm while my other three work to bring us closer to the surface. I haul her up beside me and, only when she's got her short, stubby claws dug into the hard red rock, do I release her with my upper hand and grab her with my lower. I snatch up the back of her shirt and drag her with me as I climb back onto the surface.

A moment later, we've got our toes dangling over the ledge, but we're back in safe territory, lying on our stomachs, cheeks pressed to the warm rock, facing one another. Her chest rises and falls in waves. I wonder if mine appears so dramatic. Centare, I don't think so. I open my mouth to say something, then remember she still can't understand me. Her gaze drops to my mouth and a certain *look* covers her filthy, powder and glaze-covered face. Yet, beneath the filth, I see her anger color rising again…

"What is…" I start. She doesn't let me finish.

She surges towards me, reaches around the back of my head, fists one of my spikes and yanks me to her. This female who is utterly infuriated with me shoves her mouth against mine and bites down on my lower lip hard enough to draw blood. She might be furious with me, but the too rough way she is with me has me absolutely shroving ravenous.

I grab her throat and squeeze until her teeth release my lip. She yanks back on a gasp and I lose my shroving mind at the sight of the muscles and veins straining in her neck. Her eyes roll back. I apply a little more pressure, just enough for her back to arch, and then I release and lick a line up the length of her throat, tasting so many competing flavors — the salt of her skin, the tang of the powder, the sweetness of the sticky bun, the savory gravy from the smoked geeran.

I yank down on the front of her tunic and palm her breast. "Yess..." she moans, though I hear the word in Meero, my native tongue, "*Ontte...*"

"I have to taste you *here*. Earlier, you denied me that." Hungrily, almost madly, I climb down her body, rocks kicking off over the edge beneath my boots. I latch onto her small, pale nipple with my teeth and struggle to marshal my touches into anything that isn't rough. It's hard when every one of her touches is rough. But she can be as rough as she wants to be with me. She can't hurt me. Not with her claws.

I suck her nipple into my mouth and scrape my rough palms over her sides. I squeeze. She spreads her legs under me and grabs onto my shoulders.

"Fuck...fuck, I need this," she whispers. She isn't even talking to me, but her eyes are open and she's looking at me and I feel the world come undone beneath my hands. Electricity blasts through me as I realize she isn't closing her eyes and pretending I'm anybody else. She isn't dreaming of one of her human mates, for there is no doubt that shekurr would have been performed with this female. She is *needy* and shroving ravishing. She could have a harem of mates and it would not be enough. *And yet, she won't because she will have but the one.*

"I will shrov you now," I tell her, moving up onto my knees and sliding my hands beneath hers, spreading them wide, wider still. I reach for her slit and as my hand lingers just a breath from her pretty pink gem, a lightning stick slashes across my back and a lasso wraps around my neck.

I'm hauled up, off of my female by a pack of Eshmiri patrollers. I snarl up at them and curse. It's too late. The Rekkaru she'd been chasing is hovering nearby, pointing at the female. Two armed Eshmiri drop from their gliders and move to flank her. She's still staring up at me, *want* gleaming in her werro wood-colored eyes as they grab her underneath the arms, load her onto a glider and take her away.

I shake my head, recognizing exactly how right Rhorkanterannu was. "With human females, nothing is easy." I grin at her retreating form.

4

Nalia

The manacles around my wrist are made of an electric blue energy. It radiates cool, even if the manacles themselves are a bit tight. The electric blue rope that fixes my manacles together also attaches to a metal ring in the ceiling but, luckily, the goons that shoved me in this red rock cell left me enough slack to be able to sit down.

So, I sit and frown at the goons standing at the electric blue doors to my cell, smiling in at me with their floppy ears and needlelike teeth. One of them waves at me. Feeling oddly more charitable, even though I'm stuck in another cell, I lift both my shackled hands and wave back.

The alien shoots up into the air, like he's shocked I replied, and crashes into his friend. He whispers something feverishly to the friend and both of them start to chuckle. His friend waves. I wave back. He shrieks with laughter. The two buffoons titter between themselves before eventually shuffling off and leaving me in a pleasantly giggle-free silence.

My stomach grumbles, filling the silence they left behind. Momentarily irritation flares. I threw all that food around when I should have eaten it. I haven't eaten in…since before today's tournament. *And I've done a lot of activity since then.* I can't believe I let him make me come. No, that I *forced* him to make me come. Jesus, what was I thinking?

That I was horny as fuck. Watching him struggle with that gigantic fleshlight was easily the hottest thing I've ever seen — and the filthy talk didn't help any. I had no idea what the hell he was saying, but it didn't seem to matter, my body was happy to respond to it. *It still is.*

I bite my bottom lip, grateful when the jail cell around me shudders again and snaps me out of visions…so many visions…

His hips pistoning into that orange device only this time, it's not a device at all. It's me. He's using me to empty himself. He's using me for release and he is nothing if not worshipful of the relief I provide. His lips locked onto my pale, skin-colored nipples, causing them to flush pink. His lips are hard and rough, but his tongue is pink and his teeth are white. Well, not quite. They're more shiny than that, like opal or mother of pearl. It reminds me of home and I want it… Want to swallow him whole.

The faraway sound of cheers make me hotter, make me remember how he'd looked fighting…and then after, coming to me in the bath entirely drenched in blood.

"Shit." I just bit my lower lip hard enough to draw blood. I rub it off with my thumb and, in staring at it, I shake my head. "Fuck it," I whisper. Who's going to judge me here if I want to relieve myself? Who's even going to know?

I flop onto my back, lift the hem of my gigantic tarp of a shirt and press my fingers against my clit and start to pulse them there. My body flushes with heat. I feel hotter than I should. Maybe, it's just the prison cell, deep below some kind of other, smaller arena. Maybe, it's just the excitement of almost falling to my death. Maybe, it's the way he leapt over the ledge after me, ready to do anything to keep me safe.

I close my eyes and remember the way he looked hovering over me, my thighs spread around his hips. I want to see his cock free of its fleshlight. He's an alien and I'm curious. Will it be long and skinny, or thick as a bicep? What does the head look like? Will it be veiny? Pulsing? Will it be grey or silver?

The thought makes me smile unexpectedly. This has all been too much. Every moment of waking up, first with some giants, and then again with some giants and the psychopath who tortured them, then again with some aliens of all shapes and colors, and then again as the prize in a tournament.

I'm done being scared.

I just want to *be.*

And I want to feel how totally liberated I felt when I threw that first doughy ball at an alien's head. I've never had a food fight before. *Have I?* No, I haven't. I know that definitively even though I can't remember…

I gasp as my hands are suddenly wrenched away from my legs and my whole body is propelled into motion. I'm jerked up into a seat by my shackles, and then up onto my knees and then finally I'm yanked all the way up until my feet don't even touch the ground. I hang suspended. My shoulders burn and I cry out.

My gaze flits to the electric blue cell doors where I see the four-armed male standing, staring in on me with a slitted gaze. He's shaking his head. I know *exactly* what he's trying to communicate, even though I can't understand him at all.

He's mad at me.

I've never seen him mad before. Not even in the arena.

The electric blue doors fizzle and fade, blinking out of existence like whatever's powering them is only half-working. It might be. What I've seen so far suggests that everything is a little run down around here. He steps through and they sizzle back to life with a slight snap, like a rubber band released.

I'm still flushed, nowhere near a release and horny, even with the goosebumps pebbling my skin. A chill washes over my body underneath his silent admonition. I feel...afraid? And I don't like it. I haven't felt afraid of him since... I stop and really consider. Really... Have I ever felt afraid of him? Have I ever *really* thought he'd hurt me? No, I guess not. Not really. No matter how many bones he's ripped from the bodies of his adversaries, no matter how many lifelines stolen, I still can't forget the sensation of being cradled in his arms.

That was right before I ran from him, stole the shuttle and crash landed here, where he's still fighting for me. Always fighting for me. And never once, no matter how many battles, no matter how many times I've run, has he managed to look pissed off.

"You..." I stutter. "W-what's wrong with you?"

My fear flares in time with his nostrils and, even though he doesn't have pupils, I can still tell in the movement of his vertical, diamond-shaped eyes that he's dropped his gaze to the hem of my tunic.

He rumbles something beneath his breath and his lower left hand passes over the front of his grey pants, drawing my attention to the bulge. He looked so panicked at the sight of his erection before, it had been kinda funny and strangely humanizing. Or alienizing. Whatever. It made him look like a middle school boy panicking over his very first public woodie.

I remember kissing a boy in my school at the compound and he totally freaked out when his cock got hard. I'd been a year older and had already kissed two other boys besides him — one boy even let me take a peek at it — so I pretended to know everything and told him it was probably infected and he'd taken down his pants and let me touch it because I told him my mom was a nurse... She wasn't. I never had a mom. Only an older sister...

I snap back to reality with concern. *Jesus.* Where did that come from? I shake it off, surprised by what I *think* was a memory and the fact that it didn't come with an accompanying headache, leaving me fully clear and capable of seeing the irritated look on the alien male's face.

"Te'eno hnoor, heelee," he rumbles, low and deep. He points with one hand at my crotch and I gulp audibly as he starts to prowl slowly around my dangling body. I kick with my feet, reaching for the ground, but it eludes me, so I stop.

I lick my lips and swallow hard enough I can feel it in my temples. "Are you...mad that I was touching myself?"

"Ontte."

"Ontte," I repeat. "Is that a yes?"

"Ontte," he says again and then, imitating me, he hisses, "*yess.*"

I shiver from head to toe. "It's my body. I'm allowed to do whatever I want with it," I assert with confidence I don't feel as my armpits sear and blood rushes from my head to my belly...and then lower still.

He grabs my hip and jerks me around to face him with one set of arms, and with the other, reaches above his head to the blue cable that stretches to the door. He yanks down. I shoot up. We're at eye level. He blinks from the side. I gulp down my fear, refusing to betray it — *just like she taught me.* Wait — who? A small splinter of a headache pinches my left temple but, like a needle, slides cleanly through.

I blink, not having to look up to meet his gaze for once. He doesn't speak. He just shakes his head slowly and I clench, waiting for punishment or...*or something magnificent.*

I lick my lips. He tilts his head and I feel his attention shift to my mouth. I lick my lips again. "Why are you mad? It's my pussy..."

"Centare," he sneers.

"Is that *no?*"

"Ontte," he says.

His gaze pulls down my body and he reaches for the front of my tunic. He hooks a finger into my collar and drags it down. The evidently flimsy material tears open way too easily, exposing me fully to his gaze. Warm air brushes over my body and I squeeze my thighs together. Without skipping a beat, pain flares across the tops of my legs as he slaps the sensitive between them.

"Ow!" I cry, trying to jerk my knees up higher to my chest, but he slaps them down and then uses his lower hands to spread my thighs apart.

I'm left gasping. Panting, really. We're only a couple feet apart. His chest is...so close to my nipples, which are pointed, yes, but I can't call them hard. *He's* hard. He's covered all over in thick, textured patches of rough skin, so rough it doesn't look like a sword could penetrate. I notice the plates lift in microscopic little pulses. It's fascinating. Just like everything about him. Including his fascination with me.

I jolt when he palms my left breast without preamble or warning. His hands are rough because there's that rough bioarmor on his palms, too. They feel so good against my sensitive skin. I'm *so* sensitive.

"You have an exoskeleton." I let my head fall back. "Agh… That feels amazing." I jolt when the pressure of three. more. hands. comes to join the first. "Oh my fucking god."

He laughs, low and deep. Throaty, it rumbles through him and tunnels its way through his hands and into me. My thighs try to squeeze together, but I forgot he's still got them spread. "Te'eno hnoor, heelee."

"Te-te-ono hunor?"

"Centare," he barks back, dropping to his knees. He pops my knees up over his shoulders and, even kneeling, he's so tall that my torso flops back until I'm nearly hanging parallel to the floor.

I glance down the length of my bare body and see his ridged silver pate gleaming in the electric blue light behind him, and in the orange lights embedded directly into the walls. He inhales deeply and I self-consciously wriggle back, but he uses two hands to latch onto my hips and yank me forward. His other two hands support my back.

"Centare?" I whisper, brain shorting, unable to remember what we were talking about.

He lifts up and frowns at me, his tongue retreating behind his shimmery square teeth. I squeeze his neck between my thighs and he pulls back even further.

"Centare? Re ontte?" At the word that means *yes*, he leans in and strokes his tongue up my core.

"Ontte!" I squeal and yank on my restraints, wanting to move my hands, but also exhilarated being at his mercy.

"Centare re ontte?" he repeats again, giving my labia a nip with his teeth. I jerk and jolt at every touch and caress. His hands are massaging my ass, prodding their way inward toward my tightest hole. He strokes it.

"Ontte," I shout again, tightening my ass cheeks, unsure if I want him there or not. "Ontte…"

He shoves his tongue into my pussy at the same time that he presses his finger against my clenching ass. It's a battle, one I lose, when he forces his way inside both holes at the same time. "Oh shit!"

He grumbles something around my pussy lips that I make zero effort to interpret. Instead, I yank on my chains, writhing in the only way — in every way — the position and the angle and the restraints allow. I groan and moan and whimper, making sounds that I feel I should be embarrassed about, but I can't remember why. Fuck it. Fuck that. *Fuck him. Fuck me.*

"Ontte, fuck me, *please.*"

He says something against my labia, biting and nipping at my lips in a way that hurts but in all the right ways. Meanwhile, his finger just sits inside my ass, hovering there like an unwanted guest that I've suddenly decided I want to throw down onto my bed and fuck raw. It's so *big.* It makes me wonder what his cock would feel like shoved inside so, so deep.

I'm so close, and yet… "My clit," I beg, voice torn and tortured. I don't even know if he can understand me with how hard my legs are clenched around his pointed ears. They lie flat to his head and, where my ears are curved, his are jagged up and down the back. He doesn't have much of an earlobe. All in all, a perfect combination for squeezing between my legs. I squeeze harder and he slaps my ass.

I gasp and jerk and unclench my legs reflexively as I try to pull myself away from the fleeting pain. He slaps me again, harder this time, while his hands on my hips yank me into his mouth. He devours me up and down, but he isn't spending enough time on my clit and he *knows* it. I know he does because earlier, he pressed…his palm… *Fuck.*

"Up!" I shout, voice warbled and desperate. I shout at the top of my lungs.

He lifts his head momentarily. One hand reaches up my body and kneads my left tit. He still has his thick digit in my asshole and I can tell in the narrowing of his gaze and the sudden smile that graces his wet lips that he knows what I mean and is so very pleased by it.

He licks my clit and I squeam — squeal? scream? yeah, squeam, "More!"

He shoves a second finger into my ass without warning. I start to panic at the fullness and the splitting, *magnificent* pain due to a severe lack of lube but, before I can voice any concerns or pleas, he latches onto my clit with his rough lips and sucks so hard, I can't decide which sensation to focus on — his hand in my ass, the one on my tit, his lips on my clit or the finger of yet a third hand that's found its way around my pussy lips and is stroking through them so tenderly, it freaks me out.

I'm freaked out.

I'm going to detonate.

Five.

Four.

Three…

"Holy goddamn fucking ontte!" I bellow to the cave around us at the same time that it shakes again, like explosions are rocking the surface. I can't find it in me to care. I *don't* care. There are no rules here. I don't have to care.

"Oh ontte!" I cry, dismayed when the pressure of his mouth on my clit jerks away momentarily. "Ontte, more! Please. I'm coming."

He sucks harder and a second orgasm rides the heels of the first. I spiral higher and can only feel the pain in my armpits distantly as I jerk wildly on my chains. It doesn't matter. I could pull both arms from the sockets and I wouldn't give a fuck. I shatter at the peak, like a hammer against glass. It fractures everywhere, cutting through everything, cutting through my body, cutting through my mind, but unlike the headaches, these splinters feel incredible. My skin pebbles and boils. My heart hammers and flutters. My breath — there is no breath. My eyes roll back into my skull, but I force them open. I want to watch him watch me come…

His gaze is locked on my face and when our eyes meet he groans. A mirrored moan roars out of me and I clench my soft thighs around his hard, rough cheeks and he groans deeper, the vibrations shooting through me and setting fire to the embers of the orgasms that are are left.

And then it's over, all at once. There is no come down, only a shuddering of my asshole around his fingers to the point of pain and the too sensitive sensation of his mouth against my clit that makes me cringe.

"Oh god. Stop, baby. Please, it's too much. I don't think I've orgasmed like that in…I don't fucking know. I…it hurts. My arms. Can you get me down? My ass. Be careful…" I'm mumbling incoherently, but he hears me and lowers my legs gently from around his shoulders. As he stands, he slips his hands around my waist.

Our bodies are flushed and my nipples are so sensitive, they feel like the tips of exposed electrical wires, sending shocks through me every time they scrape against his hardened bioarmor. He ducks his head underneath my bound arms and I rest my hands loosely on top of his spikes. Bearing my whole weight with one arm, he uses two other hands to massage my ass cheeks as he slowly, oh so slowly, removes his fingers from inside.

"Ohfff," I moan as the tip of his longest finger pops free. He sweeps his fantastic, filthy fingers through my pussy lips, swirling them around the entrance for a second before holding his palm up between us. He flicks my bottom lip with his fingers — his *wet* fingers. I can smell the arousal and the tang of my ass on his touch and stare up into his eyes, shocked by his gall.

"Are you serious?" I whisper.

He growls, jaw clenching and the plates along it lifting just enough for me to sense his warning. *There are no rules here, that means there is no shame. There is only want. What do I want? I want everything.* I part my lips and take a tentative taste of *me*, at first, and then I moan, fucking *loving* it. I close my lips over his fingers and suck. I suck hard.

"*Yess,*" he hisses and the sound vibrates my entire chest. He shoves his fingers down my throat and barks an order that I can't interpret, but when I bob my head up and down his fingers and choke down my own taste, I know for a fact that there are. no. rules.

And this is only the beginning.

5

Herannathon

Punished for our — for *her* — performance in the reaver market, the Eshmiri, though willing to release her from her prison, force me to leave my prize in her kintarr cell over the lunar. It's maddening, especially after what transpired between us.

I hadn't rutted the bound female even though it took every ounce of my willpower not to. I just…didn't want to rut her there. Not in an Eshmiri cell beneath a gladiator arena built for smaller creatures who can't participate in the more violent battles that take place above.

I want to rut her as Rhorkanterannu first rutted his female, in a place of honor, to worship her, to show her my value as more than just a killing machine or a male who made a mistake and claimed her when he shouldn't have.

When he really shouldn't have.

I shudder at the weight of the bolt in my pocket, and then force my mind to someplace else. To the way she shivered and shook. The way she did anything I asked. The way I had her body under my complete and total control — not just in her restraints, though those were shroving maddening, too — but beneath my touch. *Clit.* This is a special thing and I plan to worship it accordingly.

And her second hole. *Shrov, it was tight.* Mmmm. The thought of trying to seat myself inside of her *there* makes me want to squeal in delight. There will be time for this later, when she is returned to me in my tent. For now, it seems her more urgent desire is my seed in her womb. She did shout the term *kitling* several times. Unless…

I suddenly come up short, stopping dead in my tracks as I approach the arena doors. Beyond them, my prize hangs suspended in her kintarr crystal chamber. I am annoyed the Eshmiri need her up there for the duration of the games and slightly perturbed at the thought of the violence she sees all solar long. *And the violence I display. She has to know it's an act — a lucrative act that keeps her fed and me breathing.* But, I'm still a little embarrassed. She's seen me fighting at my peak, in my prime in the pits of Evernor where true champions are made.

She's also seen me kill.

I am more than this beast Evernor has created.

And yet, I must put on this act if I want to win, if I want to win *her,* and if I want to win our safety, so I firm up my fists and, when the doors open, raise them above my head towards the highest peak of the dome.

The suns' harsh rays sweep my body, pricking me like the awareness of being watched by a foreign set of eyes. And I am being watched, not by one creature but by thousands — tens of thousands. The Tournament of Evernor is the most talked about event in all the Quadrants. It was tricky to get a spot in the competition, but there were few Niahhorru entrants this year and none from Rhorkanterannu's mothership. I was a hot commodity.

And now I've got to prove why.

I take a slow turn of the arena, walking the perimeter and growling and snarling up at the stands. The higher I can drive the bidding, the bigger my wins, the better my odds of securing my prize and even potentially, the communications disruptor I'm after and, along the way, a salvation disc or two. *Not enough for the key, though. That requires an entirely separate game, one waged with Manila. Either that, or thievery…*

I hiss up at the crowd and, when an unsuspecting Oroshi lowers his tentacles towards me, I launch up, latch onto one green limb and drag him from the stands and into the pit. The crowd goes wild. I toss the Oroshi into the center of the arena where I leave him to be scooped up by Eshmiri patrols and quickly returned to his place in the premium seats.

He's swarmed by Oroshi females who gurgle and gush over him while he wipes great green globules of sweat from his amorphous jelly-tentacle face. He sees like all Oroshi see, through vibrations in the air captured by the suckers that ribbon up their tentacles in subtle patterns and swirls. I get the sense he's trying hard to avoid attracting my notice again because all of his suckers are facing distinctly away from me now. I chuckle.

Looking up at the prizes dangling there to shroving tantalize us lonely, wayward fighters is torture in itself. At least she's clothed this solar, courtesy of another shroving Eshmiri trade. Trading with them is worse than trading with any pirate.

I snort at the thought, knowing that they feel the same. No one likes trading with us Niahhorru. On Kor, *our* rules reign. I can't wait to get back there. I can't wait to get off this shroving rock. Seven more fights. Seven more kills. Seven more…*surprises.*

"Shroving reavers…"

The doors at the end of the arena roll open slowly and I groan while the crowd shrieks, the crescendo making my ears twitch. Visibly, I welcome the Egama warrior I fought the solar previous, the one who saved himself using his salvation disc. *I hope he has another. He's going to need it, the fool.* Why did he come back here? He couldn't beat me the solar previous with an opponent and now he's alone…

Ah…

I see…

Shroving Eshmiri. They gave him a weapon.

He raises an erdpremor over his head and the throngs go shroving mental. A Voraxian weapon, it translates to *star saw* and looks like a large bow with outward facing tines, similar to the hiannru growing out of my back. I squint a little harder. They *are* made out of hiannru tines, likely from a fallen Niahhorru opponent in a previous tournament. It's like they wanted to level the field. The Egama's size alone should have done that, but this? To use the hiannru of a fallen pirate against *me*? The insult.

I grin ravenously.

I don't like to kill, but this Egama warrior has asked for what is coming to him…

This might actually be fun.

I roll my shoulders back and meet the Egama's gaze across the arena. He looks at me with disdain, brandishing his hiannru erdpremor toward me with a grin of his own. This might be my only chance to fight without any restraint, like the savage that I am, certainly not anything like a kit. I glance above me at the pink kintarr cage, glittering in the light, and the scantily dressed female kneeling inside of it. She looks... concerned. I don't like that at all. Pirates fear *nothing*.

The Egama releases a battle cry and I begin sprinting towards him within the same breath. I can feel his lumbering steps through the foundations of the arena as he matches me stride for stride, his carrying him twice the distance mine do. The dome shudders and shakes and I know that, all around us, bets are flying wildly. I can see the tally in the holoscreens propped up on the fronts of some Eshmiri flyers, the patrollers shouting commentary to try to goad the betting even higher. I ignore all of it.

I focus on the brush of the filtered air on my face, the heat releasing from my body beneath my plates, the taste of the Egama on the wind. My hands flex. He cuts his erdpremor towards me, wielding it with skill even though it isn't a weapon native to his species. I bend over backwards, leaning so far back that my own hiannru sweep the sands as I slide forward on one knee before lurching back up into a crouch. From there, I don't hesitate.

I spring up, jump and claw for his throat. He dives to the side so that I only just slice my claws across the skin of his back. Egama skin isn't as tough as a pirate's and I gouge five parallel lines into his mottled green back. Darker green blood, the color of vevari tree leaves, cascades down his back with the texture and viscosity of oil. It splashes over the packed sands and my feet land in it with a thud as we square off against one another. He drags his erdpremor through the air and I leap over the blade. I latch onto his shoulder and spin, my hiannru gouging deep into the side of his face.

He howls and his one great green eye focuses with aching intensity on my feet before moving up to my arms. He charges and I skid to the right, but he anticipates the move and does something I don't expect, but should have. He *hurls* his erdpremor straight at me.

The blades catch my chest and take me off of my feet. The pain as the hiannru tines implant in my plates is *intense* — almost as bad as the pain that ripples down my spine as I land hard on my own hiannru before falling to the side.

Most of the erdpremor tines meet my plates but I can feel two places below my bottom left rib where they sink into the gaps in between. Shrov...an amateur shroving mistake...

I roar as I grab onto the bow of the erdpremor and lift it off of and out of my body. I roll onto one knee. I need to move faster, faster, shroving faster... He's almost on me now.

I slam the spikes of the erdpremor into the hard ground and I watch the confusion play out across the approaching Egama's face. He expected me to use it. I just needed to distract him. Because he doesn't expect me to cartwheel over the top of the erdpremor so that I stand directly in front of him.

I show him my back. The erdpremor I use as a brace and I need it as the Egama slams into my tines. I grip the hand holds and slam my foot against the underside of the bow, using the tines to keep me standing against the full weight of an Egama charging towards me. I roar, this time in pain. It's pure *agony*. For us both.

The Egama releases a bellowing moan that completely drowns out the sound of my cries. The erdpremor bends and flexes underneath my grip as he totters forward, threatening to flatten me. He rears back, sparing me — sparing us both — from that eventuality as he tries to avoid my tines. But, one thing I didn't anticipate? How deeply my hiannru embed in his skin… and how hard will it be to extract them.

I groan as he starts to fall back, pulling me with him. How shroving embarrassing, I think, what with my girl hanging overhead like a star in the night sky, encased in kintarr, watching this. It's embarrassing enough that I lifted my plates enough to let that shroving Egama skewer me. And now?

"Augh!" I grab hold of the erdpremor but the shroving thing springs from the ground, the hard handle bonking me in the chin as I flail onto my back on top of the Egama. I land like a beetle with all six of my limbs flailing in the air as I try to roll off of him, but can't. Meanwhile, I feel his breath shortening, his heartbeat quieting and his limbs finally going completely still. He's dead.

He's dead and I'm stuck, and though the crowd is too busy cheering my name to laugh — for now — I'm shroving sure it'll start soon if I can't free myself from this. I'll be *shroved* if I become a joke in this arena. There go all my shroving privileges, the leniency, the favors I collect after each battle…

A slim shadow appears above me, blocking out some of the oppressive light cast through the dome from Evernor's many suns. I lift my hands, expecting to see a team of Eshmiri patrollers laughing at me until their tiny heads shake off of their meaty necks. Instead, I see something wholly unexpected. *Someone.*

My prize bends down and the front of her tunic drapes open so that I almost get a glance at her lovely tits, but she's too determined to be appropriately ogled as she grabs my upper arms by the wrists and starts to pull. She doesn't make it very far, but the crowd doesn't seem to care. I thought that I'd heard their maximum volume, but apparently I was wrong. I can't even hear my own breath over the sounds they make.

They're tossing favors down into the sands — gaudy, extravagant bouquets of mok bir batons, a few bottles of undoubtedly potent alcohol, an Oosa rug, a helos staff, a hevarr hide, plus a hundred more things I can't bother to categorize.

"Are you looking down my shirt?" she blurts suddenly. *"Again?"*

I grin. "Ontte."

She's sweating under the strain of trying to lift me and, at my pronouncement, drops my arms like hot stones and shoves her hands onto her hips. The crowd seems to love it because more and more favors shower her — one, a lightning stick that nearly clips her arm. It would have had she not stepped out of the way with surprising quickness and hurled insults back up into the stands in her own tongue.

Pain ignored, I roll up into a seat and launch myself off of the Egama just as another stone — a block of kintarr — is lobbed from the stands far, far too close to her head. Her soft head. She's got a tender skull. I cradle it as I fall onto her and cover her body with my own.

This time, I actively feel things — softer, lighter things like fabric or furs — come to cover us. They pile high enough that they blot out the light from above, leaving us alone in the middle of the heap beneath it.

She stares up at me with her eyes rounded. They're black and brown and white, her eyes, but as I'm staring at her now from so close, I see that we are not wholly dissimilar. My eyes have xitrine fluid within them that creates the luminescence. Hers must be filled with the same, because even though the brown doesn't shift as her focus does, the black within it does, becoming bigger and smaller and then bigger again the longer she stares.

The brown isn't flat, either. It has such incredible depth. I want to study it more, except the black has grown larger and larger and soon, the brown is just a thin ring around it. *Fascinating*. So alien. I want to explore more of it. More of *her*. I lean forward to capture her lips with mine, but my feet slide over the ground, slipping through blood and I collapse too much of my weight onto her.

She releases a light "oomph," and I roll to the side, ripping blankets off of us. The crowd has never been louder as I roll up onto my knees and then my feet and pull my prize up with me.

"Are you alright?" she asks as I take her hand. She tries to loop my upper arm over her shoulder, but the socket is at the height of her head.

She offers no support at all and I laugh, "Never better." I kiss the top of her head and, when she grabs my lower arm at the wrist and drags it across the back of her neck, I let her. She offers herself as a crutch to support me and, even though I'm bleeding heavily from two deep puncture wounds to my chest, I stand straight, not wanting to wilt.

I raise my arms, all but the one draped over her shoulders. The crowd heaves, bodies moving like the waves of a faraway ocean. My prize bends slightly beneath the glare of their violent adulation and the rays of the sweltering suns, but I can't have that. We can't. Pirates bend to no one.

"Take your praise, piratess." She doesn't understand me, so I prod her in the center of the back, forcing her shoulders to unfurl as her chest puffs out. An Oosa contingent in the crowd suddenly blazes so brightly that their combined colors, not to mention their perfectly circular shape, make them appear like an Eshmiri torch.

A low growl picks up in my throat. I don't speak Oosa, nor does my translator allow me to interpret their colors or trills, but I know what they want. It's common knowledge across the cosmos that the Oosa have been trying to get their hands on a human ever since Reoran, their ruler, first met the Voraxian hybrid queen.

The Oosa love to mate with everyone, anyone, but most of all? The exotic, that which can't be had. And there's only one human in all of Evernor right now. Only one human outside of the protection of the Voraxians in Quadrant Four. Only one human outside of Reqama, under Niahhorru control.

And they can't have her. *Te'eno hnoor.* She's *mine.*

I push her toward the tunnel entrance and, as I do, I step between her body and the Oosa to block their view. I also slip my hand beneath her outer arm and tap it until she understands she's meant to raise it. She offers the crowd a rather strange waving gesture I've seen humans do before and I laugh — and then I choke as pain grips me and reminds me that I need to get my shroving ass to a merillian bath *soon*.

I avoid clutching my injuries until we make it through the arena's entrance and the shadows swallow us whole. From there, I crumble.

She chirps as I fall, the yeeyar glider appearing beneath me as I call it forward with the token in my ear. "Come." I gesture up at her.

Eshmiri patrollers and cleaning crews are already filling the tunnel around us. The doors remain open and I don't want to linger here, not with my black blood bleeding all over the place. I close my eyes for longer than a standard blink when she still doesn't move.

I feel warmth beside me a moment later and the piratess pokes at the glider beneath us. It wrinkles and shivers beneath her aggressive stroke. Responsive, yeeyar, it wants a command from her. She's quick to give it. "Take us back to the tent."

The yeeyar glider shoots down the hall, descending into the Below. I fade in and out for a moment and I can hear her hovering over me, making small sounds. I'm not sure if she's worried about the yeeyar or me, but I pretend it's the latter and feel myself smile as I drift in and out of dreams.

The air is warm, made warmer by her body heat. I grope her anywhere I can, wanting to touch, to ground, to be grounded. I grab her fleshy hip, wondering why it isn't so lush as Deena's, but pleased by her regardless. These humans come in so many different shapes and colors, each one astounding and beautiful.

"Into the tent," she says and the air whooshing past my ears stills, the heat intensifies as does my scent. Only now, it's tainted. Not a lot, not enough, but a little.

Enough for me to know that she was here and not just a figment of my imagination.

And she's still here, and right now, I think she's... trying to take care of me. Her hands flutter over my plates. She's got the fabric of her tunic balled up and is pressing it to the wound to try to staunch the blood flow — a kind, but useless effort.

Her voice is light as she whispers soft curses and meaningless platitudes that I think are meant to soothe me. The sensation is so foreign to me and I want to revel in it for a while longer, but not if it could cost me hours of healing, and right now, she's leading me to the wrong tub.

I issue a silent command for the yeeyar glider to stop. She squeals as it deposits us in the back of the tent. On the right and left are two separate curtains, one side for washing, the other side for wasting. I head right and peel the curtain back. Two tubs stand full and ready and waiting for me, as per my instruction — and Eshmiri protocol if they want their fighters to be able to continue to fight more than one solar. The one farther back has steaming pink water. The one nearest to me is bright purple. I groan, relieved as I sink into it the latter tub, fitting my tines through the maleable material at the back.

The merillian is thick and gooey and clings to my skin like blood-sucking micro-organisms, because that's exactly what they are. Feasting on the broken flesh, they excrete fresh cells, repairing any injury from the slightest cut to the deepest burn. And this shroving stuff is expensive. And — what the shrov is she doing?

She's followed me back here and is kneeling next to the tub, staring down at it in concern and confusion. If she could understand, I'd explain to her that it's merillian, a lifesaving substance harvested primarily in Quadrant Eight, but also a recent export of the small human planet, Heimo. I wince, thinking about Heimo and the humans I *should* have reunited her with on Reqama…but didn't. Because I wanted her, so I took her because I'm a shroving pirate.

And now we're shroving here.

Without any way to communicate.

Stuck on Evernor for the duration of the tournament.

And it's clear that the Eshmiri and the spectators have noticed her…

As my good Lemoran friend would say… Pagh!

"Is this…water?" she asks, surprising me. She stretches her hand towards it, but I catch her wrist and place it outside of the tub. Merillian works on one body at a time. To mix can lead to gene splicing in the worst of ways. The Sky are known to engage in this practice as part of their experiments. They don't always work. They don't *often* work but, when they *do*, the results are violent and terrible.

"Centare." I give her a soft squeeze as I release her and sink further into the merillian. "You can bathe there." I gesture to the tub to my left, separated from where I lie by about two long strides.

Curiosity colors her expression and her little nose twitches, yet she trusts me enough to approach the pink liquid — but not enough to jump straight in. Unlike the liquid I found her in the first time, this water is loaded with healing salves, which gives it its pink hue. She tests the water first with the back of her hand, then with her fingers. Good girl.

She sighs softly to herself when she slips her hand in up to the wrist and I try to remember my injuries at the sight of her eyelashes fluttering and her lips parting like that to reveal her pink tongue. It's about the only thing we have in common when it comes to our appearance.

She stands up fully and tucks her red hair behind her pale ear. "It's safe?" she asks me.

I groan, the pleasure of her question radiating through me like pain through a wound but blissful. "Ontte," I answer. It feels so shroving good when she nods down at the water, deciding then to step into it. Deciding then to trust me.

And then she has to go and ruin it.

She turns her back to me as she starts to slip out of her tunic. I hiss, "Centare."

The volume of my voice comes out louder than intended and she whips around, holding her fists up in what I can only assume she intends as a fighting stance. I snort and narrow my gaze at her fists and then lift my eyes to meet hers. "Centare." I drop my stare to her tunic, glaring at it with implication since we don't have words for now. We only have this.

Her lips part and her black eyes consume her brown ones. She hesitates, but I don't back down…and neither does she. She never does. And I know she won't. So, I can't be the one to break first when she slips her shoulders free of the sheathe and lets it fall to the floor. She raises one of the two furs above her eyes and I get the distinct impression that she's taunting me.

Shrov that. I break immediately.

She lifts one leg and steps into the tub and I bite my back teeth together so hard I half expect them to shatter in my mouth. Would be worth it. I'd swallow the shards happily at the sight of her perfect pink slit, remembering the taste of her essence sliding down the back of my throat.

The sound she makes as she slides in all the way up to her throat is divinity itself — that is, if we pirates believed in anything beyond the power of perseverance and wile. My eyelids flutter and my arms struggle to hold my body upright. Shrov. The effects of the merillian are working hard and fast and the results of the day are pulling me down. Pulling my eyes shut.

Stay awake.

"Are you okay?" she whispers.

I smile, lean my head against the back of the tub and exhale, "Life must persist." Sevrenn iahndru lat. The anthem of the Niahhorru. "And looking at you? You look like life itself." Her cheeks are flushed and her rounded shoulders gleam. I can't wait to take a bite out of them.

"Later," I mumble, eyelids drawing to the sides and momentarily obscuring my vision. "Ontte, later…"

"You don't look so good…"

I close my eyes and let my muscles finally release into the healing merillian pool. If I stop fighting, it'll work faster. There are platters of food in the tent. She won't have any reason to leave. She doesn't even know how. I can relax. Ontte…and when I wake, I'll find her a shroving translator and get the one thing I want most — the only thing I want right now, salvation discs and communications disruptors and Sky keys be damned.

I'll get her name.

6

Nalia

He's been asleep for hours. I mean, I think it's been hours. There aren't any clocks here. But it's been long enough for me to eat one entire tray of weird ass foods, take a nap, eat more food, go to the bathroom behind the other curtain, explore all of the chests, find things I mostly can't identify by sight, function or name, check on the alien in the purple bathtub and make sure he's still breathing…

He's still breathing, but shallowly, like he's in a deep, deep sleep. I mean…he deserves it. He's been fighting small wars every day, and then he rescued me from food fight jail, gave me the best orgasms of my life, and got gutted by a twenty-foot-tall cyclops with a bow decorated by spikes instead of arrows.

He's done so much for me.

The thought makes me uneasy. I don't really know my past, but I know my present and I know that I'm no damsel in distress. Well, I am, but I don't need a knight in shining…silver skin to save me. Well, I do a little. But I don't like the feeling that I owe him something.

I need…I need to help him.

And I can't help him if I can't fucking talk to him. I need to know what's going on.

I stand up so suddenly my head spins, a headache looming on the horizon but refraining, for once, from cutting me down at the knees. I move out of the room where I've been lurking over him in the tub like a creeper and make my way out into the middle of the tent where the black flying carpet hovers expectantly. I don't know how it works exactly, but when I gave it verbal commands — even in my own language — it responded without problem.

I clear my throat and point at the carpet. "You there. Flying carpet. Move two feet forward."

It jolts instantaneously, moving so fast it makes me jump. I lay a palm over my chest and can feel my heart beating way faster than it should be. Shit. I think I really didn't expect this damn thing to work. Then, at least I'd have had an excuse not to venture out into the great cavernous abyss beyond the tent and just stay put and wait...

"And be a damsel," I finish lamely. I shake my head and move forward, climbing onto the magic carpet. Its surface is slick like velvet beneath my folded legs. There's nothing to hold onto, so I slide onto my belly and grip the front edge of the mat, trying to disperse my weight as evenly as possible across the smooth surface.

"Lordamercy." This does not feel safe. Then again, I'm on an alien gladiator planet, fully planning on getting railed by a scarily hot silver-skinned giant who's very, very good with all four of his hands. Nothing's safe here. And I'm learning to be okay with that.

"Here goes nothing." I clear my throat. "Carpet, take me out into the cave." We jolt forward and I squeal loudly, wildly, as wind whips my face and the unfamiliar and competing smells of this chaotic world unfurl and wrap around me.

"Slow down!" The thing starts to jerk to a stop and I scream as I slide forward. "Slowly, goddammit!" The carpet responds and, after a couple more terrifying jerks, levels itself out and soon we're moving along together at a pace where I can actually breathe and also see what's going on.

This place is *insane*. Pure and perfect in its dysfunction. I find my lips tugging up into a wary grin as we pass over rocky plateaus covered in dwellings of all different styles and shapes and colors.

Tents made of bright fabric cover one surface in its entirety. A ledge jutting out from one wall has what looks like hundreds of bat-like creatures hanging from the underside of it. Creepy. Black teepees atop another platform form stalls that people — *creatures* — wander between, a market from everything I can see.

It doesn't look quite the same as the market where I started the food fight, but it looks similar enough, and that's where the alien had been taking me to find a translator… Maybe, they'll sell translators at this one.

"Descend to the surface of that rocky ledge there." I point, though the carpet is already in motion. It seems to know what I want the moment I think it and I wonder if my thoughts are what it's responding to, more than the commands I give it. Fascinating.

Carefully, I dodge other flying crafts making their way on and off of the rock. Some are more like those metal cage things the announcers in the arena use, but others are just as baffling as the contraption underneath me. Some are flat and clear, like flying plates, others have undulating surfaces that make it possible for the occupant to maneuver into small crevices.

The strangest of the bunch has to be the one the jellyfish-looking creature is riding. He's — she's? — all tentacles, no face at all, and the thing around it is a gelatinous blob that makes it impossible to distinguish where its jelly body ends and the hovering machine begins. I think it's watching me as I pass by to the right of it. Unsure of what to do, I wave at it. It lifts a tentacle in response and the suckers suck at me. I smile and, for some reason, that little gesture more than anything settles the raging tattoo of my heart. Then the jelly man speeds off towards the other side of the market below, moving past me, acting like the sight of me is totally normal. Like I belong here.

I can do this.

"I can do this," I whisper under my breath as I touch down onto the surface.

I draw far fewer stares than I expected to. Instead, people — beings — seem to be pouring down the street, urgently headed somewhere I can't quite see. A foot above the ground, I step off of the carpet and look down at it, remembering that the alien in my corner had managed to make it fold up and store it.

"Make yourself smaller," I tell it and it shrinks about a foot in every direction. "Something I can hold in the palm of my hand or, better yet, wear like a bracelet." *Whoosh.*

In an elegant flourish, it molds to fit like a cuff around my left wrist. I smile at it. "Good carpet." And give it a little pat. Then I make my way down the street, wondering if I might also be able to buy some shoes…

Hmph.

A few stalls in, it becomes apparent to me that this isn't actually a marketplace. The stalls, most of which are empty, seem to be hosting some sort of tournament of their own. But it's not a *fighting* tournament. I think…I think it's a *game*…

I like games.

Hm. I wonder where that thought came from.

Large crowds gather around just a few of the tents on the road and periodically the crowd bucks with roars and shouts and howls and clicks and whistles.

Hands and tentacles and paws and fins exchange what look like some kind of currency — flat silver, sometimes black discs. I frown, recognizing that I don't have anything to trade and that I probably should go back and hunt around my four-armed friend's tent for some discs, but I'm too curious about the game to go back now, and worse, I want to play, or at the very least, gamble on the outcome.

I like gambling.

Oh boy.

I'm one of the shorter creatures in the crowd and most of the creatures shorter than I am can fly so that doesn't help me much. Nope. If I want to see anything, I'm going to have to push my way to the front. Navigating tentacles and smushy round balls of beings that glow from the inside out, not to mention the giggling thugs wrapped in patchwork linens that run this whole operation and the flying creatures shouting insults from above is…kinda fun.

I'm smiling a little devious smile by the time I manage to shove up to the front of the crowd overlooking the table. I watch two rounds — identifiable only as such by the way the crowd releases two bouts of collective roars, and in the way two contestants leave the table only to be replaced by two others.

It's these rotating people — beings — that I know are the players. All of the players are identifiable by the sticks they hold in their hands. Some sticks are large and ornately wreathed. Others are small and stocky. Some look like they've got blades on the sides while others look like they might be electric. Some definitely *are* electric by the way other sticks sizzle when they bounce off of them.

It takes another six rounds before I decide two things:

One — I *think* I know how to play the game.

And two — I want in.

Winners take home huge sacks of chips. Okay, maybe not huge, but some chips anyways. And some is better than none. I *need* a fucking translator, shoes, and a freaking comb would be nice. Not that I'm trying to impress the four-armed alien I left behind, or anything. No, definitely not that. It means absolutely nothing at all that the mere thought of him makes my pussy pulse like it has its own heartbeat. It's definitely got its own mind. A one-track kinda mind.

As the cheering dies down, jittery nerves rattle up and down my spine. I've got to say something *now*, if I want to say anything at all, and if I want to be noticed, I'm going to have to say it *loud*. Now that I've been standing here as long as I have, it's like I've ceased to be something surprising to these creatures. They're more interested in the game and I…I like that.

I clear my throat. "I want to play."

The table is matte black, located about hip height and, when I lean forward and press my palms into it, I can feel energy vibrating through it like a current. Across the table, another tentacled creature with no discernable eyes or mouth wriggles three green liquid-looking limbs at me. They're speaking, but I don't know what they're saying, only that they sound pissed.

I lift up my hands, showing both palms — as *if* that gesture translates — and repeat just a little louder, "I want to play."

My voice cracks. The beings closest to the table hush a bit. There's a bunch of glancing and limb throwing, sticks raised in the air and used to make even more compelling gestures. Everyone seems to have an opinion on the subject when one voice cuts through the others, loud and crisp.

I turn and watch the female saunter through the crowd, surprised and a little annoyed to find that I recognize her. *That's* the female my alien was attempting to negotiate with. Friend or foe, I couldn't really tell. More than friend, maybe? Well, I don't like that a bit. I lift an eyebrow and watch her skeptically as she reaches the head of the table.

She smiles at me and lifts her cyborg wrist to her mouth. "So, you want to play?" Her voice comes out mechanically, gravelly and awkwardly chopped together…and it's the most beautiful sound I've ever heard because for the first time in however many days that I've woken up here, I can fucking understand someone.

"Uh, yeah," I stutter.

She grins. She makes me nervous. The devious way she watches me begs consideration, but, I'm here.

"Ontte," I repeat, "I want to play."

"You don't know how and I have no time to teach you," she says, like she doesn't care one way or another.

"I do know how."

She tips her head to the side, long black hair swirling around her shoulders like she's underwater. It moves all on its own. It's lovely and fascinating. "You don't have any batons, and mok bir batons can't be given out or traded. Not here anyway. A player must come with that, at least."

My mind fires. I'd been considering this and my solution is a risky one. But I don't see any other way. I move my hand to the bracelet on my left arm and I'm surprised to feel it move without me having to speak to it. The bracelet drops down into my palm and separates, forming two separate black sticks, each about a foot long and an inch and a half thick.

The crowd oohs and titters and clicks at that. A winged being points at me as it speaks conspiratorially with one of the creatures dressed in rags. My pulse beats harder. Shit. Maybe, this wasn't a good idea.

"I've got batons," I say instead with a confidence whose provenance I can't place.

The female blinks her large, glittery black eyes at me — she blinks from the side, just like my alien does. I don't know why that surprises me. It's certainly not more surprising than her orange face or the buzzing fly-looking creature hovering near her left shoulder.

She waves it away and narrows her eyes. "You have nothing to bet."

I've been thinking about that, too, and that's where I've been stumped. I literally don't own anything, not even the batons-slash-glider I borrowed — *stole* — off the four-armed alien back in the tent. I lick my lips when her eyes twitch. I can tell where her gaze is pointed by the way the light glints off of the round orbs of her eyes, even though she, like most creatures I've seen so far, doesn't have irises or pupils. And right now she's looking down at my oversized tunic, reminding me of my savior and captor for the second time.

"You want to fuck me?" I ask, genuinely confused.

The crowd goes wild, bodies pushing into mine from the back. I can feel a sticky, round ball of a being push right up against me, a probe separating from the rest of the blue ball and poking the backs of my knees. I turn and bang the blue ball over the…the head?…with one of my batons, winning a gale of cheers and cries from the crowd surrounding it.

The blue ball falls back and I turn to face the female. She's smiling widely, wildly now, revealing all of her pointy white teeth. She runs her cyborg hand up through her hair. Away from her mouth, the word comes out alien when she says, "Centare." Then, she drops her arm back to her lips and repeats, "No. Not *me*. But you are… exquisite. If you offer yourself to the table champion, I'll waive the participation fee." *The ante. I know that, because I've gambled before.*

I grit my teeth. "I'm already with…" I don't even know his name. Fuck. "I'm already with a champion. The gladiator. You might have seen him? He's got four arms and harpooned a cyclops today."

"And where is he now?" I didn't think she would care about that flimsy half-truth, but she does pause, her eyes do dart across the crowd, searching…

"He's…resting."

She shakes her head, smoothing her free hand down her gorgeous, silky black dress. "Pity." She smiles again, not sounding the least bit sad at all. "So, do we have a deal?"

"If I lose, I have to have sex with the winner?"

"Ontte."

"And if I win, I collect the winnings of the table?"

She nods. "Centare. You collect the winnings of your round."

I nod. Makes sense. "Fine. But I want something else."

"What?" she snaps.

"I want a translator."

She makes a gesture with her fingers, sweeping two through the air in a way that sort of makes me think of an eye roll. "Centare…"

"I'm betting a lot more than a few chips."

"Chips? You mean tokens?"

"I'm betting a lot more than anyone else." I point my batons at her chest. "I'll come back to play tomorrow with tokens. These are the stakes today only."

The crowd intervenes, shouting at the female, overwhelming her. I notice that the bots floating over her head start puffing gasses out of their bases that cause the crowd to edge away from her, discontent and grumbling. She holds up her free, orange hand and I can tell she isn't happy by the twist of her expression, even as she forces a smile.

"Three games of six. That's how you win. You take over for whoever is struck out next."

"We have a deal, then?" I ask her.

She hesitates, glancing down at my tattered, threadbare dress and the lack of shoes on my feet. She snorts, "Deal." *She isn't the first to underestimate me.*

I can do this.

The crowd cheers and I'm jostled into position between one flying creature who stands grounded at my height — a female with a broken wing — and the blue rolling thing beaming light from within. They hold a baton that glows a luminescent green, reminding me of a lava lamp. *A lava lamp?* I can't even picture it, but I can feel my mind pushing, pushing, reaching for some long-lost memory and scraping at my headache in the process. No no no no no. Stay *back*. Now isn't the time for the past. Now is the time for me to take what I want.

Everything.

I grin around at the other players and, to the orange-faced female, nod once. "Let's play." I lift my black batons up.

7

Nalia

The game is like a cross between table tennis, jacks, and full-blown anarchy. Cheating is allowed, stealing other players' chips — tokens — is allowed, flinging things that aren't your sticks — batons — is allowed. The only thing that isn't allowed is getting hit. And getting hit with your own baton? Ooph. That'll get you laughed off the table right quick.

I manage to bat someone's baton away using my own and I hit so hard, my aim shockingly true, that it rebounds and nails them in the forehead. The winged creature tumbles from the air, falling into the crowd, and even though he only had one out, he was ejected from the game instantly. A new rule, I guess, one of the many — or maybe one of the few. It's hard to say. All I know for sure is to dodge every baton flung my way.

I duck the first baton fired at me from across the table. The second is deflected by a side baton that's tossed in. When that baton hits the first, it constitutes an out for the thrower, too. In the frenzy, I throw my right baton down as hard as I can, towards the table. It hits the table and springs up high, arching over the top of the head of a short, rag-wearing creature and poking an orange-skinned being in the eye.

A baton is coming at me at the same time. I bat it from the air with my own, but the freaking thing *splits* and I don't manage to hit the second one. I take the baton to the chest on the bounce and the crowd shrieks.

"Fuck." It's my second out. I have two outs, two wins.

The game goes on for some time, me not hitting anyone, but also deflecting every hit. Tokens are traded and passed around and I can feel creatures close at my back, crowding me in. An attractive blue-skinned male stands behind me. He has horns and I can feel him lowering his head and brushing them against my back every so often. I think it's getting him off by the way he's grunting. I wait for my opportunity.

Yes — or rather, *ontte*.

The flying creature launches its spiked baton at me. I turn around, grab the male by the horns and wrench him forward. He takes the baton to the cheek, howling in pain, and the crowd loses its ever-loving mind when I fire both my batons at the same time, throwing them in opposite directions.

My aim is extraordinary. I mean, even I can say that it's really fucking good. Too good. Hm. Maybe, I was a professional some-kind-of-thrower in my previous life. Whatever the case and whatever or whoever I was, I wish I could remember more, because this skill is working for me in this universe.

I hit a cyclops giant that looks a lot like the one my alien fought in the ring. I hit him on the back of his gigantic hand when he's too slow to deflect my baton's trajectory. The other baton, meanwhile, manages to land a bounce off of one of the floating discs — because, of course, the table is rigged and additional elements occasionally sprout out of it seemingly at random — and hit the tentacle creature in one of its many baton-wielding limbs.

The two hits come as my third and fourth, winning me everything on the table at that time. It's a tricky business, winning, because I realize as I see two new players approach the table — a horned menace with a stack of chips half as big as I am and a tiny flying creature that looks like a giant golden fly — that it's not enough just to win this game, really. Because *when* to win is important, too.

Dammit.

I didn't win half as much as I could have, I muse as I'm escorted through the crowd and away from the table by a group of four rag-wearing, laughing creatures armed with batons that look electric and shoot lightning in various shades of blue. They wield them wantonly, zapping beings with every step they take whether those beings deserve it or not. I chuckle under my breath and shake my head at their recklessness.

My bag of winnings is still heavy enough to cause a stagger in my step. I let this console me as I try not to think about the riches I left behind. *Next time.* Next time? *Ontte*...now that I've gambled once here with these aliens, I want to do it again.

My, er...*guards*...take me to a big cone tent illuminated on the inside by more of those floating balls of light. They're beautiful, really, and cast everything in an ethereal glow. Every*one*. I wave my free hand around at the other creatures assembled before me. There are four of them, me making five, not counting the band of baton-wielding brothers.

I recognize a couple of the others as earlier winners from the table and frown when I note that *all* of their bags are much bigger than mine. Boo. *I want to win.* The four gathered winners wave enthusiastically back.

Two of the winners are giggling creatures, both male. At least, they *look* male — *all* of the giggling ones I've seen look male so far, making me wonder if I'm missing something. An orange creature with fins on the side of his face is another victor. Then there's a grey flying creature that looks female, I think.

I sit on what looks like an upturned crate between her and the giggling ones. She smiles at me to show all of her sharp, jagged teeth and I smile back, not fazed by them in the least.

She says something to me and I shrug. "I don't have a translator," I tell her and she rises up from her seat on wings that look paper-thin and gestures angrily at the ones with the batons.

They reply and I feel annoyed that a conversation is being had about me without my intervention, but I fully expect the orange female with the pretty eyes and the cutting tongue to hold true to her promise. I wonder if she'll tell my alien what I bartered in order to get a seat at the table. The thought makes me nervous and I chew on my bottom lip. I hope not.

I really, *really* hope not.

Time trickles by. The others make conversation and I sit by dejectedly, watching it unfold, unable to take even the most rudimentary stab at what they're saying. Eventually, we're joined by two more creatures. One is a huge being, shy of my alien's height by a half-foot but just as broad. He looks totally unlike anyone I've seen before.

The male that saunters into the tent is bright green with pink and gold hair that falls straight to his waist. His chest is bare and he's got abs and pecs and eyes and a nose and yeah, there are bumps on his face, too, forming little hills where his eyebrows should be, but holy *hotness*, he's beautiful.

I blush when he looks at me and I gawk when I see what he's dragging behind him. He's got not one, but *two* huge black sacks and they're so heavy he has to heft one high over his shoulder and drag the other behind him. He takes the upturned crate directly across from me and is still staring directly into my eyes in a way that makes me super glad my alien *isn't* here because I feel like I'm doing something very wrong, even though the male hasn't even said anything to me yet.

A breeze passes through the tent, pulling my attention away from him in time to see the ringleader of this here operation sweep into the space. She takes inventory of the rather, errr…odd group before her before settling her glare on me.

Her hostility falls away the instant she takes a step. She's grinning as she comes up to me and slaps her left hand over my right ear hard enough that I think, for just a second, this might be an attack. Then, she does the same with her right.

I feel something *wriggling* against the sides of my face and then a splitting pain cuts through everything, reminding me that it's been a while since I've had a headache. Sharp and sudden, I tuck my head, bracketing my temples between my hands and collapsing my elbows onto my knees.

"What the fuck?" I murmur harshly under my breath as my vision fades to black for a second before it starts to clear.

"*Fawk*,...hm. A new expression. I like it…"

"Holy shit!" I lurch up and look at the orange-faced female as my headache continues to pound. It doesn't matter. I'm ecstatic. I grin at her wildly. "Was that a translator or something?"

"Or something." She sweeps her black hair over her bare shoulders and juts her chest forward. She's wearing a black dress of sorts, the material delicate enough that silk would be jealous. But, like her hair, it seems to move with a mind of its own, sometimes clinging to her skin, other times ballooning out, like it does now when she reaches her hand into her pocket and produces a fistful of gold tokens.

"Take these and present them at the tournament table in three solars. Until then, try not to get robbed of your winnings." She returns to me as she finishes distributing the rest of the coins. "Though, you shouldn't have much worry there." She glances down to my pitiful little bag with a sorry smirk and the giggling ones burst out laughing beside me. The winged female next to me laughs. The fin-faced guy or gal hisses, and across from me, hot guy smirks.

I narrow my gaze at the orange woman and spit, "It was my first game, you ass."

She laughs and so do the other players. "I know. I'm impressed, but you'll want to do better than that if you really intend to make it to the final table. That's where you'll play *me*." She blinks both eyes rapidly. What a cocky bitch.

I half grimace, half grin. "I'll clean you out."

"Clean me out?" She shudders. "That sounds horribly unpleasant."

This time, I'm the one to laugh. I run my hand through my hair, at least as far as the tangles allow for, and shake my head. "It's an expression. A human one." I gather my winnings into my lap and give the mostly empty sack a happy pat. "I just mean that I'm going to take *everything*."

She makes that dismissive gesture again with her hands. "Human." She shakes her head and steps back, then crosses her arms over her chest. "We've never had a human at the tables before."

"Or on Evernor," the giggling one closest to me says. "I'm Tintin."

"I'm Nalia." I wave at him again, for lack of a better idea of how to greet him. He seems to find that fucking hilarious because he doubles over laughing while his friend waves back so ferociously, he knocks himself off of his own stool.

"Jesus," I whisper.

"Don't mind him. Eshmiri reavers take everything lightly. They think our very existence is a joke." The leader turns and heads to the exit while the others gather their winnings and start to stand.

I shout after her. "Wait. What's your name?"

"Manila." Her hair lifts from the back of her neck and seems to *wave* at me as she walks. She disappears with one parting piece of advice — "Don't be late," though I have no clue what the hell tournament I just signed up for, where the next table is, or where to find out.

The flying female takes pity on me and approaches while Tintin and his giggling friend turn to leave. "My name is Olanora." She waves at me jerkily in a way that suggests that the gesture is as foreign to her as it was to the laughing creatures.

"Nalia," I repeat.

She nods, looking a little confused. "I know. I heard you before when you were speaking with Tintin and Gibli."

I feel my mouth quirk and nod. "Right. Gibli, that's his name?"

She nods. "That's Silini," she says, gesturing to the fin-faced creature just as he hurriedly disappears out of the tent. "And that is Rhogan." I notice her wings flutter even faster as she points him out to me.

He seems to be struggling with his winnings as he drags them towards the exit and pauses, likely because he can sense both Olanora and I staring. "Rhogan," he says, tipping his head towards her.

She responds by clasping her hand into a fist and placing it over her heart. Caught a little off guard when he turns his gaze to me, I mimic the gesture Olanora made. At least, I try. His lips tip up into a smile and I catch a glimpse of pearlescent white teeth, like my alien's, only his are square in the front and filed near the back. I look up into his eyes. They're brown with flecks of fire and gold sprinkled throughout. I gulp. Holy hell. I decide definitively then that he's the hottest male thing I've ever seen. Maybe, the hottest *being*, gender be damned. Not even Manila can give him a run for his money. And he's got plenty of that. Whatever's in those bags is clattering like it's living.

I wince when Olanora's wing suddenly flutters my hair. I tear my gaze away from the sight of Rhogan's too-gorgeous face and look up at her. She's laughing. "Her name is Nalia."

"Oh. Oh shit. Yeah…Nalia. I just…err…" I've never been tongue-tied like this in front of a guy before. I mean, I don't *think* I have. "I've just never seen…um anyone that looks like you before."

He nods, as if this is a totally acceptable reaction to someone seeing him — it likely is. He probably has creatures falling over themselves to catch a glimpse of him on the daily. "I'm a hybrid. I suspect my father is from Quadrant One. My other half is Voraxian." He gives a nonchalant shake of his head. "Who knows. Like most of the beings here in the Below, I might never know my ancestry for certain."

"The Below? You mean here, underneath the, uhh…" I point up like an idiot.

He gives Olanora beside me a wary look and I feel my face heat even hotter. "The world under the arena. Evernor's true colors. Where we are now. A world where *anything* goes." He grins at that and his expression gleams in a way that makes me distinctly aware of every place the warm air caresses my bare skin. My nipples tighten. "If you're bored, I can show you around."

"She's an arena prize," Olanora offers — a confirmation of what I'd already guessed.

"That so? Pity I didn't throw my name in then." He grins at me and I'm caught in his gaze for so long that a small realization sweeps me.

I open my mouth to voice it out loud, but Olanora says, "Herannathon's claimed her already."

He has? And wait — his name is Herannathon?

My thighs tighten and I feel my lower lips pulse, an unexpected reaction. Because I know that what I should feel is moral outrage that I've been claimed like some wilting, weeping vixen by a barbarian who beats his chest and plants his stake in the ground and tosses me over his shoulder and *takes* me, but that's suddenly *all* I can envision and now…now everything's different.

Now, I'll be able to understand his voice and all the filthy things he says to me. Well, hopefully filthy. For all I know, he could be telling me that he hates my freckles and thinks I stink. I shake my head, caught in the vision and wondering why it's so…alluring, especially when I have the hottest guy in all the galaxies standing just within reach. But I'm not picturing him stringing me up. I'm picturing the four-armed gladiator who's laid claim to me. And now, when he does, I'll know what name to scream.

Rhogan starts to nod, but hesitates. Slowly, he says, "But has she claimed him?"

"I…" I choke. I *actually* choke. My throat gets all clogged and my face floods with fire as I drop my hands onto my knees and try to clear the pipes.

The other two are laughing, saying something that I can't hear over the sound of my embarrassment. By the time I finally right myself, the other two are both making their way towards the exit, but moving slowly and looking back over their shoulders at me as if waiting for me to follow. It makes me feel like I'm a part of this…and my heart gets just a little fuller.

As I waddle to catch up, feeling pitiful holding my dinky little bag next to Olanora's big one and Rhogan's two massive sacks, Rhogan shoots me a wink. A *wink*, like a human might. "If you change your mind, you can always find me at the mok bir tables. I'll see you in three solars, if you don't find me before then. I *promise* I'm a good time."

Three things shock the words out of me as I watch Olanora fly off and Rhogan ride away on what looks like a glimmering metallic flying motorcycle. The first — that he's clearly a male slut and wants a piece of me. The second — he *winked,* such a human gesture. And the third? His eyes. He had white eyes filled with brown circles ringing black *pupils.* Human eyes. Huh. What a weird coincidence. *There are no coincidences,* I hear, but the voice isn't mine. It belongs to another female.

I shake off the strange memory and sense of déjà vu and form my bracelet-turned-batons back into a hover craft. Giddiness floods my belly as thoughts of the hot dude roll into visions of someone else. Someone with eyes that are more insectoid than human, someone with an overabundance of confidence, swagger and limbs, somebody with a roughhewn torso that's got both the texture and build of a sturdy tree trunk and somebody whose name I finally have, but whose voice and answers and body and *everything* I want.

Herannathon.

"Herannathon, I'm coming for you." Wind whips past my ears and I grin as I spy his tent on one of the platforms and arrow towards it.

8

Herannathon

"…hear me? Wait, what am I saying? Do you understand me? Shit, you could understand me before. I need *you* to talk to *me*. Herannathon? Herannathon? Am I saying that right? Are you even awake? You look awake. Herannathon?" She mumbles to herself about how my injuries look healed and what the purple goop is doing to me and whether it's killing me, but I can't reply to any of that. Not quite yet.

My limbs come slowly to life at the call of her voice. It feels nice, waking from the merillian to the sound of her voice. Her presence. Knowing that she's safe with me on my ship, in private quarters where my brothers can't interrupt us when I bend her over and take her in that tight rear hole where Niahhorru females only have a slit that would be impossible to penetrate. *Shrov.*

"Shit! I can hear you. But it's not translating. Maybe curses don't translate," she hisses. "Say something else." She touches my shoulder and I moan under the contact of her fingers. They're so warm. And soft. They shouldn't be so shroving soft. But I know how soft she is all over.

She touches my neck and I growl, "If you don't stop touching me, I may have to finish what we started in shekurr…"

"Shekurr? And yes, it's working. Ontte, the translator works." She squeals in glee.

"Of course it does," I groan, rolling the stiffness out of my neck as my tines straighten.

The merillian has worked its way through me and I feel reborn. Groggy, but made anew. With the severity of my injuries, it wouldn't ordinarily work so fast, but I'm on a merillian regimen nearly once every three solars. As it stands, I'm so full of it that I don't think I'll get it fully out of my system for at least a dozen solars after the tournament ends.

I moan and shake my head, trying to get grounded. "Yeeyar tokens are the best. And this is Kor. You think I'd have gotten anything less than the best for you?"

"Why would you get me the best? And what's shekurr? What's yeeyar? And I thought we were on a planet called Evernor? That's what Rhogan and Olanora told me. And holy shit! The translator works! Next time I see Manila, I'm going to kiss that female on the lips."

"Manila?" My thoughts flicker with my vision as the skein lifts from my eyes and lets in the light. The light is…odd. It's orange but that can't be. The light on the mothership is a pale yellow-white. And we don't use Eshmiri torches — why would we when we have yeeyar? And my female speaks of Manila, a female who I know spends most of her time on Evernor running various gambling tournaments in the Below now that she's free of the Sky.

My female's voice is crisp and clear through my translator, but it's also odd…I get the distinct feeling that

I shouldn't be able to communicate so well with her. "Yeah, Manila. She and I made a wager on whether or not I'd win my first mok bir tournament. I did. She gave me the translator."

My skein lifts fully and I stare straight ahead at the canvas tent domed over my head and the glittery, velvety objects within it. This is not the mothership. This is not Pleasure Alley. This is not Kor.

It comes back to me in a rush and I snarl. My hands curl around the smooth edges of the tub, my claws clacking against the wooden exterior as I drag myself up. I don't stop, but rise all the way to stand, merillian sluicing off of my body as I stare down at the female, watch her start and drop back onto her ass on a carpet made of tumtum feathers. It's a winning. One of many I've earned as a gladiator in the tournaments of Evernor. Because that's where we are. That's where my female crashlanded. And that's where I followed her with the vow to keep her safe, retrieve her from Evernor, and take her back to Kor a few tokens — and a Sky key — richer.

My gaze rakes over her form. She's still in a shoddily patched tunic given to her by the Eshmiri patrol. It's clear it was meant to be worn by an Eshmiri because it gapes around her chest and drops to her shins. It's hideous, but that doesn't matter at all.

Her ocean of flame-colored hair is fanned around her face and cascades over her shoulders all the way to her hips. Shrov, she's lovely. The small spots dotting her skin make her appear almost an entirely different color. There are speckled species, which would lead me to think she's a hybrid, human mixed with one of them, if I hadn't pulled her from one of the human tanks myself. *Robbed her of it.*

She's giving me a human expression that I can't decipher, the small furs above her eyes pulled together, her lips twisted and turned down. "What's the matter with you?" she shouts up at me and I about lose my shroving mind.

I sweep the merillian from my limbs, the individual particles eager to return and rejoin the larger whole, and step out of the tub. My shadow draped over her, I watch her expression flatten and reform, becoming even angrier. Where has the skittish female gone who cried every solar, hanging above the arena? This is the female who started a food fight in the reaver markets. This is a female who, if I'm hearing her correctly, *left* the safety of my quarters and ventured out into the Below without so much as a shroving weapon or warning!

"Are you meaning to tell me that you wagered with Manila at the mok bir tournament?"

She scuttles backwards, moving away from me into the larger tent. She knocks into a closed chest and then into the leg of a table, yet the expression on her face does not change. No contrition to speak of, the insolent human female.

"I *won*." She points at a dirty sack that, spread open on a nearby net, is leaking the tokens of various species. Gold for Quadrant One. Pink for Lemoran. Silver for Eshmiri. Black for Niahhorru.

I feel the muscles holding my tines flex, my hiannru rippling in response. Her eyes widen, flashing over my shoulder at the sight of them appearing over the top of my head before settling back down. She swallows hard.

"You entered the shroving tournament?"

"I didn't exactly have a choice, now did I? I needed a translator. I saw my opening. I took it..."

I cut her off. "You did have a choice. I was bartering with Manila for your translator when you started the shroving fight with the Rekkaru!" I punch my fist through a stack of soft pillows, useless things, and they scatter across the decorative kintarr-encrusted table they were stacked on, knocking over a pile of crates filled with useless and expensive trash and tipping their contents onto the floor. She squeaks and scrambles away from me, the mess, the sound, weaving through towers of junk while I hunt her across the carpet, prowling, never letting her out of my sight.

"I..." Her hand comes down on a decorative mok bir wand stacked in a small pyramid with several others. She picks it up, gives it a surprised blink and then the little wench throws it at me. I snatch it with my lower left hand and toss it aside hard enough it topples or breaks whatever it crashes into. She releases a high-pitched squeak that I find strange and alarming and arousing and shroving adorable.

My blood starts to heat. Shrov, I was hot already. But the heat begins to transform.

"You're being an asshole!" The word out of her lips makes me think of *her* tightest hole and I choke. My plates lift from my skin, releasing heat in the same precarious way they did before, but I don't shroving care. Not here. Not when we're alone. Not when she's looking up at me with such defiance. I won't be floored by a little female with no plates or tines to speak of.

When she edges back, her tunic rides up to her hips. She doesn't seem to notice *but I do* and as she turns over and scrambles onto her hands and knees, she gives me a perfect view of the pretty pink slit below the curve of her ass cheeks.

Perhaps, I will be floored by her.

I stoop down, grab the hem of her tunic and wrench back, pulling her off of the floor. She releases another adorable squeak that preempts my lower plates shifting, the protective shell around my cock sliding back as the softer, sensitive flesh pulses with the beat of a heart that's all its own. I will it back, fighting, remembering my rage and allowing it to supplant my lust. *Except it isn't rage, is it? It's fear.*

I haul her up against my body and rope my arm across her hips. The soft curve of her bare bottom presses up against my lower plates. "I had no idea you were trying to find me a translator! How could I? We couldn't communicate!" She kicks her feet into the air and tosses her head back, hair cascading across my chest and catching on my tongue as I wet my lips. I bite it and pull, wrenching her head back and winning a breathy cry from her that disintegrates my focus.

I walk to a large chest propped against the wall and fling the cabinet open. Inside, I shove aside artifacts, each more precious and rare than the last, until I find rope. Synthetic fiber woven rope. It's crass and cheap and I could use a Droherion model that would be more secure, but the synthetic is softer and I don't want to hurt her.

I sweep my hand over her forehead, pulling the back of her head to my shoulder. I nuzzle my way past her thorny curls until my nose is pressed against her cheek. I can feel her heartbeat thrumming through her entire body and it's beating fast. Lust or fear? For a moment, I just hold her against me as I war with my urge to please and my desire to punish. It's a moment that lasts too long as I press my nose against her jaw and nip at her throat with my teeth.

She gasps, further unraveling me. I snarl, "We couldn't communicate, so you decided to leave the safety I've *killed* to provide to wander around a dangerous subterranean planet alone...and unarmed..." I squeeze her throat with one of my free hands while the hand I have roped around her waist crushes her tighter to me. My lower plates peel back and my lust presses forward and I know that I'm slipping...

The vibration of her heart pulses against my tongue when I lick a line up from her collar to her jaw. She tastes like sweat and salvation. It's a taste all her own. "And then you joined a tournament run by one of the most ruthless creatures in the Below to play a game you've never played before..."

"I still won," she pants, the insolent creature she is.

I move up to catch her breaths with my mouth and kiss her hard, unsure if any kiss has ever been delivered with more aggression. I invade her mouth with my tongue, bite her bottom lip between my teeth and pull hard — hard enough to make her whimper, just not hard enough to make her bleed.

I notice as I kiss her that she's stopped fighting me.

Her desire for this makes me grunt. My hips piston into her backside and my cock slides forward, free of its sheathe, just a little more, and it's so shroving satisfying when I yank up on the hem of her shift and my sensitive flesh meets soft, soft heat.

"Did you also know that now that you've entered and been moved on to the final tables, you can't back out?"

"Wh...what?"

"You can't back out. If you do, they take all your winnings and put a bounty on your head. Being you, they'll try to *sell* you."

She freezes and doesn't speak.

I worry that I've scared her and then I decide that scaring her is not a bad thing. "Now, you have to play."

"I want to play," she breathes, surprising the shrov out of me. A small torch lights in the back of my mind and I think of the mission and what we need to get. She's already gotten something *impossible* from Manila. Perhaps, the ex-assassin has a soft spot for my female. One that any pirate would exploit. *But she's not a pirate.*

Yet.

Elation wars with frustration and I hiss, "You don't have a choice."

"Good." She nudges her back into my pelvis and I see stars. I squeeze her neck tighter. She moans, "I'm going to win."

"You're cocky now that you can talk…"

"I could always talk…"

"Shh." I lift my lower right hand into her plane of vision and watch her gaze drop to it, feel her throat muscles work underneath my upper left palm. "You seem to have forgotten our lesson in the reaver pit. I think you need a reminder."

She doesn't answer and I don't know what to make of it, but she also doesn't resist when I bind her wrists together and toss the rope over the thickest support beam crossing over our heads. I loop it around her right ankle, then toss it back over and loop it around her left. Finished, she dangles in an inverted arc, her stomach hanging towards the ground. She's supported by the restraints at her hands, which are bound together, and her feet, which are bound apart.

I step behind her and spread her legs, moving between her thighs. I watch her ass muscles tighten as she shifts, trying to relieve what's certain to be pain in her shoulders and upper back, but she says nothing and continues to say nothing.

I'm waiting for her to complain, to fight, to say something, but her breathing only turns harder, her coloring shifting again to anger… *But she's not Voraxian… Perhaps, her anger color means something else.* Curiosity overpowers me and I step out from between her legs and prowl slowly around her body.

I drag a claw down the arch of her foot, down her shin, over the back of her thigh, across the arch of her back up to her shoulder. I watch the skin beneath my claw pucker with small bumps everywhere I stroke her. I don't understand the reaction, but I like it because it's accompanied by an increase in her pulse. I can feel it throbbing in her neck when I pull the mass of her hair over one shoulder and come around to her face.

I drop onto my haunches and look into her eyes. Centare, there is no anger here. There's *lust.* Pure, blinding desire. My hand twitches towards my cock as it painfully protrudes half a hand's length from its protective shell.

Her gaze drops to it and she licks her lips and swallows, and I imagine stuffing the full length of my cock down her throat. I hiss, "You think you need another lesson?"

"*Yess…*"

"Tell me in Meero."

"Mee-meero?"

"My language."

She pauses, pupils dilating as she fights against her restraints. I can tell she's in pain. Why doesn't she ask for reprieve? I like that she doesn't. I like everything about this female. *But I knew that already. I knew that the first time I saw her in the pods and decided she belonged to me.*

"Uhm…" She says a word that doesn't translate before stuttering, "Ontte."

"Ontte." I touch her cheek with my protracted claws. Grey and shimmery as stalyx, they look like knives against her flesh. "Good girl."

She sucks in a short breath and our eyes meet and I feel shroving mad. Standing abruptly, I tap her cheek with my claw. "Open your mouth," I order her gruffly, the skein over my eyes fluttering wildly as if my body can't decide whether or not this is a battle I can win even though she's half my size and chained up.

Her jaw unhinges, her pink tongue lolling out eagerly. I smirk, "Good girl."

I comb my fingers through her hair, but my hand is shroving shaking and I don't want her to feel it. My erection is at half-mast, desperate to free itself from its sheathe and *painful* every place the outside air touches it. I hiss and turn from her, quickly grab a short bench and stack it high with pillows — high enough that her belly can fall softly onto them and her arms can lower around her face. Still tied, her hands dangle off of the front of the bench. I push them down and grab her jaw, then I feed the flat head of my erection down her throat.

I start to come the moment she begins to suck and shout a curse up to the ceiling. My hiannru flex and quiver and, in a dangerous display of vulnerability, all of my plates lift away from my body. "Shrov," I growl while she bobs her head on my length — the little of it she can reach.

It takes all of my concentration not to fully impale her, because as much as I'm enjoying this, I don't want to choke her to death. I feed her only the first half a hand's length while the rest of my cock remains safely hidden.

I have one hand fisted in her hair, arm muscles fighting not to pull, and another resting along the column of her throat. I love the feeling of her throat working around my length as I keep coming. She starts to choke.

"Shit...do you ever stop coming?" She looks up at me with grey cum smeared across her chin while I continue to leak across the seam of her lips.

My skein drops halfway. I'm breathing harder than I do in the arena as I say, "It's safe to consume."

Her gaze glazes, losing focus. "You want me to swallow?"

"Every shroving drop."

She gasps a little and, behind her, where her feet hang half-suspended, I see her little toes curl. She nods jerkily, *eagerly*, and I push my cock past her lips and watch her work with renewed vigor. Even though she's only got a fraction of my length inside of her now, the warm, wet heat of her mouth sends sensations traveling through me from the root of my plated cock to the tips of my hiannru. I can't shroving take it.

I'm in a full-out pant, thighs quivering as she attempts to follow my commands and fails. My seed spills everywhere, off of her chin, down her throat to the pillows, dripping onto the floor between us. She chokes and I pull back on a hiss, pain needling through the pleasure as my exposed cock begs for her heat. It hurts to touch it, it's so tender, and I'm not finished. I'm going to have to get the synthetic.

I practically lunge for it, but the moment I lift it up, she mewls, "Wait."

I wait.

She licks my seed off of her bottom lip and spreads her thighs around the pillows propped under her legs. "Don't use that. Use me."

I black out for a split instant, imagining what it would be like — and then immediately shake my head. "I don't want to shrov you here. I want to shrov you on Kor."

"What's Kor?"

"Home."

She mouths the word so sweetly. Then she looks down at my cock and the synthetic in my hand and curses in her own tongue. "Please," she whimpers.

I shake my head, refusing to budge. "I will shrov you when we're off of this filthy planet. I'll fill you with seed then." I let my cock protract fully into the synthetic and groan. "I want to see you swollen with it."

She gasps, whatever words she was about to say forgotten. I hold her gaze — I try to — as I work the bright orange contraption over my cock, even though its wet pressure is *nothing* in comparison to her heat. I grunt as I feel my body nearing its final release and I go to my female and topple the bench and pillows beneath her. I grab the strap at her wrists in one of my upper hands and hold it high, high enough that I can bend down and capture her lips with mine and feed her my tongue as a surrogate for my length.

"Mhmmmm," she moans into my mouth, our breath tangling, her heat a shroving intoxicating thing. My upper left hand reaches forward to fondle her chest and its pink-tipped mounds. She whimpers when I squeeze her tit, panting and writhing in the air where she hangs suspended.

"At my mercy," I moan, using my lower hands to move the synthetic.

"Ontte."

I kiss her even harder, bruising her softer lips with mine, but she matches me stroke for stroke, tongue dancing around mine in a rhythm I can't hope to match. I'm getting lost, pushing my hips into the synthetic, frustrated and fumbling with the shroving machine, wishing I was holding onto her hips and emptying, emptying, emptying...

"I want you to finish in me," she begs, sounding as desperate as I feel as she jerks on her bindings. "Finish in my mouth. I want...want to be swollen, too, just *not* with...kits, or whatever."

It is my species' biological imperative to covet kits above anything — everything — but in this moment, I know exactly how she feels. I want to do wretched, wonderful, wild things with her across the known Quadrants and in the unknown cracks in between them. And, in the future I have envisioned, I don't see a place for little ones either. Not yet. Not until I fulfill my every fantasy and, more importantly, hers.

"I can't fit in your tightest hole. Not...like this." I glance down and she follows my gaze, and I show her the inflated root of my semen-slicked cock, beating like a bloody heart for her. "I don't have the...restraint to be careful."

She moans, mewling, twisting her hands, squeezing her knees... "In my mouth..."

"Too long."

"I can take it..."

I shove my tongue *fully* into her mouth, sliding it against her own, nearly hitting the back of her throat. She gulps and jerks back, proving my point.

"I'd kill you."

"Come *on* me."

Hm... That, that I could do. My back muscles tighten. My thighs shudder. My hiannru lift and I clench my teeth together so hard needles of pain shoot through my temples. I rip the synthetic off of my throbbing member, the pain killing me for one precious heartbeat before I gather the female to my chest, jerking against her restraints until I've got her right up against me, her knees still bent, but her soft stomach the perfect cradle for my need.

I bury my face in her hair and bite down softly on her neck as I roar out a moan and endlessly release. I pump against her belly and chest and she clenches and parts her upper thighs wildly. I know she's hurting. That knowing is the only thing that keeps me from collapsing the moment I feel the fever break and the tide part and my feet touch back down to reality.

I pull back enough to kiss her forehead. I do that once softly, softly.

She begs, "Herannathon, please..." And it's too much, the sound of her begging me, calling me by my name when I still don't have hers.

I wait long enough for my erection to shrink back behind its short, thick plating, at least mostly, before I cradle her cheeks.

"You're hurting, aren't you?" I whisper against her temple.

"Please." Her voice comes out as a pant.

"I need something first."

"What? Anything." The black of her gaze has fully consumed all color.

"What are you called?"

"Wh-what?"

"Your name."

"I…" Her cum-stained lips quirk. "Nalia. I'm called Nalia."

"Nalia," I exhale. I step around her, line my lips up with her swollen wet core and dive forward.

I lick her clean and keep licking her until she's filthy. I wrench orgasm after orgasm out of her until she begs me three times to let her go, but I only let her go when I'm good and ready. Sometime later, after she's gone almost entirely slack, I finally cut her free and carry her to the net where I have no intention of cleaning her off, but where I bring her to two more orgasms with my fingers and one dangerous orgasm with the exposed head of my weeping cock pressed right up against her soft folds.

I rut her without penetrating her until she shakes and shivers apart twice. She passes out and, while she struggles to recover and find the light, I cover her in another grey coat.

I'm shaking by the time I douse the lights and try to climb up onto the net beside her. I say try, because I fail the first two times, clipping my shin on an upturned bench and tripping over a pillow. She laughs lightly when I finally fall down beside her, the net swinging precariously beneath us.

"Don't...don't you think I should clean up, Herannathon?" She breathes sleepily, teeth shining in a soft smile even in the dark.

I swipe a claw through the sticky sheen covering her chest and bring it to her lips. She licks it clean, the good little piratess. "Not unless you want me to tie you down and bring you to another orgasm, Nalia."

She laughs and it's the sweetest thing, because as she laughs, she reaches for me...like she trusts me. She doesn't even know me. "No way..."

"Centare," I tell her. "In Meero."

"Centare," she repeats, already lost in dreams.

I pull her body over mine, my cum an adhesive between us, and against the shell of her curved ear, I say, "Do you think you've learned your lesson?"

"I don't have any idea what my lesson was...but I was happy to learn it and wouldn't mind learning it again."

I laugh and know then that every battle I've had to fight to claim her here on Evernor, and even before this, was worth it. I just hope she knows that I didn't come all this way just for her pretty pussy. I came for her. I came for forever. Convincing her of that may be a battle — it will be, I know it, because this female is far more strong-willed than she initially seemed.

But this strong-willed female and I also have something in common.

I play to win. And so does she.

9

Nalia

"Your aim is good, but you need to be prepared to defend against the different kinds of mok bir batons your opponents might use."

I nod, watching Herannathon across the mok bir table. He's been practicing with me since the close of his battle earlier today. It was an easy one in the sense that it was over quick and he left it unscathed without having to use more of the purple healing goo, but he also mortally wounded one opponent and killed the other, and since then, he's been off.

It's a curious thing, one that's been demanding more of my concentration than his explanation of this game, which feels like small potatoes, by contrast. He killed someone — he's killed loads of creatures, but...what if he doesn't want to?

He pauses. "Are you okay?"

I frown at him and bite my bottom lip, not wanting to come across as cruel. "I should be asking you that."

He glances down at his chest, his severe expression made more severe by the fact that I can't see his silver swirling eyes well beneath the matte grey shields that cover them. They blend in with his skin around the edges, making it even harder to tell if he's looking at me and, if he is, where. I don't know why he wears his shields now when normally he doesn't in my presence.

"I'm not injured," he finally blurts.

"Not on the outside."

"I have no internal injuries or bleeding."

"That isn't what I meant."

"Then what did you shroving mean? Because you're not paying attention to this and you need to be if you want to win." He throws down the baton in his hand and it springs back up from the worn wooden tabletop in a flurry of spins and whirls. Like a boomerang, it whips in a circle and I only avoid getting hit in the face by blocking it with my forearm.

"Jesus Christ."

He frowns at me even more severely than before. "Herannathon."

"What?"

"My name. It isn't Jesum Crips."

"Jesus, I know that. It's just a curse, like shrov."

"Then why don't you say *shrov*?"

I plant my palms on the table and lean forward, heat crawling up the back of my neck that I have a surprisingly difficult time batting down. "Because I'm not a Niahhorru space pirate."

His shields flutter, twitch, do whatever they do. He leans forward onto his palms, too. Onto all four of them. Over the top of his head, the tips of his brutal, slate-colored spears appear, causing goosebumps to prick the tops of my bare arms. I'm in another crudely patched together shift and I'm getting kind of sick of them. Herannathon was telling me that the ultimate prize up for grabs at the mok bir tables is some kind of key that

Manila holds, but right now, I'm feeling less than charitable. I'd rather win a tee shirt, a pair of shorts and some sneakers. I'd kill for sneakers. Instead, I've got on shoes made out of this blue goop. It does the job, but feels slimy around my feet.

"You think I haven't realized that?" I feel the sting of his words like an insult that doesn't make a lot of sense. I'm *not* Niahhorru. I'm not of his kind. Therefore, I'm not a pirate. But…it still smarts worse than getting hit in the forehead with a mok bir baton. One of the electric ones.

He goes on, "If you *were* a pirate, then you'd have known better than to steal a shroving Eshmiri escape pod, from Ashmara no less, and even if you had, you'd have known how to program a different shroving destination into the star map, and even if you *hadn't*, you'd have been able to land on Evernor and fight for yourself."

The heat along the back of my neck intensifies and spreads to my chest. My lips part and I wait just one baited breath for him to apologize because his words ring *harsh* to me…but he doesn't. He just continues to lean forward and stare at me with his shield-covered eyes and his dark grey lips clenched into a razor-thin line and his spikes glittering over the top of his head like a deadly promise.

I slap my hand down onto the table. "You're an ass."

"Centare, I'm a Niahhorru shroving pirate. What are you?"

"I'm a human. You knew that when you chased after me and decided to fight. Why did you, if you clearly aren't happy about it?"

He scoffs, "Maybe, because I didn't want to see you *used* in ways so many of these beings would love to use you."

"Maybe, that's *exactly* why you followed me — to use me in all the ways *you* would love to use me." I throw the baton in my hand at his chest. He catches it easily, making me wonder how I won a single game at all. He's fast — way faster than I am. If there are any competitors with half his hand-eye coordination and a tenth of his speed, I might as well just prepare the shackles for my sale now.

His eye shields peel to the sides, but only a little, just enough to reveal a sliver of silver. He whips the black baton up, like he's flinging it backwards over his wrist, but instead of sailing through the air, the baton flattens, transforming into a forearm brace. He does this without breaking my eye contact and without breaking his stride as he approaches me slowly around the table.

The heat in my throat, a latent anger, is the only thing that keeps my feet rooted as he prowls towards me, looking as dangerous as any predator. I feel hunted by him even though I'm standing perfectly still.

"Don't try to intimidate me. It won't work," I lie, because it's working. His size alone is enough to intimidate me without adding in the fact that my body seems to want to submit to his in every way. The feeling goes beyond normal want. It's...almost supernatural. I lick my lips and try not to shuffle my weight between my hips. "I'm serious, Herannathon..."

"So am I, *Nalia.*" He elongates my name, overenunciating each vowel and making it sound like *Nahleeahhh.* I refuse to swallow — I don't want him to see my tells — and let my mouth fill with saliva and heat.

"You think I'm not? You think you know anything about this place, these creatures, what they'd do to you if they had you at their mercy?"

I bite my front teeth together and clench my fists by my sides, standing steady and stiff. "Whatever it is, I'd endure it."

"Bwa!" he barks out, voice sounding less like a laugh and more like a dagger cutting through flesh and finding bone. "Have you seen an Egama? Their cocks are the length of my thigh. But that wouldn't stop them. They'd rip you open." He touches the center of my chest and drags his claws down. "Or maybe you want to try your luck with a Rekkaru horde. They mate in groups mid-air. It's a shroving frenzy. The chances you wouldn't plummet from the sky, half-impaled on a stumpy grey cock, is almost nothing.

"Or the Oosa. Their amorphous forms can take to any shape and they love to shrov. They'd shrov you until you suffocated. And still, all of these would be better than if you were won by someone interested in trading you to the Sky. They'd breed you with one of their death machines, and that's only if their mechanics didn't reboot your brain, erase your memories and turn you into one of their assassins, first. No one would ever shrov you then, but it doesn't matter, you still wouldn't survive it.

"Endure it, ontte. You would. But centare, Nalia, you wouldn't survive it. You wouldn't survive any of them."

I'm clammy and cold, despite the sweat on my skin. I don't like this. I don't like the way he's talking to me. A surge of rage and energy blasts through my arms and I karate chop him in the side — a move he easily blocks —

but it distracts him enough for me to be able to take the remaining baton in my hand and strike him with it.

I make contact with his jaw. His head tips to the side and though the movement is a micromovement, the baton in my hand is reactive to my touch in ways that suggest it's somehow learning from me — and it grows barbs. Thorns sprouting from the end of my baton scrape away the softer skin around his mouth, cutting into his bottom lip and drawing black blood.

Satisfied but still seething, I turn my back on him, recall the black magical sheath from around his wrist and am surprised when it actually comes to me. I toss it to the ground along with the other baton, step onto the platform they merge to create and sail off without caring if — or how — he'll follow.

10

Herannathon

Nalia and I haven't spoken since she left me at the damn training table to hitch a ride with a passing Lemoran. Now, we sit on opposite sides of the tent — me, at my makeshift weapons depot polishing a massive anka blade won off of a Mormora opponent — one of my first in this tournament — and her, at the small eating table, picking apart the last of an eebi bird, a delicacy I traded for at the markets last lunar before returning to her.

I was harsh with her. I should say something. I clear my throat.

"I know. I'm a slob." She drops the bone she's holding and wipes her hand on a piece of cloth lying on the table beside her. "Must be the human in me."

Her sneer sets me on edge. I try to remember that she must be afraid — she's been afraid this entire time. I try to remember what it felt like to hold onto this shaking female after I found her with the Lemorans. She'd been so scared. It had shaken me to my core. Remembering that female now feels strange. That female feels so far away.

This female, this one here, this one…*is a pirate*. I told her she wasn't — I've been trying to convince myself she isn't — but only because I don't know what scares me more, seeing her shivering in her human skin, or knowing that she might be shedding that skin and adopting Niahhorru tines and Niahhorru claws *mentally*. But no matter how much her mind may harden, the reality is that her skin is still soft. Too soft not to break.

"There is no other way to eat eebi." I grunt, speaking through clenched teeth. "You're a natural." I exhale the rage burning within me. Not rage. Centare, not rage. *Fear.*

Her hesitation doesn't go unnoticed. Her gaze drops as she notices me noticing. "It tastes good. Much better than that other sludge."

The corner of my mouth twitches. "You don't like Ebo nut paste? It's highly nutritious."

"That gunk the giggle freaks were feeding me every day in my cell? It's a nut?" She frowns. "Doesn't taste like it."

"To you, maybe. After all, you are human."

She gives me a strange look and tucks her hair behind one ear. It's bushy, her hair. I like it. Adore it. I want to see it wrapped around all four of my hands while she's on her knees. "Thanks for the reminder."

I refocus on the blade before me to ward off the growing stiffness between my legs, pushing against my protective plates, and mumble, "It's not a bad thing."

"Isn't it? Makes me the easiest target here. It's why you have to fight for me, isn't it? It's why you think if I compete in the mok bir tournament, I'll lose."

She shoves away from the table and takes her dish to the refuse area in the back. It's picked up by Eshmiri patrol every solar — well, every solar they remember. I find myself slashing my ion sharpener harder against the edge of the blade while she's out of sight. I like to see her, always. Even if she makes me want to punish her. Maybe, especially then.

She reappears a moment later, still wrapped in rags. I'll have someone at the markets stitch her something after the tournament this solar. Something beautiful. Maybe, I'll ask the Walrey to make her something out of their silk. It'll cost me an arm and a leg, but it'll be worth it… I shake my head. What am I thinking? I need the key. *I need salvation discs.* I cringe at the memory of killing that pair of Oroshi. I like Oroshi.

They're wily and conniving, as slippery as each of their limbs. They're shroving reckless gamblers and always bet at the highest stakes. The pair of Oroshi I fought entered the tournament willingly and I…I knew one of them. Not well, not by name, but I recognized the weapon he carried — an axe with an ionic blade that was almost weightless.

I tried to bribe it off of him once. That was back on Kor in the Cosmos Dome, back before I'd heard anything of a species called *human*. Instead, he managed to gamble me out of some mok biz winnings over jugs of Lemoran hibi. It had been a good lunar. A memorable one. And in the tournament here on Evernor, I'd tried not to kill him…but they were tough opponents and his axe…he was good with it. Too good.

I cut his teammate in half and severed three of his nine limbs. Oroshi bleed fast. They weren't able to save him — either of them. No amount of merillian could have. And the shroving Eshmiri, what did they do? They gave me his shroving axe as part of my winnings.

I glance at it leaning against the wall with the other weapons I've collected. My stomach sours. All thoughts of touching Nalia are spoiled like bad meat.

"What is it?" she says softly, voice tender in a way that I'm not used to. Niahhorru pirates turn everything into jokes. I wouldn't ever consider telling them what I'm thinking…because they would never ask.

I look up and wince, seeing her face and its softness, the slight crinkling of the fur above her eyes that makes me think of pity or maybe something akin to it. I open my mouth, prepared to joke with her, but…that expression. The spots on her face. Her large dark and light eyes. So much white.

"I knew the Oroshi, the one I killed. I knew him…"

Her lips move. Words come after a beat of silence. "Oroshi?"

"The one who wielded the axe." I cock my head towards the wall, my fingers curling around the hilt of the blade in my lap. "And I never said you wouldn't win the mok bir tournament."

There's another lengthy quiet in which I can hear, but can't see, her move. I don't want to look at her. I don't want to hear her joke. I don't want to feel her anger towards me. It would be deserved.

I'm forced to look up when I hear her slight "oomph" and the sound of her feet dragging over the carpeted floor. She's rubbing her hip absently with the heel of her hand as she skirts a wooden table and continues to approach. She can't come to me though, if that is her intention. There are crates of crap we don't need stacked between us. Crates that won't buy me salvation discs because, across all of Evernor, there aren't any left. *I'll have to kill again.*

I switch my gaze to hers and her lips part. "Herannathon, I…" Her face flares with color. She stops moving. "You…you don't like killing them, do you?"

I laugh. It isn't a pirate's laugh or even a reaver's. It's a glib and scathing thing. "You think I *like* killing creatures? Creatures who may not be here willingly, but are captured and thrust into the tournament? Creatures I know?"

Her face turns a brighter red. Her shoulders tense.

"Of course you do. You're a soft human and I'm just a savage pirate, after all."

Her eye furs crinkle together and her hand bunches into her ratty garment, forming a fist. "That isn't…"

"They're here. Let's see who I'll have to kill this solar." I push up onto my feet and go to the entrance of my tent at the sound of rickety Eshmiri flyers drawing closer. I drop my sword behind me. I'm the favorite, so I'm never allowed a weapon in the arena. The spectators pay more to watch me rip Oroshi apart with my bare hands, limb by limb.

I close the flaps behind me with a flourish and look up, a little saddened by Nalia's perception of me. I don't know why. I wanted her to think me the killer capable of protecting her. *But maybe I also want her to think me more than that.* And to want me beyond my capacity to kill for her.

As the glider approaches closer, all rickety red metal, my sadness morphs to surprise. "What are you doing here?" I ask Uuni. He's usually traveling with Gibli and Tintin's crew — it's also Ashmara's. *Shroving Ashmara…* "I didn't think you'd docked."

"Yeeshee," he replies in Eshmiri, hoisting his blaster higher on his shoulder as he tries to peek past the barrier of my tent and see the stores within. Likely plotting what he might try to steal — *try* being the operative word. No one steals from a Niahhorru pirate and lives to speak of it. No one. *No one except* him.

Jerrock the killer.

I roll my eyes when Uuni doesn't elaborate and hold out my arms. "Why? Didn't think your crew liked watching the games, what with Ashmara's whole save-the-unwilling bit."

It's a known fact in the Quadrants that Ashmara will rob anyone blind, but she takes a special delight in stealing the stolen and freeing them. Her crew's intercepted so many poor souls destined for Sky experiments, it's earned her head a nice fat price and a host of Sky assassins interested in claiming her bounty. Only one holds her contract though, and he's held it for rotations.

Jerrock, Sky's prodigal son.

Somehow, she's managed to avoid being caught. I don't know how, though. She may be a slippery sucker, but she's also reckless sloppy and a known muuir addict.

Uuni nods vigorously. "Prize is too good to pass up this time."

I squint up at him and tense when I see a pod of Eshmiri speeding towards us in their gliders, a clear kintarr case traveling between them. I exhale, remembering that I only have three more of these shroving battles. Three more and then I collect my prize, contact the mothership and get the shrov out of here. I feel for the metal bolt in my pocket and exhale shakily, knowing that the rift between us is repairable, just not here. Off of Evernor, I can prove to her that I'm worthy and that I don't think of her as just a human. Because I don't think of her as *just* anything.

She's everything.

Glancing back at Uuni, I refocus. "What prize?"

"Come. You can't be late and your challenger's already on the field." He cocks his head to the side, his lips curling into a grin that reveals all of his pointy teeth. "I'll tell you on the way."

Curiosity gets the best of me and I vault up onto his glider just as he starts to pull off of my island and into the Below. As we pull away, Nalia steps out onto the landing and into her kintarr prison. She looks up, trying to find me, perhaps, but she doesn't succeed. There are already too many gliders zipping back and forth between us.

"There's a Sky key here and they say that Manila has it."

Shrov. Reluctantly, I tear my gaze away from Nalia and turn back to the reaver before me. "How the shrov do you know about that?"

Uuni giggles high and loud as he swings the glider wildly to the left, just barely dodging a hive of flying Walrey, bulbous-eyed creatures from Quadrant Eight. Nasty things, but the honey they create is coveted across the cosmos and so is their silk. They come to the Below to play.

"Everyone knows. They say Manila has it and that she'll give it up as a prize to the champion of the mok bir tournament."

"Why the shrov would she do that?" I ask, though I know this information already. I just want to know how much *he* knows.

"Because only some can win the battle tournament, but mok bir is equal. Anyone can win. *Anyone.*"

"That's not what I mean," I huff, frustrated, sure that he's speaking in riddles. Of course he is. He's a shroving Eshmiri. "I mean, why would she give up a prize of such great value? One she's carried with her for *rotations*?" Since she became the first Sky assassin to break free. She made *history.* And though I've known about the key since the solar I entered the gladiator tournament, this is one question I haven't been able to answer.

"Not for nothing." His head bobs to the sides in little wiggles. "Makes for better competition and she gets a cut of the profits, you know. It also transfers her risk."

"Risk?"

His large, oversized eyes glitter like gems. His small mouth reveals needles for teeth. "Yeeshee." His forehead, covered in a light sheen of small hairs, wrinkles. "Everyone knows that Manila carries the key. *Everyone.*"

Shrov. My skin prickles. I glance around, half expecting metal-bound cyborgs to leap at me from the chaos here and now. "Assassins are *here*?"

"We suspect."

"That's your only shroving job, you blasted Eshmiri. You keep the peace by keeping *them* out."

"The Sky assassins have new weapons. They can cloak themselves and they want their key back. Only with the key can the Sky planet be found. They have orders to send not just one assassin for it, but *many.*"

"Shroving comets." I rake a hand down my face, furious and fearful, for once. It doesn't surprise me that others know of Manila's key. Since I wasn't planning on joining the mok bir tournament, I was planning on trading her for it. *Or stealing it.* But to know that I won't just have the creatures of the Below to deal with, but that the Sky have sent their killers here for it?

"But we've caught one."

I tense, attention snapping to Uuni. "Caught? You *caught* a Sky assassin?"

He just giggles.

"Why don't you kill it?"

His eyes sparkle, all bulbous and glowing a pale cream. There are small points of light within his gaze surrounded by darker and lighter cream-colored rings but, like his giggle, his gaze gives away nothing.

"Shroving reaver," I hiss as the gates approach. "Why do you even want the key?"

"Lemora is willing to pay a high price for it. Clan Chief Raingar is still upset about what the Sky did to his miriga."

"What they did to *his* miriga? What they did to *my* female!" I grab Uuni by the collar of his tunic and give the smaller creature a sturdy shake. The butt of his blaster slams into the plates of my upper thigh and I groan. It's a cheap shot — one that, without protective plates covering my cock, might otherwise have sterilized me. And we can't have that. I have seed for Nalia yet.

I grab Uuni around the throat with my lower hand and give the smiling bastard a threatening squeeze. "If the Lemoran Clan Chief thinks to rob the Niahhorru of their vengeance and you help him, I'll be coming for *you*, personally."

"Threats, threats, threats," he says as his glider finally comes to a stop. I disembark in the tunnel, booted feet landing on Evernor's hard surface with a thwunk. His glider lifts again into the air, hovering low to avoid hitting the roof of the cavern. Just before he whooshes away, he leaves me with a very human wave and parting words, "Threats weigh less than kintarr."

"Shroving Eshmiri…" I shake my head as I watch him leave, his rusty glider nearly crashing into the right wall, causing the Eshmiri cluttering the hall below to laugh riotously.

The Eshmiri are going to be a problem. They have eyes aplenty and they're skilled in all the games of the Below. If they've sent their best to the tables, Nalia has no shroving chance of competing. The fact she made it to the next round at all is frankly a miracle. And if there are assassins here…

Shrov the key and the mission and our vengeance. I need to get her off-world. I grip the bolt tightly in my lower right fist before dropping it back in my pocket. *After all, I'm the reason she's here.*

The doors to the arena floor creak and clang. I face off towards them, weaponless and wondering what the shrov the Eshmiri have planned for me this solar. The battles have been getting more and more intense, the opponents more savage. But when the gates peel open and I see a short, thin creature staring me back at me from across the packed red sands, I don't understand…

At *first.*

And then I register her face, her markings, and see the chains hanging off of her small frame, all Droherion and radiating a vibrant, almost blinding blue.

Shrov.

Her hair hangs to her waist in a braid that rips down the center of her head, almost in cruel imitation of my own hiannru. It glistens an unusual and fluorescent pink. It *glows.* To either side of her braid, silver plates gleam along her skull, likely made out of stalyx. Her eyes are missing, replaced by flat yeeyar sheets. I'm not fooled by her lack of orbs for eyes — I know she can see ten times as far and a hundred times as well as I can with those Sky modifications.

I forget about everything else. Forget about the kintarr chambers dangling so tantalizingly above me. Forget about the argument I had with my female — a female currently angry with me and who's likely to be angrier still when she realizes that I've been lying to her from the start.

I know why she has no memories. I know it as well as I know that I've got a metal bolt in my pocket.

The crowd's roar is overwhelming, louder than ever. I'm the favorite, but there's never been an assassin on Evernor's soil. I glance up at the bets illuminated on the holoscreens of the Eshmiri flyers. Centare, I'm not the favorite anymore.

I glance up at the stands towards the Eshmiri booth where I see Uuni's craft hovering. Below him, clustered together on the bench seats of the rocky red arena, are the other members of his crew. They appear as a brown mass that's disrupted only by the darker swatch of brown among them. Crowned by a shock of white hair and a smile to match it, Ashmara grins at me wide enough to show all of her teeth.

Her eyes flare with color, a wild and satisfied silver followed by a flash of green amusement. She has no control over her colors at all, but even if she did, I doubt it would matter. The female is as relentless as she is shameless. She claps her hands and makes a face and points at the Sky assassin, as if I'm not aware I'm about to fight this creature to the death and likely lose. *Centare — I can't afford to lose.*

I glance up at the kintarr boxes floating amidst so many Eshmiri pods. Together, the prizes and the announcers almost blot out the shimmery grey curve of the dome and the blazing sky above it. A pirate versus an assassin. It's a fight that, were I in any other position, I'd have paid good credits to see.

I find Nalia's box, glittering pink. The protective skein over my eyes is already in place. Through it, I see her more clearly — clear enough to make out the confused expression on her face. She's glancing between me and my opponent as if she doesn't understand. It makes me smirk. To her it probably looks preposterous.

A zing rips through the scattered thoughts in my mind as the chains slough off of my opponent. As she steps forward, I turn my attention away from a laughing horde of Eshmiri and away from my confused prize, determined to prove to her that she's absolutely right.

I am a killer and this will be a preposterous fight.

//
Nalia

Ho. Ly. Fuck. The female Herannathon is fighting is a beast. Monstrous in her intensity, savage in her bloodlust and fast as can be. She takes a beating better than a practice dummy and, when Herannathon spins and catches her with his tines, she deflects with her metallic forearms without sustaining so much as a scratch.

Her forearms are glittery silver-white. Above her elbows, her skin is a matte blue. Her legs are the same, only the metal bits below her knees are cut to have an extra joint. They help her jump high, like she does now, but Herannathon jumps, too. He jumps high enough to catch her ankle, whip her over his head like a flail and slam her into the ground. The tail end of her braid slashes at his wrist, drawing blood. I wince at the sounds of pain that thunder out of him.

Her pink hair looks neon and electric and may very well be because after her braid lashes Herannathon across the face the very first time, he works hard to avoid its strike. It reminds me of Manila's hair, moving with its own autonomy. It slashes almost like a tentacle, making me wonder if it is even hair at all. It moves like all the rest of her limbs, which all move seemingly out of coordination with one another, like Herannathon's fighting four opponents at once — well, including the hair, five.

She kicks him in the chest and he flies off of her, skating back over the sand. He charges her again and she dives out of his path. He slips and she jumps onto his back, and from her arm — out of *nowhere* — she produces a blade. She stabs down, spearing him through the back, through his upper right shoulder.

I gasp and pound my fist on the bottom of the cage and I keep pounding. He needs help. *I can help him.* The thought blazes through my brain with urgency as I watch him stand and attack and defend and attack again, over and over and over. The fight seems to last an eternity. I know he can't make it forever. And worse, he's flagging while she isn't. She doesn't seem to be tiring at all.

"I want out!" I shout towards the Eshmiri flying in the little craft nearest to me. "Hey!"

The little brown being standing in what looks like a rusty metal bucket glances at me quickly before turning his attention back to the fight. He leans forward and shakes both his fists with such violence that he almost spills out of his flyer. He tosses some flat silver and black tokens down to the surface and shouts across to the other Eshmiri.

There's an announcer hovering in the crowd somewhere holding the alien-equivalent of a leaderboard. The Eshmiri closest to me has been betting on the Sky assassin and now substantially increases his bid.

"Fucker!" I shout. "Let me out of here!"

A whistle from below pulls my attention down and around, but I don't let myself be distracted by it.

"Hey! I want out."

And just as I open my mouth to shout again, my entire cell goes plummeting to the ground. My scream lurches up into my throat and, before I can catch my balance, I'm tumbling out of my box and onto the hard, packed dirt. My head whacks the side of the hard box on my way out, and for a second a headache splinters into my thoughts and everything goes grey. When I open my eyes, I stagger up to standing.

I tilt my face towards the breeze and open my eyes. The pink cell is floating away from me, back up to join the rest. A second whistle yanks at my attention and, even though I have more pressing issues to attend to, I still look up.

I look into the crowd while everyone else looks down at the dueling pair…everyone, except for one person — being. There's one set of eyes, bright white in color with no pupil or iris, focused entirely on me. She's grinning as she points a finger slightly to my left and I turn to follow her stare to see a staff half hidden beneath some gaudy gems, worthless-looking rocks and shimmery pieces of fabric.

I lunge for it immediately and scoop it off of the ground. A two-sided blade, I know how to use it the moment I fit my fingers to the holds. Something beyond instinct is driving me as I race over the hard ground amidst a thunder of screeches and screams. Something that feels an awful lot like *memory*…

I'm wielding a machine gun like a staff because I'm out of bullets. There's a knife attached to one end, like an old-school bayonet, because in this world we're running out of bullets and knives are what we have left.

I'm confronted by not one but three buff dudes as I round the next building. It's a secret reservoir, one they shouldn't know about but that I let slip the coordinates to at the bar last night. I was playing poker. I always liked cards... I stab the first guy in the gut when he hesitates at the sight of my weapon...

A shadow flashes before my eyes. I slam the blade down with every ounce of force that I have, a small thrill rippling through me as I make contact. *There you are, you crazy bitch. Finally.* The voice in my head is *mine*, I know that, but it doesn't sound like me. That woman sounds like an asshole, somebody I don't care to be. *Oh, sweetheart, but you need me. Look.*

I peel my eyes open as my weapon hits the packed soil, colliding with it and bouncing up because my arm's gone completely slack — this time in shock. I just cut off the killer woman's arm. *No. I did. Remember me? Remember* you.

I blink as the female rounds on me, her terrifyingly blank eyes shifting beneath whatever covers them. Red seeps into her gaze a second before she lunges. I manage to deflect the blade on her arm with my staff, using the two-handed grip to block her forearm the next time she attacks. But I don't retreat. I press her back.

The female hesitates, like she's shocked — hell, that makes two of us. I lunge at her, like a fucking madwoman, and jab with one of the thick cylindrical blades on either end of my weapon that seems to cut no matter which way I turn it. She jumps out of its path, but when I whip the other end of the weapon up, I'm too slow. I don't see the damn braid coming. It whacks the outside of my arm and hot *damn.*

Damnnnnn.

The pain is shocking enough to cause me to lose my hold on my weapon and the little bits of coherency left in my brain. I know I'm down, but I'm not conscious of hitting the dirt. All I can feel is the burn of the hair that's definitely not fucking hair against the entire right side of my body. *I've been tased before.* It feels like getting zapped by a taser the size of a goddamn truck. Electricity flows through my veins, freezing me where I've fallen.

"Ho…ho…ly…fuck," I curse and suddenly I can't help but think of Herannathon and how hot as fuck I find him now that I know exactly what he's been up against this whole time. He's been flagging? *Flagging?* Jesum H. Cripes! I'm *dying.*

I open my eyes when I feel a cool shadow pass over me. I look up at her face. *Remember who you were. Remember.*

The flat sheets of her eyes have turned completely black. Her mouth is tight and lipless. She hisses something at me that not even my translator manages to catch before lifting her remaining arm. A sword extends from her wrist that's half the height of her entire body. Meanwhile, the blue stump of her left arm drips blood, little metal wires and electric cables.

I struggle against my own inertia and the spasms coursing through my veins…but I'm down. How Herannathon has been getting up after each hit is entirely beyond me. Now, all I can do is watch as she aims for the center of my chest…

Remember and fucking move!

I gasp and roll towards her legs, trying to knock her off her feet, but I don't roll far enough to clear her sword entirely. She stabs me in the left side — straight through the stomach. Pain inundates me but my adrenaline and shock keep me conscious for just a few more seconds. Seconds are enough to watch her stumble back as I collide with her weird goat feet and fall straight into Herannathon's arms.

He catches her like a lover against his chest, trapping her one whole arm, blade and all, between her breasts. He grabs her by the braid on the back of her head and roars in wild pain while electricity fires up and down his left arms, *visibly* skittering over his silver skin in shades of neon pink all the way up to his tines, which start to shimmer bright pink, too.

He pulls. I don't realize how hard he's pulling until the woman's mouth opens wide on a silent scream. I don't realize how *extremely* hard until her eyes — or whatever they are — start to sink in at the centers like... like...

Holy fucking shrov.

He's pulling her eyes out through the back of her head using her braid.

He rips her braid away from her skull and doesn't just scalp her — he completely removes the back half of her head, everywhere that silver plates don't cover. Blood and flesh and cables and wires and little electrical things that I'm too alien to name come gushing out.

Lying on my back, I reach beneath me and press my hand into the sand, intending to push away from the carnage...but there's something already wet underneath me. I lift my palm. Red. Bright red. *Yeah, that's me.* Fuck me, I shoulda moved faster. *I coulda moved faster.*

I slump back and remember passing out — not now, *before*. I remember stepping into a tank. I remember fighting, telling them I was ready. *I'm not ready. I'm not ready.*

"Herannathon," I croak.

The thump of a body next to me makes me jolt. I breathe in something sickly, like chemicals and poison, but sweet. The taste crawls up the back of my throat until hands — four of them — grab hold of me and lift and I'm suddenly being cradled against a chest that smells like sand and leather and tastes like butter and feels like he'd do anything for me. I've never had that. *No, I've never had that.*

I wrap my bloody palms around him and, as he races with me off of the battlefield to the tune of creatures of all kinds shouting his name *and mine*, I hold him back.

12
Nalia

Remember…

Hands are on my body, multiple sets belonging to different people. One woman with hair just as red as mine shakes her head as I'm fully submerged.

"You're supposed to be my sister!" I shout up at her.

She glares, her expression as hard as the steel she wears strapped to her chest. War. We're at war over water and she's part of an elite team meant to save humanity, or earth, or both. "You were supposed to be a soldier. Instead, you gambled your life away. You compromised the mission. You risked everything we've worked for."

"Don't let them wipe my memories. I'm supposed to be doing this with you. We're supposed to save the world together." I grip the edges of the tank as my lower half seeps into the freezing cold gel. It's not the gel that worries me, but the man standing to the woman's left. "Don't…" I stammer. "Don't do this. I can still be a part of the Sucere Project."

"No. You fucked up. If you make it with the others on board the satellite, you can try to save humanity with them. But you can't join us. You could have, but you can't. Not after everything you've done." She steps back, letting the dark-haired med fucker take her place.

He crouches down beside my tank and wields a syringe like the hangman wields an axe, ready to fucking end me. "This won't hurt," he says, as if that's some sort of consolation.

"Fuck you." I glance up. "And fuck you, too. You're not my sister."

"You're right, Nalia. Because when you wake up, you won't remember that I ever existed." I don't even feel the syringe. The sadness in her eyes is the last thing I register.

A moment later, goo wraps around me along with hands, two sets belonging to one body. I open my eyes, see the alien and scream.

I open my eyes, see the alien and grin.

"Shrov," he curses, his eyes blinking rapidly from the side as I take in his blurry face. "What's wrong with you? Nalia? Are you hurt?"

I'm not awake. I'm still caught in the goo, lost in the dream. "I remember."

His lips part. His tongue slips out to wet them. It's pink. So very pink. "Remember what, Nalia?"

And then I forget. I swallow, the taste in my mouth odd and unlike anything I've ever experienced. It feels like I'm sucking on the sun, a muted warmth that rumbles through me like pure energy. "What...what I said...before."

I slump backwards and feel hands cradling the back of my neck tenderly, so tenderly, too tenderly for an alien made out of sharp cuts of wood and thick, blade-like thorns. "I don't think you're a killer, Herannathon. That's what I was going to say before. I thought you were, but I know you're not and I feel...I feel *bad*. I shouldn't have run. Any of the times. I shouldn't have run. I should have stayed…trusted…waited to hear…stopped trying to find, to search…"

"Nalia, shhh…the merillian hasn't finished healing you. Just sleep." His hands gently smooth the sides of my face, thick thumbs rubbing beneath my eyes.

I lean into his grip and nod. "I just…I'm sorry you have to fight for me."

"Centare." His voice is a deep rumble. It soothes me. "It's an honor to fight for you, Nalia. But it is a greater honor to fight *with* you."

With my eyes closed, I can feel the tension shoot through his fingers a split instant before he drags me forward. I feel a hard pressure against my mouth and a tongue — a pink tongue — gently part my lips. I moan into his tenderness as he kisses me. I didn't even know aliens knew how to kiss. Maybe he doesn't. Because I've never been kissed like this. Brutally and beautifully, lips like stiff pieces of leather with a soft, satiny tongue in between. He worships my tongue with his own, moving mine when it doesn't respond to his immediately. I'm slow and syrupy, lost in the abyss. I'm not ready for it to end though, either.

"But Nalia?" He pecks my lips as he pulls back and I slump down even further into the goop, lost…lost in time and lost in space.

"Hm?" My eyes flutter open only long enough to see him grinning at me rakishly.

"Don't do that again."

I grin back. "No promises…"

13

Herannathon

It takes Nalia too long to recover from her wounds. The merillian works slowly on humans but, fortunately for us both, the Eshmiri were so thrilled with her shroving performance in the tournament that they delayed the mok bir tournament an entire lunar just so she could participate. Which she did. She survived her matches, too.

Her pot wasn't the largest, but it was large enough for her to advance to the final round. Watching her play was magnificent and a little alarming. It's like... somewhere in the merillian tub, she forgot that she was afraid and became utterly fearless. Maybe, it happened before the tub. Maybe, it happened when *I* was lost in the merillian and she acquired a translator through wiles all her own.

Now, she fights savagely.

And I couldn't be shroving prouder. Or am I more terrified? Certainly, some cruel combination of both.

"Here, drink this. You've earned it." Manila steps around me and slaps my female on the back. Any other lunar, I'd think she was trying to rob Nalia, but not this one, not with that mischievous expression on her face. If she were truly trying to steal Nalia's winnings, she'd be smiling a lot more.

Instead, she thrusts a cup of bubbling pink liquid into Nalia's hand. Smoke wafts from the top of its gooey surface and it smells sweet and heavily spiced all at once. Nalia lifts it immediately to her lips and would have drunk the shroving thing, too, if I hadn't swiped it away from her.

"Hey, that's mine," she pouts, pink lips twisting into the cutest shroving expression. I want to bite her lips. I want to swallow her tongue down my throat. I want to bask in her every freckle, feature and flaw.

I clear my throat and glance at Manila. "What the shrov is it?" I take a sip, the sensation like a match set to oil and poured straight down my throat.

Nalia reaches for it again while Manila kicks a Hypha off of their seat on Nalia's other side. The creature's too drunk to complain and topples onto the patchwork metal floor among peals of laughter from their friends, a melee of creatures with not a commonality between them. That's the Revel.

Strung between five different platforms, the Revel rooms are some of the few built structures in the Below, though they aren't rooms at all, but open platforms made of whatever odd materials the Eshmiri and other traders had lying around.

We sit in the densest part of the Revel now, drinks thrust upon us at every turn by the last tournament's spectators, excited by our performance in the games. Well, her performance, I can begrudgingly admit. Because far more drinks are going to Nalia than to me.

"It's not meant for you," Manila says, her metal arm stretching forward and whisking the drink from my grip. She hands it to Nalia, who marvels over the concoction.

"How'd you do that?" she says, eyeing Manila's Droherion and stalyx-enhanced arm. Maybe, she's not admiring the concoction then, but rather, Manila's speed.

"What? This?" She tosses something into the air — an object I can't quite make out because she's so quick in catching it again.

"Ontte, that." Nalia nods. "Is it your arm? It looks like the other woman's."

"That was no human female," Manila tsks. She reaches across the rocky bar and hails the Walrey behind it. A few moments later, a different Walrey buzzes over and sets three Walrey honey meads down before us. "That was an assassin of the Sky order. New, if I had to guess. I haven't seen some of her enhancements before."

"I hadn't either."

"The yeeyar they used for her eyes. It surpasses even Niahhorru yeeyar, would be my guess." Manila's black eyes flash to mine and though her smile remains fixed, I can see a slight fear beneath her expression.

"We make the best yeeyar, you know that," I snort, masking my mirrored fear with confidence.

She shakes her head. "They keep coming out with new models these solars. Since I was an assassin, the updates have become near unrecognizable."

"You were like her?"

"Once," Manila says tossing back her mead and hailing the Walrey for another.

The bar itself is made of red rock stitched through with golden streaks of ioni, so that it shines like a golden snake slithering across the platforms with no reason or order. Manila wipes her mouth with the back of her other hand, this one yellowish-orange and a testament to her Hypha heritage, before setting her glass down and hailing the Walrey for yet another.

"Manila is the only Sky assassin to break free of their chains," I add, bumping Nalia's hip with my knee.

She's wearing a Walrey creation, made of their silks. They had it tailored to fit her while she was out in the merillian and it shimmers a brilliant, brutal red. It's all bands of silk wrapped around her thin, pale frame. It encircles her throat and covers her breasts before wrapping down to meet a long, flowing skirt. It looks so delicate. I can see all the lines of her body pressing against the underside of it. The peaks of her breasts…the thatch of curls between her legs…

"She is?"

"She is." I clear my throat and ignore Manila's teasing glances. "The Sky architects — the ones who create the assassins — implant two things in each new assassin they make. A Sky key, which is a beacon for all Sky assassins to find their way back to the Sky planet…"

"I thought that, but I was wondering," Nalia interrupts. "Did you get the Sky key from the female we fought in the arena?"

I shake my head. "The key is only active while the assassin has a pulse."

"It's a safe guard," Manila adds. "Otherwise, it would make sending assassins out with a key at all too risky for the architects. They have a lot of valuable technology on their planet, a lot of slaves with allies that would like to liberate them, and have as many vendettas against them for their crimes and cruelty as there are stars in the quadrants."

Nalia nods soberly though, judging by the color in her face and the newfound gloss to her gaze, she's anything but. "What's the second thing they put in Sky assassins?"

"A tracking device. It's made of yeeyar, the same substance your mok bir batons are made of, only it responds to commands issued from Sky itself. The Sky architects thread it so thoroughly throughout the body that usually the body can't survive the process of disentanglement. Manila is the first, the only to have survived. And because she survived the process, so did her Sky key. She defeated them."

"Not me. Ashmara," she says to Nalia. "I was an Ashmara experiment."

"Ashmara?"

"The Eshmiri reaver who pointed you to the Andalinian sabre."

Nalia slams her pink goblet down onto the rocky ledge and shivers all over. She wipes her mouth with the back of her hand, makes a face and sputters, "Whew. Again!" Three beverages appear before her, thrust there by a Hypha, a Mormora and a Tinkana, respectively. I sample all of them before letting her try any. I don't think she notices. She's enrapt with Manila's story.

"The Eshmiri reaver?" she asks, shaking her head. "I thought all Eshmiri were male."

"Except for Ashmara."

"She was adopted," I add, "but don't let it fool you. She's as reaver as it gets. The story goes, she'd been hunting for a Sky assassin to liberate for rotations — "

"Why? That woman...female...I've never seen anyone fight like her. To actively track one seems dangerous."

"Extremely. And who knows? She's nuts. All reavers are. It was probably a passing fancy…"

"Her greatest challenge," Manila interrupts. "It's what made her famous."

I correct, "*More* famous. She'd already made a name for herself by the time you came along. Don't flatter yourself."

Manila laughs and sweeps her black hair back from her shoulders and I watch the way the tips animate slightly, bending against the foul-smelling wind that rolls through the place on the heels of the Egama contingent stomping towards us.

My muscles remember the pain of holding onto that assassin's braid, holding and holding longer still, knowing that I needed to be rid of it in order to save Nalia. Knowing that I'd never let go for that same reason. Even if it killed me. And, for a moment, it felt like it just might.

"Anyway," Manila picks up. "The reavers on board her ship, Tintin and Gibli and Uuni and the rest, managed to trick me or something — at least, that's how the story goes, my memories from that *transitional* period are funny."

She takes another drink. "According to Ashmara, it took the whole clan six solars to perform the surgery. They did it on board her ship. They had a Walrey healer with them, a Voraxian scholar on all things Sky, and they even enlisted the help of a Niahhorru pirate, an expert in yeeyar and a harvester at that. Cost them a fortune. Ashmara had to trade her ship to be able to do it. That's why she runs the skies in the decrepit machine she's in now."

I open my mouth to add something about Ashmara's muuir addiction, then decide against. I take another draught from my mead, letting the sugar more than the booze go to my head.

"Hey!" I call out to a Lemoran behind the bar. "Have any lobba?" The female grins at me and slides over a jug of the stuff. I toss her a token, which she returns.

"My clan hates the Sky. You did us a favor," she says. "You and your female. Once the tournament ends, you'll have to come see us in Quadrant Two. I know Clan Chief Raingar and his miriga would love to meet you both."

I grin. "Perhaps, for the right quantity of kintarr, we'll consider it."

I wink at her and she rolls her eyes at me, grey horns twisting away from her forehead like arrows to the stars.

Behind me, Manila is still speaking. "They found a way to extricate the yeeyar from my muscles and bones. They couldn't take it out of my skull, but they found a way to deaden it by blasting a highly concentrated dose of ionine directly into the yeeyar itself. After that, I regained control of my body. I got my…not my memories, but my consciousness back. I owe Ashmara and her crew everything I am."

"Wow. She sounds like an impressive…well, I don't actually know what she is."

"A hybrid of some kind. No one knows which species, for certain."

I do. I clear my throat. "She's a reaver. It doesn't matter what planet she was born to."

Manila smiles and Nalia lifts her black goblet. "Cheers to that."

"Cheers?"

"Oh." Nalia laughs and shakes her head. "Sometimes, I forget I'm not on Earth. It's a human custom. Lifting your glasses and clicking them together in honor of something. It's called a toast."

"You said it was a cheers," I say.

"It's both."

"Confusing species."

I nod, agreeing with Manila. "Confusing language."

"You're welcome for the translator," Manila says lifting her cup and mashing it against Nalia's. I do the same and Nalia laughs as we drink our fill. Manila's cup now empty, she slides from her stool. "Speaking of equipment, I heard you may be in need of a disruptor so you can communicate with the mothership."

My ears perk. "You know where I can find one?"

"I know where you can *buy* one, ontte. And with as many tokens as you and your mate earned during the last battle, you'd be able to afford two." She gestures over her shoulder absently. "Rekkaru domes on tier eighty-nine, eleven, two. A female with a broken wing, she sells rarities but don't expect to be able to negotiate with her. She's a menace." Manila frowns, leading me to believe that she's been negotiating with the female for some time over something she wants and losing. I laugh. Manila doesn't like to lose.

"Thank you." I nod at her.

She nods back. But before she can disappear into the crowd, Nalia says, "If you owe Ashmara so much, why not just give her the Sky key?"

Manila freezes. Her expression flutters, wavering as she turns to look my female over. My *mate*, as she called her. I feel the same surprise she does, or at least an echo of it. It's a smart question, one I'd not been bold enough to ask.

Manila's lips work. "How…did…how did you know Ashmara was looking for it?"

"Uuni," I answer.

Manila nods, albeit gravely. The boisterous crowd around us seems no match for the solemnity in her gaze. "It isn't a question of honor or price. I want whoever takes the key to be able to take on a Sky assassin in wit and in cunning — not in strength, because assassins can't be matched in that — because whoever does claim it will be hunted for it. It's a heavy burden to bear and after what Ashmara did for me, too high a price for her to pay even if she may be clever enough. Only just clever enough."

Manila takes another step, but Nalia's words hold her in place. "You really care about her, don't you?"

With Manila's smirk, some of the tension around us dissolves. "Ashmara is one of the least likeable creatures in the entire galaxy and yet, she has friends everywhere. I count myself among them." Her gaze switches between Nalia and I, and I feel myself, for whatever reason, sliding my lower arm around Nalia's waist, as if claiming her. "As I do both of you. I'll see you both at the final mok bir tournament. For the same reasons I just mentioned, I hope you lose.

"But if you insist on winning, good luck. You'll need it. Rhogan and Olanora have been cleaning house. There won't be any tokens of value left if you don't manage to outmaneuver them. Just a hint — Olanora's weakness is Rhogan. And Rhogan's weakness may just be you. I've seen the way he looks at you." She waggles her fingers over her shoulder and is gone before I can ask her what the shrov she's on about.

"What in the shrov is she talking about?" I say at the same time Nalia says, "How do you know Manila?"

And at the same time, we both answer, "Errrmmm."

Weaving between the hovering stalls in the Rekkaru marketplace, I learn of the males and females Nalia played her previous mok bir tournament against. And I also take the time to tell her of the shekurr.

"So, let me get this straight," she says, slowing and turning to face me fully. "You have eight males…"

"Or more."

"Fuck. You have eight or more males and one single female and you put her on a table and you all go to town trying to breed her?"

"Centare, not at all. We don't go into any towns. We breed her right there on the breeding table. That's what it's for."

Nalia barks out a laugh that makes my chest tighten along with my tantu leather pants. "That isn't what I meant. I meant that it seems impossible that you'd all… rut all over her and that she'd survive it. I've seen the size of your…package."

"My cock?"

Her skin turns a startling pink. "Ontte."

"The longer the reach, the better the odds of impregnating the female. But Manila didn't want to be impregnated, she simply wanted eleven males to worship her."

"Eleven," Nalia whispers quietly. I'll admit, I'm surprised by her reaction. Centare, not only surprised, but also aroused.

"You aren't angry?"

"Centare." Her brow scrunches. "Why would I be?"

"Deena. Rhorkanterannu's female. She is a human and she was jealous to hear of her mate participating in other shekurrs. That's why they only breed each other."

Nalia simply shrugs. "I can understand why other people get jealous. But I didn't know you then. If you were in a shekurr now, without me, I wouldn't..." She stops, voice catching, body temperature rising — I can feel it. "I wouldn't like it," she says.

My throat is tight and I can't shroving help it. I lash out and catch the back of her neck. I drag her against my chest and she stumbles, catching herself against my plates with her small, soft hands. *Soft hands made for grabbing sensitive cocks, and fisting them.*

"And if you were ever in a shekurr without me, I'd slaughter every male involved."

Her breath hitches, her eyes close longer than the other blinks I've seen her take before. She licks her lips. Her tongue tastes like victory and sweet malt. I want more. *More.* To slake my thirst. "But with you?"

My heart thrums. Power buzzes through me like an ocean current, ready to drag me under. Ready to take us both. "Would you like that?"

She shrugs, her eyes slanting to the side. "Maybe. I... I don't know. Honestly, it sounds a little scary."

"You'd have no reason to fear. I'd kill any male who did anything you didn't like, even unintentionally."

She laughs, but it dies quickly. "You really mean that, don't you?"

"Ontte."

"Even though you don't like killing."

"Ontte. Even then." I lift her hand from my chest and bring it to my mouth. I sweep my tongue across the backs of her knuckles, marking her with my scent. "In every shekurr, there is one lead male who keeps the others in line. If you wanted, I would be yours, leading you through endless fields of pleasure until you were sick with it, your belly swollen with seed, stars bursting in your eyes."

She sways forward. I slide my lower hand across her stomach. She whimpers against my pectoral, little chin tipping up as she rubs her face against me, like she's scent marking *me*. The thought makes me absolutely shroving feral. "Ontte. I'd like to do that with you. I just…don't want to get pregnant from some random male."

"Never. Not some random male. My brothers. And not from them, either. They will drink the sterility draught. The only seed that will take will be mine," I lean down and whisper against her cheek. "And it will take. After all of my brothers finish rutting inside of your body, you'll be so slick with their seed, so primed and ready for me there will be no other option. Would you like this, Nalia? Eight males worshipping you, all under my control, my direction?"

She gasps, whimpers slightly when I tug on her hair, rakes her dull claws roughly over my plates — rough enough I can just barely feel them. "I thought you said it would be eleven."

I hiss, "Naughty little human…" I grab her waist, but she pushes herself upright and sweeps her hair back from her neck, revealing its fevered flush.

She takes my hand — my lower left one — and gives it a tug. "Let's get this over with fast and go back to the tent."

A growl I have no control over purrs from my throat. Her eyes widen. She licks her bottom lip. I lean in and swipe my own tongue across it, tasting her sweet, salty flavor. She smells of flowers — centare, their thorns, dripping in blood. "Savage thing. You are not what you seemed in the beginning."

Her blunt teeth sink into my bottom lip, sending sensation scorching through my tines, making my plates lift as I expel heat. I want to work her over. I want to feel the sweat slick her skin in a way it doesn't ever slick mine because I have plates and she doesn't. She pulls back and I find myself leaning forward onto the balls of my feet.

"I'm not what I was in the beginning." She pulls me forward, leading me through the crowd as I follow behind her blindly.

"What do you mean?"

"I mean, I think something's been happening. I'm starting to remember who I was before."

"Before?" My skin prickles. Cold sweeps my skin, freezing some of the warmth. "Before what?"

"Before I woke up. I'm starting to remember certain things from Earth."

"Earth? Is that the name of the human planet?"

"It *was*. I…I have this feeling that Earth doesn't exist anymore."

"Do you remember anything immediately after you woke up in the blue box?"

She shakes her head. "Not really. I remember Jerrock. That's my first real memory from after, and even that's more or less vague up until the point that Jerrock kidnapped Essmira and you and the Lemorans came to rescue us."

I swallow hard, plates lifting again but this time in anxiety. "That's…good."

She gives me a strange look over her shoulder. "I guess? So far, the memories haven't been good. I like the new memories I've made much better." She closes one eye at me, an expression I've seen Deena make many times and always in jest. Always with affection. Rhorkanterannu has an affectionate female. I don't. It makes her one-eye blink mean even more.

"I'm honored to be a part of them," I tell her. She smiles. I cock my chin to the left. "I think we're here."

There are very few Rekkaru who ever bother to walk, so to see one grounded stands out. Nalia veers to the left as she spots what I do — a female beneath the awning of a square tent made of white sticks crudely patched together.

"It looks like a nest," Nalia says. I nod and approach the female who's currently haggling with an Avmar, an eight-legged creature with a glistening yellow carapace. The creature is intimidating as it rears up on its back four legs and snaps its maw down at the much smaller female, who does nothing but hold out one grey-hued hand. She curls her fingers towards the creature when it snaps at her again.

A moment passes before the Avmar reaches one pincer beneath a scale hidden along its underbelly. It produces a single glowing yellow stone and drops it into her hand. She hands the Avmar a mok bir baton. A shroving good one. One that doesn't just ward off incoming mok bir batons, but that incinerates them. Not even yeeyar is immune.

"Shrov," I curse.

"What?"

I shake my head and plaster on a smile. "I'll tell you later. Ishitengram," I announce — a formal greeting in Rekkaru. The female looks up at me, nonplussed and unamused.

"Mok bir batons are fifty thousand credits."

"Fifty thousand!" We're not even here for mok bir batons, but that's still an outrage. "You can buy pouches of kintarr for less than that."

The female shrugs, her left wings fluttering reflexively while her right wings hang at a lower angle than they should. "Then play mok bir with a pouch of kintarr. What do I care?" She turns and starts to waddle back towards her tent.

"Whatever broke her wing must have also broken her sense of humor," I whisper to Nalia, who smirks.

"Wait." Nalia steps forward, moving back immediately when the Avmar drops forward and slither-scuttles past. "What about a disruptor?"

The female stops and turns and gives Nalia a once over with her dark grey eyes. "Communications disruptor? You want to speak off-world?"

"Ontte."

"That's not allowed here on Evernor." She blinks rapidly, her wings fluttering more feverishly, disrupting the loose and lacy fabrics she wears. They look expensive. As do the stones dripping around the female's neck.

Nalia just shrugs.

The Rekkaru female looks at me. I follow my mate's lead and shrug, too.

"Hungh," the trader grunts. "One hundred twenty-five thousand. Not much good it will do you, though. No ships can dock here, so your friends can't save you from the final battle or from competing in the mok bir tournament." Her gaze flicks from me to Nalia and back again. "Unless your friends happen to have a certain machine I've heard rumors about."

I just grin. "Machine? What machine?"

"A machine capable of pulling living creatures off of planets Quadrants away? Hm?"

"Why, that does sound impressive, but this is the first I've ever heard of it," I lie effusively through my teeth. "We just want the disruptor to be able to chat with good friends. They'll be missing us by now."

She gives me a dour look, one so dour it makes me laugh. She shuffles back into her tent, muttering all the while, "Shroving Niahhorru pirates, think everything is a joke." Inside, under shadows, she shouts, "I found it. It's in good condition. The price is one thirty."

"Shroving female," I bark back. "One twenty."

"One fifty."

"Pagh! Fine. One twenty-five…"

"Wait!" Nalia steps towards the entrance to her tent and lifts a hand. She holds onto the edge of the awning, fingers curling into the lattice vines. "What about a salvation disc? How much would that cost?"

"Nalia…" I stutter. So does my heart. I slip my hand around her elbow and pull her back, away from the tent. "Nalia, you know I'm not…angry with you…our fight before. I was being…an anal hole."

She grins. "Yeah, you were. A big one."

"I'm sorry for that."

"Don't be. After I experienced what you're up against every single solar…" She takes a deep breath. "It isn't easy. You make it look easy. And I know you don't like to kill. I don't want you to have to."

My chest…it aches with a sudden emotion I've never experienced. So strong, I can't even give it a name. "Nalia, we could use the disruptor to get a ride out of here. We wouldn't need the disc at all."

"And leave without the Sky key?" She smiles, as if lives aren't on the line. As if hers isn't. "Leave without all our winnings? When we could take it all? That doesn't seem very pirate-like."

I smirk and pinch her chin with one hand. With another, I rope her into my chest. "Revenge isn't as important as living."

"A wise pirate once told me that if we tried to cut out before the finale, there'd be a price on our heads."

"It wouldn't be the first time and it won't be the last."

"Herannathon," she huffs. "Why are you chickening out now? Let's finish this."

"What is a chicken?"

"It's a bird and that's beside the point. I'm serious. You think I, of all people, don't want to seek revenge against the Sky? Of course I do. Not just for locking me up on that ship, but for what they did to those giants." She shivers, her gaze unfocusing. "It wasn't right. And if they're enslaving people — beings — and forcing them to commit tortures like that, then they need to be stopped and the enslaved, freed."

I smile as I stare down into her eyes, glittering with passion that sparkles as bright as greed. "You sound like Ashmara now."

"Maybe, we should band with her."

"Reavers and pirates don't work together."

"Good, then, that I'm not a pirate."

I smile. "You're *too* pirate for your own good. And besides, it's unlikely that she even has a salvation disc. Rumor has it, they've all been used…"

"Five hundred thousand credits." The Rekkaru female steps out of her tent holding an orb. It glows green, but that's only for show. The raw, liquid Droherion inside is dormant. It's only when dormant that it glows. "It's my last salvation disc. You want it or not?"

Shock. My heart hammers and all twenty of my fingers flex. I slip one hand around the back of Nalia's neck. Another I extend towards the Rekkaru trader. "Let me see it."

"Need collateral." She tosses the rock up and before it lands, Nalia swipes it from the air. Fast. Too fast for a human. I feel the prickly sensation crawl up my spine again, same as I did when I watched her wield that Andalinian sabre. She held it well, as if she'd handled weapons like that before, and when she struck the Sky warrior, she didn't hesitate. *She's fought before. Maybe even killed.*

It makes me wary of her, even more wary when she shows me the stone with a smile, as if moving so fast is something she does all the time. *Maybe, she's an assassin herself. A skilled one. What if Jerrock embedded something in her skull and is watching me through her eyes, even now?*

"What?"

"Nothing." I take the stone while the Rekkaru female grumbles behind Nalia, but makes no move to sic any of her kinsmen on us. "This…" I tilt it up to the light and watch as the Droherion inside clings to the inner hollow. I grin. "This is a fake, isn't it?"

"Centare," the Rekkaru answers.

I give her a look. "Truly?"

"If you have to ask, then it's not."

She has a point. And Eshmiri won't know the difference. Well, they will, but they don't care. A fake is almost as hard to generate as an authentic one and cheating is not only tolerated in the games, but encouraged. The only problem is that, well, I don't have five hundred thousand. I'll have to rob this female and then the other Rekkaru will send their drones to skin me in the lunar. That won't work.

I grit my teeth. "Two hundred thousand."

"I don't negotiate."

Nalia jumps in. "Two hundred thousand and I'll give you ten percent of my mok bir winnings."

Surprising me, the Rekkaru hesitates. "I've seen you play. You play well, but unstrategically. You don't take home many winnings. Would be a bad deal for me."

"You've seen me play *once*. I noticed you in the crowd." Nalia nods. "That was my first time playing. I didn't know the rules. I know them now."

"Hm." The female strokes her long grey hair. It falls thick around her shoulders, betraying her age. The older Rekkaru get, the thicker their hair. Hers is shiny and glistens like finished stalyx, falling to her elbows. "Your first match?"

Nalia nods.

"How many have you played since?"

"Only one other, but I've been playing in the interim with Herannathon."

The female is quiet. I don't flinch as she looks me over. "You think she will win?"

"Ontte," I answer without hesitation. "She will."

"I *know* I will. And I'll bring you far more than five hundred thousand chips."

"Chips?" the Rekkaru says.

Nalia stutters. "Credits. I don't know why I said chips. I think we gamble with chips where I'm from."

"Gamble," the Rekkaru says slowly, stroking her hair more feverishly, as if she's never heard of the word before. "Two hundred and fifty thousand and fifty percent."

"No way," Nalia interjects, luckily before I can slam my fist through the Rekkaru's jaw. Fifty percent. *Fifty* percent? Has she lost her senses? No wonder the Avmar was so furious. "Fifteen percent."

"Forty."

"Twenty-five."

"Mehh." The Rekkaru waves a hand in Nalia's face, dismissing her. "Fine. But you better win."

"I won't let you down." Nalia beams and looks back at me. "You okay with that?"

"Ontte. You're a natural." *Too* natural at this. I reach into my pocket and produce a flat yeeyar disc, one with all of our credits on it.

Nalia has one too that she produces from her robes. She hands it to me. "I don't know how this works."

I nod and press the two discs together and numbers appear on either surface. In shifting black, like sand or smoke, I see that Nalia's disc holds twenty-six thousand credits — not a bad haul from two mok bir tournaments — so, I transfer exactly two hundred and twenty-four thousand credits onto Nalia's disc before tossing the flat yeeyar token, no larger than Nalia's palm, to the Rekkaru.

"We'll be back with Nalia's winnings."

"You must be mad, pirate. I'll be there to collect *my* winnings myself." She points at Nalia's nose, which doesn't stand much higher than her own. "You better not fail me or it'll be your mate's winnings I'm after. If he survives."

"That's a guarantee now, isn't it?" Nalia asks, rather than answer.

The Rekkaru shrugs. "You should know better than anyone, anything can happen in the tournaments."

I slide the salvation disc into my pocket, along with the few tokens Nalia and I have left. "Come on, Nalia. Let's get some food and get back to the tent."

Nalia looks up at me without a smile this time. She looks concerned. Because the Rekkaru is absolutely right.

And I have a bad feeling about all of this.

14

Nalia

I've never been so sick in my life. Whatever I ate last night was apparently too alien for my stomach. Serves me right for insulting the Ebo paste the Eshmiri were feeding me before. Ebo always treated me right.

"Euhhhh," I moan. Herannathon has been alternating between laughing at me riotously and being in a full-blown state of panic ever since I threw up the first time last night.

Now, it's the middle of the night — the lunar, as he calls it — and he's holding my hair in one hand and rubbing my back with another. "Here, drink this. The shroving Eshmiri healer finally showed up. He says this is a cure-all for any species."

"You…believe him?" I groan into the rocky basin. It doesn't echo, *not like a toilet would*, because it's all made of rock and disappears deep into the ground. The ground smells nice. *Smells like Georgia red clay. I used to play in it when I was little. I'm a Southern girl.*

"Unfortunately, I do believe him."

"Why…unfortunately?" I say as my stomach heaves again. Nothing comes out this time. Thank god. He hands me the plastic-feeling cup and I take a large swig of the slightly sweet, eerily salty liquid. My stomach starts to churn almost immediately.

"Because he says the only way to purge the uhh... delicacies of the market is to purge everything all at once."

My gut clenches. *Fuccckkkk...*

15

Nalia

I'm dead asleep when I feel claws against the side of my face. They scrape tenderly around my hairline before trailing back into my hair. I shudder and moan at the unexpected spark that thrums between my legs.

"There is food for you when you wake. You should make sure to eat something." His mouth brushes my forehead, which is cool and dry, thanks to all the sponge baths he's been giving me.

I mumble, "What time is it?"

"Early still. I'm just going to the tournament grounds early to tell the Eshmiri why you won't be in attendance."

"Centare. Centare, I can make it."

"Shh."

"Don't shush me." I prop myself up on one elbow, surprised by how much better I'm feeling. No longer sick, now I'm just beat. My abs are sore as hell, but I don't feel like throwing up anymore, at least. "I *want* to make it. I need to make sure you actually use that stupid disc on yourself and not on another sorry soul."

Herannathon chuckles, but I can still feel him moving away from me. His warmth is replaced by a different warmth, less…thrilling and more…normal. I frown. Normal is completely overrated. I fight to open my eyes and, when I do, I see him standing at the foot of the net watching me with a fondness that makes my bones hurt. An unfamiliar energy courses through my body, making my toes curl…

I gasp just a little and Herannathon flinches, like he's been jolted by a very, very small taser. He hisses, "You shouldn't look at me like that."

"Why not?"

"Because I'll stay here and submerge myself in you when I should be concentrating on the battle."

"Mhmm. I'm okay with that." I roll onto my back and watch his gaze slip over the pelt that covers me. I'm not wearing anything else. Sometime in the lunar, he undressed me. He'd been purely clinical in his ministrations, but I can still remember how it felt to have four hands caressing me. Slowly, I push the top of the fur down and show him my breasts.

He growls and jerks forward, then rubs his upper left hand roughly over his face. When he looks at me again, his protective eye shields have dropped into place. "You're sick. Don't tempt me, female."

"I'm not sick. That poison water helped."

He laughs, but keeps his back turned to face me. I find the spikes *hot. Dangerous. I've always liked playing with explosive things.* "Stay put. Stay safe. And eat something." He reaches the doorway and lifts a tent flap. Light outside filters in, all reddish-orange. It glints off of his silver skin, making him glitter. "You'll need the energy when I return."

"Change your mind about waiting to shrov me until we reach Kor?"

My empty stomach flips — and growls. Herannathon must have good hearing because the little flaps that I suppose he hears out of twitch and he laughs loud. "Eat, female," he barks, ignoring my question, my taunts and my desires.

He leaves me in the lurch but it doesn't seem to matter. He leaves me smiling. It doesn't last. It takes me about two seconds of lying on my back smiling up at the ceiling before I start to imagine Herannathon's last opponent and his next fight.

I picture all kinds of terrible, twisted things. Too worried to do anything but give myself an anxiety attack, I roll off of the net — literally, roll — and manage to make it to the bathroom, or well, the room with the water in it.

I bathe more properly, a little annoyed that I don't have a razor to shave my pits and the giant red bush growing between my legs, but whatever. I move past it, grateful at least to be clean and not feeling like a bucket of bolts rattling around, especially after I manage to get some more Ebo nut paste in me.

There's some dried meat on the tray Herannathon left me that I sample and that seems to settle right. There's also some creamy looking substance that I avoid at all costs because it looks like the cup of what I *thought* was ice cream, but tasted more like meat and cheese and that I think made me sick last night. I eat the fruit, the white brick thing that I can't identify at all, and I down all the water in sight.

I've just emptied the second pitcher of sweet water in front of me when I hear the distinct sound of flyers whizzing outside. They sound louder than they should.

"Hello?" I say stupidly, as if I expect a response from the furniture.

When I don't get one, I quickly pull on a fancy robe that fits me — a gift during Herannathon's last tournament — and knot it around the waist.

I walk towards the exit and slip through the tent flaps only to see an Eshmiri face that I recognize and two that I don't. "Gibli?"

Gibli and the other two Eshmiri wave both hands at me in the strange human-not-so-human way they seem to be fond of. I wave back with both hands because why the hell not? They simultaneously burst into fits of laughter.

"Come, come," Gibli says as their giggles die down. He gestures me forward.

"Where?"

"To the Above."

"I thought Herannathon talked to you guys about me staying here." I plant both hands on my hips, not sure about this. At all. The Eshmiri can't be trusted. Herannathon's said it enough, but even without his warning, I'd never trust anything that smiles so much.

"He did, but there are others who want to see you Above *more*." His tan-colored eyes glisten and gleam. This can't be good.

"Who?"

"Oosa."

I cross my arms and step forward, the surface of our little rock dry and dusty and warm under the soles of my bare feet. "Why do they want to see me hanging in a box in the sky while the fighters fight below? What do they get out of it?"

The Eshmiri turn towards each other, giggling and whispering too low and too fast for my translator to catch. They're up to something and I want to know what.

"Gibli, tell me what's going on. You don't even have the box here with you."

"Kintarr isn't needed today," he chuckles.

His friend says, "You won't be on display."

And then his other friend elbows him in the gut with the blunt end of the strange spear-looking weapon he carries. The elbowed friend buckles and produces a spear of his own. It crackles blue on one end when he jabs it towards his other friend, who yelps and jumps three feet into the air, causing the flyer they're standing on to sway dramatically and all three males to plummet into one of the rickety railings.

Gibli releases a squawk-screech and takes out a blaster and hammers the handle on his friends' heads until they all devolve into a fit of giggles and turn their collective attention back to me. "Come. It's a special tournament today," Gibli says, wiping his eyes.

"That sounds dangerous. I think I'll stay here," I bluff. There's no way I'm staying here. If there's something *new* happening up above, it's undoubtedly dangerous, and if Herannathon's involved, I want to be there. My fingers twitch. *Where's my gun?* I shove them under my arms.

Gibli doesn't smile, which transforms the strange shape of the Eshmiri face even more, turning it from a flattened circle to a near perfect triangle. Their mouths almost disappear when they don't smile, their large eyes appearing as huge as moons. "The Oosa are willing to pay lots and lots of tokens to see you Above. Herannathon will get them directly. And you, too."

"At least two hundred thousand!" one of the Eshmiri shouts.

Two hundred thousand? My ears perk. That's enough to buy the comms disruptor off of the Rekkaru trader. Or get us closer to being able to buy the salvation disc outright. And then I think about it more… They wouldn't be offering to pay us directly unless the risk was high. Higher than high.

Slowly, I shake my head. "Nah. Sounds like trouble."

"No trouble," Gibli says.

"No fighting."

"Guaranteed win."

I frown. "You're lying."

"Not lying."

"Never."

"Eshmiri never lie." Gibli grins.

"What am I missing?"

Gibli shares a look of mock disbelief with his friends. "Nothing. We're not keeping anything from you. Come Above. Make lots of credits. Return right after. No risk."

His friends nod. "No risk," they say together.

I take a step, hesitate, then take another. The Eshmiri release a collective shout of glee and clap their pudgy, multi-fingered hands together. One of the Eshmiri looks like he has twenty fingers strung across both hands while Gibli only has eight — not evenly dispersed, either, but five on one hand and three on the other. He beckons me forward with his three-fingered hand and the contraption they ride tips forward as he helps me on.

"Whoooooowwwweeec!" One of them screeches. I turn towards him as wind whips my face and we lurch along.

"Was this flyer built for four?" I ask as the machine beneath me sputters and dips.

"Oh krakaw." The friend shakes his head as he mutters a word that comes through my translator as *no*. It must be another language, then. "I am Hunhun."

I hesitate, then hold out my hand. "Nalia."

He giggles wildly and pokes the center of my palm. I smile at him. "In human, we do a handshake. Here, like this." I shake his hand, finding the texture of his palm pleasantly furry and warm, which sends him spiraling into peals and rivulets of unending laughter.

His friend butts forward and says, "I am Dogo! Shake my hand!"

I do and Dogo laughs just as hard as Hunhun had. Finally Gibli shoves him off and repeats the action and soon they're all laughing and I can't help but laugh myself as we zip dangerously low to the market stalls, clipping the underside of our rust bucket on one conical tent, and then dangerously high, towards a glowing blue Oosa glider, clipping one of the rust bucket's rickety barriers on a glowing blue ledge.

"Jesus Christ!" I shout as a blue blob tries to grab at my hair from above.

"Chesumkripppees!" the Eshmiri shout all around me. Soon, they're laughing again and then clapping and then shaking both of my hands and each other's.

I roll my eyes, excited to get off this damn flyer by the time we make it to the black hole — it looks like the entrance to Hell, even though it leads up rather than down. The darkness that washes over us hurts my eyes, compared to the brightness of the Below, which is luminous. We zip into the tunnel that leads to the arena gates. They're closed now.

"What's going on with the tournament? Is it underway?" I ask when the gates to the arena draw close. I glance around. The tunnel is curiously empty. Too empty. Normally, there are some Eshmiri loitering around, drunk and gambling and very occasionally working, not even bothering to watch the fights going on outside, but today… Today, there's no one.

It's *quiet.* I mean, not quite, because it can't possibly be with how loud the crowd outside is roaring. I can feel the vibrations of tens of thousands of bodies in the stands through the rocky walls around us.

"Is the fight still going on?"

"Yeeshee, yeeshee," Hunhun says.

Dogo and Gibli shake their heads. "Krakaw. Hasn't started yet."

The glider dips and Dogo jumps to the ground and heads to the controls on the wall. There's a black box that he speaks into and then shoves one hand inside of and, when he finishes doing whatever he's doing, he waves us forward and the gates open.

"I don't understand. I thought you said no fighting." I cross my arms, feeling heat and nervousness climb up the back of my neck as I glare down at Gibli, who isn't even my height though he's ten times my breadth. "If there's no fighting, why are we even here?"

Gibli smiles up at me with his little sharp teeth. "No fighting. Pinky swear." He holds up one of his five fingers — not a pinky either, because it's the thickness of three of my fingers. But I loop my pinky around the thick digit anyway and nod.

"How do you know about pinky promises? That's a human thing."

But he just giggles and, as heat and blinding light wash over us, he guides the glider forward.

The minute we're out under the dome, the heat intensifies, becoming searing and making me wish I'd worn something other than this thin robe — because I'd like to take it off. "Shit." I start fanning myself while the throngs go absolutely mental around us. "What in the…" I glance around the packed red sands and up at the dark grey metal and red rocky arena bench seats. They shoot up like enormous shards of glass stabbed down into the planet's surface…and I don't understand. "There's no fight here…"

"Krakaw, there isn't. We said there wasn't and we Eshmiri never lie," Gibli says, and then he shoves his stupid hand in between my shoulder blades and gives me a sharp push.

I squeal as I tumble towards the edge of the glider, grabbing onto the rails for support. But Dogo just reaches for my hand and forces it into a shake, and when he lets go, I stumble backward. We're low enough I don't fall, but manage to stagger off of the platform and onto the hot soil. Swaying like a clever drunk, I stay upright and shout up at the glider, "Jerks!"

"Shurks!" they shout back at each other before zipping up above to hang out with the other Eshmiri gliders usually hanging like Christmas ornaments from the dome's translucent grey arch.

"Holy shit…" I say as I follow the path the trio take up to the tippy top of the dome. It's *full*. There are just as many gliders and crystalline boxes containing prizes up there as there were the last time, and the last battle was meant to be the most epic of all. Even with her bright orange skin, I can't identify Manila among them. I glance at the stands. I can't identify anyone. "What is…"

I look forward, gaze ripping around as I hear a high, sharp sound. I pad forward, farther onto the field, aware that there are literally hundreds of thousands of eyes on me now and *all* of them seem eager and pleased. I don't understand anything. All I know is that I'm not alone.

A weight settles in my chest like a stone, feeling like an anchor rather than a burden, as I spy a familiar set of sharp grey spears shooting out of a male's grey back. He's all the way on the opposite side of the arena and hasn't seen me yet. Instead, he's shouting up at a cluster of creatures riding a flat, glowing blue glider.

Most of the creatures definitely form an Oosa contingent, though with their completely bulbous and amorphous shapes I can't tell how many of them there are — or how many Eshmiri are riding with them. I wonder what they're arguing with Herannathon about.

The dirt is hot under the bare soles of my feet as I step forward, the edges of my robe gathered high like a damn princess'. *Not exactly the war getup I'm used to.* The red dust clings to my legs and to my dress, looking oddly sinister, and beautiful. I have this strange sensation that I'm in a dream — *gunfire sounds all around me, and I'm not afraid but I'm angry.* It reminds me of a dream I've had before — *not a dream, a reality* — but I don't feel the way I did then. Not at all.

Here, I feel the same heat, the same fire burning through my blood, but none of the anger, the rage, the fear. Here I feel *freedom.* Pure liberation. And my heart starts to pound and my stomach exalts when I come close enough to hear exactly what they're saying.

"...what the shrov is this? You can't change the terms of the tournament..." Herannathon shouts.

"We're not changing terms. It's still a battle," an Eshmiri I don't know, but that I've seen presiding over the games before, shouts back. He gesticulates wildly with his short arms and the electric spear he carries. Several times, he shocks the Oosa standing next to him, winning harsh *glows* from them. I can only assume the glowing and the chirping are insults because my translator picks up absolutely none of it.

There is an interpreter on hand, though, a Hypha. He clicks and whirs just like the Oosa do before speaking down to Herannathon. "They want to offer you a gift of your choosing, and you will automatically survive to the final battle. They will offer your companion a gift as well. They just want to watch you two couple…"

"Out of the shroving question!" Herannathon roars. The violence of his response damn near makes my heart trip. I feel a huge rush of insecurity that's wiped clean the moment he continues, "I'm not involving her in this. I don't want her to touch these shroving sands!"

"Too late." I swallow hard and pitch my voice loud, though it's hard to speak. My words, like my insides, all feel as dry as the surrounding wind, which smells of an ancient desert, so many battles fought and lives lost. Metal and smoke. A dash of gunpowder. And above all that, alien spices I've never smelled before.

"Nalia!" Herannathon whirls around to face me and his expression, the little of it I've learned to decipher, completely transforms. The shields in front of his eyes drop into place and his fists all clench, his upper shoulders jump high and his ear flaps twitch wildly. His nostrils flare.

"You bastards!" He turns back towards the platform, this time lunging at it. He jumps high, a good ten feet, to latch onto the edge of the glowing blue glider.

The Eshmiri holding the electric stick jabs it down into Herannathon's neck. It doesn't faze him.

"Hey!" I shout.

He jabs again.

"Hey, asshole!" There are small rocks around my feet. I swipe a few and pelt them at the Eshmiri, hitting my mark every time.

He scowls as he lifts his taser and shakes it at me. In the meantime, Herannathon drops down and approaches me, spikes first. His arms splay out to the sides, as if in a defensive stance, as if he has something to defend me from this strange, motley contingent of horny creatures who evidently want to watch us bang.

My skin sizzles and prickles. My blood heats. My gaze travels over Herannathon's backside, settling on the tight round muscles of his ass casting shadows in his grey leather pants. *Yummy…*

"I'll battle whoever you like. But I'm not debasing or defiling my mate."

"I don't mind." My voice breaks. Did he just claim me as his mate? My heart. My little stupid heart… *No one has ever claimed me before. Not like that. No man has ever wanted me for more than a night.* But…maybe *men* were my problem. Maybe…I just needed to meet the right pirate.

My face forms a smile, though it feels a little shaky, as all of them — Herannathon, the Eshmiri and presumably, the Oosa, though I don't know where their eyes are on their faces or if they have eyes or faces at all — turn towards me in slow motion.

"*Nalia*," Herannathon heaves. He rounds on me, blocking out the sight of anything behind him, drowning out the heat of the suns, blotting the arena's noise. He grabs the outsides of my arms. "We do not have to do this. The Oosa are being unreasonable. They're rich — the second wealthiest species in the Quadrants after the Lemorans — but, unlike the Lemorans, they're more than willing to abuse their positions."

"It's fine." I shrug, trying to play it off like I'm not nervous. Not at all. Just preparing to exhibit myself in front of fifty thousand screaming aliens. Just about to have sex with my...*mate* for the very first time. Strange, that the latter should freak me out a hundred times as much as the former. We've done so much already. But we haven't done this before.

Herannathon balks, "It's *not shroving fine*. I haven't... we haven't..." He seems flustered, which only makes my heart squeeze again.

"What? You were prepared to share me with ten of your brothers in a shekurr. This is kinda like the first step?" I laugh lightly. It sounds forced.

He frowns and clenches his teeth. "This isn't how I wanted this to go — to be. I wanted to honor you. To worship you..."

"And you can." I step up against his chest and place my palm on his abdomen. The Oosa behind him seem to like this and flare bright with colors that distract me momentarily. "Just do it in front of them."

His lips part, but I can't decide what expression I think he's wearing. He seems surprised most of all. "Why would you want to do this? Humans are private beings."

"Humans are all different. Every one of us. And I don't mind this. Especially if I know that it means you don't have to fight anyone. That you don't have to hurt anyone…" I make a face and take a step back. "Unless you don't want to. Unless you don't want me." I take another step back and Herannathon's reaction scares the piss out of me.

He slashes forward, grabbing me by the front of my robe and dragging me up against him like I'm a mugger in an alley. My toes barely touch the ground as he bends down and snarls against my cheek, "Don't say such stupid things. Don't try to manipulate me."

"I'm not," I stammer. "It's just…you've had me in your tent now for *days* — for solars — and we've done other stuff, but you haven't tried to fuck me yet. And I don't know why. Why haven't you?"

"Because." He exhales, hand coming against my neck as he lowers me to my heels. "I wanted to make you gifts, introduce you to my brothers, buy you a ship of your own, take you places, show you the universe… I wanted to *fawk* you somewhere safe, somewhere mine, somewhere *ours*."

My heart. My little shaky heart. I smile up at him, emotion knotting my vocal cords as I whisper, "You can do all of that once we're off this lousy planet." I smirk, "But first, let me do this for you. Let me take you to the finals. Let me *please* you."

A snarl barrels out of his throat and one of his lower hands reaches down to the front of his pants, which have begun to bulge. "*Shrov…*" He hisses.

Feeling an urgency that leaves me weak in the knees, I extract myself from his grip, step around him and shout up at the glider. "Herannathon will choose a communications disruptor for his gift." The Oosa colors begin to spark and flare as they start conferring among themselves. The Eshmiri try to insist that that's not allowed, but they're giggling as they try to assert their edict.

"The Oosa accept," the Hypha translator says.

"And I want a gift, too."

More giggling, glowing and whispering. "The Oosa are prepared to offer you a gift, as well. What do you want?"

"A mok bir baton shield."

"That's against the rules!" the Eshmiri shout again, and again they're overruled.

"The Oosa accept, *if* they are satisfied."

"I'm not worried about satisfying them," I say as I turn my back on them and return to Herannathon, whose neck is twisted as he watches me over his shoulder while wearing a pained expression. "I'm worried about satisfying *you*." I scrape my fingernails over his plated abdomen, fingering between all the grooves as I trail my touch down to the top of his trousers. I yank on the ties roughly.

"Nalia." He swallows my name. I watch his throat work. "Nalia, I can use the salvation disc. I can get you out of this…"

It's my turn to balk, this time. "After what we paid for that stupid thing? Are you crazy? Besides, if you save it and this advances us directly to the finals, then there is no risk that you won't survive the tournament. And if you win, you won't have to kill anyone. Please. Let me do this."

"Nalia…"

"I want you. I want to."

"Nalia," he gasps again as I pull his trousers down his ass, exposing it to the sun. His cock comes into view, but only barely. It's a weird cock, that's for sure. It looks like a tree stump, rough and plated on the outside around the base, but the longer I look at it, the more the flat, light grey head presses forward. Already it glistens with cum. "My cock can't be exposed to the elements for long."

"I figured. And trust me. It won't be." I undo the tie around my waist and before I can consider one more word of dissent from him, I tug it free and toss my robe onto the ground behind me.

He half growls, half gasps and reaches for my breast. The rough pads of his fingers glance my nipple, but only for a second before I sink to my knees. His cock pushes free and I look up, straining to reach it from this position. It gets easier when his cock pushes forward, out of its protective shell, as thick around as my wrist — maybe thicker. Cum sprays over my chin and chest.

"Comets, Nalia, you know you can't take all of me…"

"Between my mouth, my two hands and all four of yours…" I wink up at him. "I think we'll be just fine."

He hisses as I pull his cock down to my mouth and take it between my lips. I swallow as much of it as I can down my throat, my hands clasping together where my lips don't reach. His lower two hands fit around the base of his cock, matching my strokes, overlapping my fingers while I suck hard.

His head flings back towards the sun and the dome and the hundreds of creatures hovering above us. They screech and scream and roar, louder now in their excitement, or maybe I'm just projecting my own. My pussy is hotter than fire as the many suns' ubiquitous rays strike through the outer dome and caress every inch of my bare skin.

The heat from below radiates up through my knees as I swallow his cum, every single drop of it, regardless of its strange, alien taste. It feels like whipped cream and tastes like Ebo nut paste and musk and comes in thick bursts.

He groans and grunts, and doesn't stop groaning and grunting. The Oosa are in a frenzy on their little platform, hovering just a little ways away, but I don't care about their pleasure.

Only his.

My hands work in rough strokes as his cock keeps unraveling from its plate. It's long. So fucking long. His strokes atop mine start to slip, moving unevenly, and I can feel his knees start to buckle. "Nalia...I can't... prepare you with my mouth...not without a synthetic..."

I nod and moan around his cock, understanding what he means. He can't leave his cock that exposed, which means it'll be a tight fit inside my body. I can't fucking wait. "I love...your taste," I gasp around his girth, cum spilling out of my mouth and dripping down my chin onto my breasts.

His eyes blaze down at me, shields fully lifted. His hands clench in my hair, pulling swatches of it away from my face and wrapping them around his fists. He tugs me back in and I unhinge my jaw, letting him shove his cock hard into my mouth, letting it slide deep, deep down my throat until I gag on it. Then he pulls back. He does this again, six or seven more times. My eyes roll into the back of my skull as he takes over, using my hair like fucking reins as he fucks my mouth how he wants, all up until the moment that he stills, gasps, makes a sound like a gutted boar...

I didn't really understand how coming worked for Niahhorru pirates up until this moment. I kind of thought they were coming the whole time...I guess they are, but I'm not prepared for what an orgasm is in the pirate universe. He freezes, going completely rigid, his body tightening as a sudden surge of semen fills my mouth and explodes out of it. I choke and he pulls back. His fists coming around mine and jerking as he sprays his seed over my face and hair and stomach.

"Shrov, Nalia," he curses again and again, grabs my hair and pulls me back in, emptying what he has left inside my mouth, along my tongue, down my throat. I swallow, throat burning as it works around his length. I want to take it all. I want to take *him* all. I moan.

The world falls away, curtains dropping from the heavens and blocking out everything but the scent of his skin and my rising need. I whimper when he finally pulls free and my right hand fumbles over the fresh slick coating my stomach. I look up and meet his gaze, gathering his cum from my belly button and bush and swirling it around my clit. Then I push my cum-slicked fingers inside my body.

He roars and before I know what's going on, I'm up off of the ground and in his arms and his cock is right at my entrance, prodding its way past the barrier of my lower lips...

"You're ready again? That soon after?" I gasp.

"Ontte. Always. Forever. A thousand times will not be enough," he growls, gathering a wad of grey cum from my left nipple and from the crease underneath my tit. He holds it in his hand — it damn near fills his palm

— and I watch, fascinated and elated, as he brings that palm down between us and cups me. I whimper at the roughness of his skin, wanting more, wanting friction. I start to dry hump the cum in his hand, but it isn't…

"It isn't…"

"I know."

"I need…"

"I know what you need. Quiet, and I'll provide it."

I shut the fuck up, ready and eager. My thighs are fucking shaking as they grip the sides of his body, my shins tucked up underneath them, because I can't circle them around his back without turning myself into a human skewer.

I'm sweating, even though we haven't even started fucking, and my eyes are glued to his cock between us as he slowly slides it through my thick red hair. "Herannathon," I whimper. I slam the flat of my fist down onto his shoulder. "Quit teasing. *Please.*"

His lips quirk before tightening. His jaw clenches and he nods. "A pirate never begs," he whispers and then he slams inside of me, only making it in about an inch — at least, that's what it looks like — even though it feels like I've just been impaled with a brick.

I scream, my neck rolling to the side and then forward as I look down in the shadows between our bodies and pant, "Good thing…I'm not a pirate, then."

"Oh, but you are," he moans, yanking me down deeper — roughly, brutally, causing flares of pain to light up inside my body as I try to relax and make space for him that simply does not exist. He shoves again and I shout, "You're too big."

"You'll take all of it," he says through clenched teeth. He grabs my hair and jerks my head back. He leans in and breathes along the column of my neck. "Because you're a pirate." And then he pistons his hips up and I feel cut in half in the best way fucking possible. Over the sound of me screaming his name, I hear him say, "I've never been more sure of it."

16

Herannathon

I can't stop shroving her. I've lost my mind. There is no tournament, there are no spectators, there is only this — her brilliant, white speckled flesh wrapped in red sand, stained in the blood of the fallen.

I roar and slam my claws into the dense soil beside her left shoulder as I arch back and release. I pump my hips, slamming them against hers, using my lower hands to hold her hips in place. She's screaming in wanton abandon, hair tossed across her face, stuck to her skin with semen and sweat. She's sticky all over and I love the tastes of her body. She tastes like carnage. She tastes like no battle I've ever waged before, a victory I've never felt.

I grab her breast with my last free hand and flick her nipple roughly. She bellows out a moan. I know she likes this.

Her cunt squeezes around my shaft, shroving blinding me as I empty into her wildly. Grey globules of my semen spurt out from her body. Her belly is bloated with my seed. She will need to drink a shroving gallon of sterility draught this lunar if she does not intend for it to take. I don't care if it does or not. The decision as to what she does with her own body is all her own. I will accept whatever she chooses to do, and be for her whatever she needs me to be.

Sexual slave or breeder. Pirate or father to her kits. Both. Nothing. Everything in between.

I can't think. My mind is a chaotic haze. I can feel her clenching around me as I rub a finger roughly over her swollen nub. She cries out that it is too sensitive for her to take, but I don't care.

"You'll take it," I warn her. "You'll release for me again…" I slam into her. "When I want." Again. "When I say." Again. "Te'eno hnoor, Nalia." You're *mine*. "Come for me, pirate." Now. *"Now."*

She wails and grabs hold of my arm, fingernails cracked and broken from how she's scratched my plates to pieces. We've been at this for an eternity. Long enough that I've felt the position of the suns change, shifting around us. The crowd's cries, however, haven't waned. They've become white noise in my ears. The items they've been throwing down have become more and more grandiose and more and more lewd.

I reach for a mok bir baton that's landed near her right shoulder and lift her limp body from the ground. She fights her way back to consciousness as I slip some of the semen from around my protective lower plates to her back hole. It's puckered as the waves of her orgasms trickle off, pulsing as I prod it with my knuckle. I don't have the dexterity now to retract my claws. My capacity for control is thinner than water.

Thinner than blood.

"What are you…" she whispers, half coherent. Her eye skeins are weighted, each blink more languid than the last. I don't care. I don't need her coherent for this. At least, not fully. Not for what I have planned.

I hoist her high onto my body, smearing her wetness across my abdomen while two of my hands work around her ass cheeks, massaging them firmly. "I need to prepare you," I growl into her damp hair. "Because I will take you here."

"Oh god, yesssss," she wails in her own tongue. The yeeyar token in my ear translates her words and spits them out, but I turn the volume lower. I want to hear her pleas to her own creator, knowing that whoever he is, he cannot save her now.

"Your god cannot help you, Nalia," I whisper, petting her hair with one hand while sliding the smooth, rounded end of the glowing blue baton through the crease between her cheeks. "Not while you are with me."

"Fuuuuuck… Herannathon."

"Do you want me to enter your back hole?"

"Take my ass," she answers immediately. "Take me anywhere. I'm yours."

The words burst in my chest like a flare and I clench my teeth and steel my bones, fighting for restraint so I don't impale her completely as I slip the blunt end of the baton into her tightest entrance. I worry for a moment that as she starts to move she's trying to outrun it, especially given that my cock is much, much larger than the baton, and I pause. But I'm rewarded for my patience when I feel her shaking thighs clench around my hips and her trembling arms clutch at my neck as she tries to bounce up and down on my hard length and the mok bir baton.

"Ontte…" I growl against her neck, biting down on the soft flesh there.

She cries out and I start to jerk the smooth, glowing mok bir baton in and out of her more quickly, timing the movement to match that of her bounce and my thrust. "Oh my god, yes. Yes, Herannathon, fuck me." Her head falls back, exposing the long column of her throat. I lick her sweet sweat clean, tasting the woodsy aroma of my own seed on my tongue. "Kiss me, Herannathon. Please…"

I dart forward, sliding my tongue into her mouth, shoving it down her throat, feeling her battle my tongue with her own, but she's losing and I know that she loves to lose this battle to me. I can't stand it and wrench back. "Enough."

I'm not half as careful as I need to be as I lower her to the ground and pull my cock free. The good thing about having released a dozen times already is that my cock is less sensitive to the atmosphere and the heat and I can stand having it outside of her body the few instants it takes for me to get her rolled over and balanced on her hands and knees.

"Hold for me, Nalia."

She heaves out each breath, throat sounding ragged. A tingling awareness that she needs sustenance visits my conscious mind, but I ignore it for now, with every intention of returning to it, but not now. Not yet…

"You aren't holding."

"Sorry," she breathes, and then she laughs. "I didn't remember you being so demanding…"

"Elbows and forehead on the ground, ass up." I pull the mok bir baton out of her puckered ass and toss it aside to the sound of her squeal. I spread her cheeks and grab fingerfuls of semen sliding down her thighs to wet her rear entrance. I shift my knuckles inside, one and then two at a time, feel her tight ring stretch. "It's going to be tight."

She doesn't answer, just moans and mewls for me.

"My prize," I whisper, leaning forward and arching over her as I line my cock up with the tight ring of muscle I fully intend to breach. I pull her hair off of the side of her face and watch her slowly blink up at me over her shoulder. She smiles. "You'll tell me if it hurts."

She pushes back against me, sending my cock sliding between the softness of her cheeks. They grip my cock lovingly and I love every moment of it. "I'm not your prize," she murmurs, sounding half asleep. "You're mine."

I laugh and snarl, my lower hands slip underneath her hips, fully supporting them so that her knees only just barely graze the red world below while my upper hands work on parting her ass cheeks and feeding my cock into her tightest hole.

"Why can't it be both?" I thrust forward, breaching her entrance, and she moans like a beast. Perhaps, the moan is my own.

It takes an eternity for my cock to push into her body and, even then, I don't make it far. I have to use my lower hands to cover what of my cock doesn't fit inside of her body as I pump shallowly in and out of her tightest hole. Shrov, she's tight.

"Shrov, you're tight."

No reply. Only another wild moan. I laugh up into the sky — the dome — and drop my skeins into place as a defense against the bright light. Here, it is never dark. I don't know how much time has passed, only that one sun has moved into the position of the other and that more Eshmiri gliders have moved into place, while others have left. I cast my gaze to the stands where I can see several creatures coupling or jacking off with whatever appendages they have and I couldn't care less.

I push into her a little bit farther, only fitting in a hand's length — her hand, not my own — and curse when she tightens. "Touch…touch my…"

She doesn't need to finish. I know she's ready to come again, but she can't reach the source of her pleasure, not with how hard I'm rutting into her. She needs both forearms planted on the sands to brace herself.

I reach around her body and touch her soft nub and she combusts almost instantly. The pressure of her orgasm spirals around me and is, frankly, too much. Much too much. I hiss in pain and pleasure, unsure about whether I'm terrified of the sensation or terrified of how much I need it — crave it — *desperation. This is desperation.* I erupt into her tightest pleasure center while her body contracts around my length in jerky waves. But it's still too much. I can't take it. She has defeated me in every way the arena opponents who came before her could not.

I pull out of her on a roar and collapse on top of her body, flattening her to the sands. I capture her body in my arms, but I can't resist the pleasure as it reaches its peak and I rut against her back. The warmth and the softness and the pressure are enough to keep me coming endlessly.

I finish against her skin, spasms rocking through my body in ways they never have. I've never felt like this. Never. I'm panting against the back of her hair, doing my best to cradle her head as I roll our bodies to the side. I notice her shivering — centare, her quaking, too, spasms coming so fast that it feels like she's trembling all over.

Her legs keep twitching, tangling in my own. I fight for wakefulness when I notice that her eyes are closed. I want to fall asleep. I'd kill to fall asleep right here…but I can't. Not under the sun which bakes her pale and soft and sensitive skin. Her human skin. With her pirate heart. I vow to protect both as I gather her off of the tournament floor and carry her back into the Below, into the dark.

17
Nalia

I sleep for two days — well, whatever passes for days in this place — waking only when Herannathon tells me I need to eat, shit and pee and then go back to sleep. He sleeps next to me on the net, a strange bed that I could see myself definitely getting used to, especially when I'm wrapped in soft, warm linens and rough, warm arms that cradle and touch and stroke me whenever possible. And rut me, too.

He's insatiable. I wake twice to the feeling of his mouth on my cunt and once to the feeling of his tongue in my ass. I love his cock and spread my legs, taking him willingly and letting him take me willingly whenever I can. I've never had a cock like this before. A little voice in the back of my head whispers things that I don't like to hear. *He only wants you for this. He'll leave you as soon as the two of you are out of here...*

But I don't have a lot of time to think too hard about them, because when I wake next, Herannathon isn't touching or fucking or feeding me. He's staring across the room at me from his seat atop a wooden chest. He isn't sharpening his weapons this time, but fiddling with *my* weapons — well, my mok bir batons.

"What's going on?" I croak, stretching my arms over my head and arching my back. *Like a cat.* Strange that the word comes to me, but I can't picture the object. I wonder if it's a stringy thing like an Oroshi, based on the wild contortions of my body at the moment.

Herannathon makes a face. It isn't a happy face, either. "Mok bir tournament is in two lunars. And we haven't practiced at all."

I smile and shrug. *Ugh. My breath is awful...* "Doesn't matter. We'll still win. Do you have any more of that tooth washing stuff?"

"The gamma wand?"

I nod and get up — awkwardly rolling off of the net — and go to the box of supplies he indicates. I hold up several sticks until he acknowledges that I've found the right one, then I pass the red laser-y thing over my teeth. It tingles.

"What?" I say. "Why are you smiling? Do I have toothpaste on my face?" I chuckle.

He looks confused. "What is tooth paste?"

I roll my eyes and go into the back, into the wash room where I pull on the plug in the bottom of one tub and watch it begin to fill from below with water that has a slightly purple hue. It seems to constantly change colors.

"Just a human joke," I call back. "I just wanted to know what was so funny."

"You said *we*." His voice is much closer. I glance over my shoulder and see him standing at the curtain that separates the front room from this back area. "But it won't be like the last battle. I can't fight this battle with you."

I wink at him and grin, heart kicking as my gaze takes in his broad chest and all four of his muscular arms and his big hands, tipped in grey claws like stainless steel. I look at his crotch and he covers it with one hand, rubbing himself through his leathers. "Pity."

I slip into the water as he hisses out a series of curses and disappears around the corner. "I can't look at you without a synthetic ready," he grumbles.

I laugh. "I'm available," I offer, spreading my legs against either side of the tub. He peeks back around the edge of the wall and curses more loudly.

"You're a menace," I hear him mumble.

I laugh wildly, feeling like an Eshmiri as I finish cleaning up. Nothing can weigh me down. Nothing at all. Not the soreness radiating throughout my body or the threat of another tournament.

"Rhorkanterannu, are you there?" I hear Herannathon's voice and lurch out of the bath.

"Is that the pirate king?" I ask as I wrap a large red cloth hastily around my body. I pad out into the main room to find Herannathon standing in the center of all of our winnings. It looks fucking *nuts* in here.

After we fucked in front of the thousands for hours and hours *and hours,* we woke up to Eshmiri unloading buckets and barrels and baskets and crates of stuff into our tent. It spreads out through the doors, completely covering the platform. But the most useful thing we got? The small black box Herannathon's holding.

"Did she just call him a king?" A female's voice cuts through the line, speaking a language I've never heard before — *one that sounds eerily familiar* — but that the translator in my head has no trouble deciphering.

"Centare," Herannathon says, a smile touching his lips, making me wonder if he and the female were ever *friendly*. "She did not."

"I thought so…" The female laughs. "So, are you ready for extraction? Quinti has the machine up and running. We could bring you both out now."

"Centare," I say, strutting forward until I'm at Herannathon's side. I speak down to the box, though I feel a little silly doing it, knowing that the actual communication is coming from the device in Herannathon's ear. The box is only disrupting the frequency that prevented him from communicating off of this wretched planet. This wonderfully wretched planet. "We're not ready. Herannathon still has the final and I still have the mok bir tournament. Let me win the Sky key for us, Herannathon can clean out the Evernor stores and then we'll be up in a jiffy."

The voice that cuts in is dark and menacing, a brogue that's undercut only by his words when he says, "A jee-fee? Is this some human contraption?"

The female laughs, like she isn't speaking with the most intimidating voice in the world, and says, "Probably. Though I'm not sure what. You know humans *are* pretty diverse. You've heard how many different languages they speak on Reqama and how tricky it's been for Svera to upload them all to the universal translation databases…"

"Ontte, ontte, my pirate. Come here, take your daughter. She's hungry."

Shock. I hear the soft sound of a baby babbling and the female speaking to it in hushed, soothing tones. I look at Herannathon and he grins, and I'm reminded of our conversation. *Mating has produced successful kits between Niahhorru and humans before.* This must be the human mate of Rhorkanterannu. The pirate queen. The one who doesn't like to share. The one who gave birth to hybrids. I place my hand over my stomach and swallow hard. Shit.

"Don't worry," Herannathon says. "I have sterility draught you can take. It still works up to seventeen solars after rutting. I'll take the next doses, until you ask me not to."

I exhale, feeling warmth fizzle through me, reminding me of the sensation of drinking too much ale and feeling light because of it. Lighter than a glider. "Thank you. And I promise, I will be ready. Just not yet. I still have more worlds to explore."

"To ravage." Herannathon lowers one shield, like he's winking at me and I laugh.

Through the sound that echoes between us, I hear the female voice say, "I don't remember you giving me that option, *Rhorky bear.*"

"And I won't. I'll fill your belly with enough kits to occupy the next planet I purchase for them, *Deena,*" he calls her, using the same patronizing tone she used.

Herannathon looks at me. "He means it."

"Sigh," Deena says, followed by an audible sigh. "I suppose that's a fair compromise, then. After all, I do have to *share* my beach now."

Rhorkanterannu laughs, low and deep. "It was your idea."

"I change my mind. I want my own beach planet now."

"Which one should we steal?"

"What do you have in mind?"

They devolve into a conversation over planets I've never heard of, bickering like they've been married for decades before I hear the unmistakable sound of a female's breathy giggle and a male's deeper moan.

I start to laugh, "Well, if you don't need us for anything else, I think I'll go get ready for my mok bir tournament now."

Deena says, "Nalia, are you sure? We can pull you out. You've been through hell. You don't need to fight anymore."

"I don't know what you mean," I tease, surprised she knows my name but at the same time, warmed by that fact. "I'm having the time of my fucking life."

"Spoken like a true pirate." She laughs, "And *fuck*, I love hearing that word. But I was more talking about getting woken up from your sleeper tank early by Herannathon and getting captured by Jerrock. You shouldn't have done that, Herannathon. You know Rhork and I are still pissed about that. Sheesh, I don't know how Nalia got over it."

Beside me, I feel Herannathon tense. I glance up at his face, see that his shields are in place, and frown. He never has his shields lowered in our tent, not when it's just us two. "Sorry, I think I missed something. He woke me up early for what?"

"Shrov, Herannathon, you didn't tell her?"

"Deena," he growls, as if in warning.

"Centare. Shrov that. She has a right to know." Shuffling. Then a heavy breath. "Nalia, we found a whole host of humans locked in these blue sort of stasis tanks. They were on board a satellite and had been for generations. Hundreds of rotations. We agreed with the Voraxians to open the human tanks one by one and integrate the humans into society, answer all of their questions and help them adjust from their pasts to their new reality.

"Herannathon got greedy, saw you and knew he wanted you. He opened your tank early. It sounded like that might have caused some trouble with your memories. Did it?"

I nod, mute, unable to categorize the emotion stuck in my throat. "Ontte, I don't remember anything from before. Others do?"

"Yeah. Most. Not all, but those that don't have uh… well, not everyone survived stasis. The Voraxians have supremely good medical technology, and that's helped, but not everyone recovered as well as the rest. If you lost your memories and that's the worst of it, that's not bad at all. It wasn't so *wrong* that Herannathon pulled you out early. The problem was *when* he pulled you out.

"We were under attack by Egama giants and they got hold of you on board our ship when you ran. They pulled you onto their ship, but they were soon after boarded by a bounty hunter who'd been hunting them. That's how you ended up locked away with Jerrock. I… I'm sorry, Nalia. No one should have to spend time with that monster. I can't imagine what you experienced."

I shake my head. "It wasn't what *I* experienced. It's what I was forced to witness. What he did to those giants… They never hurt me. Maybe they would have before he boarded, but they never got that chance. He… the torture." I shiver, my skin getting cold and clammy as I remember it. As I remember all of it…and nothing before.

Herannathon cost me my past.

I frown down at him as he looks up at me from his seat. I wonder what sort of life I missed out on, what sort of skills he's cost me. I was an analytical thinker with a solid aim, maybe even an okay fighter, too. *I was also a drunk and a degenerate gambler with a high sex drive and the will to use it.* But that can't be all. There must have been more. A mother, a father, a family. *A sister with hair just as red as my own.*

"Makes sense that you want to stay and get the key, then," Deena says.

I nod. "That fucker needs to go."

"We're behind you. You get that key and, once you do, that'll be priority one — killing Jerrock. The Lemorans'll be too nice. They want him alive. I want his heart."

"If he has one," I mutter.

"True."

"I'd like his eyes. There's good yeeyar in there," Rhorkanterannu adds, ever practical.

I smile, but I don't really feel it in my chest. "I got you. I'll bring the key up and we can cut out his eyes together."

Rhorkanterannu laughs, "You chose well, Herannathon. This human has more spirit than the rest on Reqama."

"What human?" Herannathon says quietly, his voice betraying no emotion at all. "There are only pirates here."

"My mistake, brother."

"I'll see you soon, brother."

"Keep that disruptor on you. We'll be close and waiting to extract you at your call."

Herannathon nods and the line cuts, somehow. All I know is that I don't hear their voices anymore, or the sound of background shuffling or babies or any other white noise coming through. "Nalia, I…"

I shake my head, cutting him off. I feel…deflated. Not mad, though that emotion would perhaps be easier to process. "Just…" I huff, "you should have told me."

"I know."

"Especially before we…"

He winces dramatically. "I know. It's…one of the reasons why I didn't want to mate with you yet. I wanted a chance to get you off of Evernor, show you Reqama, introduce you to other humans, and explain to you…" He swallows hard. "What I did." He reaches into the pocket of his pants and removes something small and made of metal. He holds it out to me and I take it.

Some kind of washer or nut, it's smaller than a token and much thicker, too. Made of pocked dark metal it has a hole in the center lined in groovesI don't understand. "What is it?"

"It's from your tank. When I took it apart. You fell out into my arms and I thought everything would be alright…until the Egama showed up and you ran."

I scoff and throw the metal rivet back at his chest. He catches it with one hand, annoying me even more. "I've been getting headaches this whole time, wondering who and sometimes even *what* I am, where I came from, why I don't remember, how the shrov I ended up with that psychopath…and this whole time you knew. You claimed you didn't. You lied to me and I don't get it. Why? I wouldn't have even been mad."

The muscles at the curve of his jaw clench. His eyes twitch beneath his shields. "I didn't want you to use that to decide which male to choose." He reaches for my shoulder, or maybe my tit.

Regret barrels through me, an echo of an emotion I previously felt often, though I have no memories to accompany it. "Right. Not until you fucked me first."

He frowns. "That has nothing to do with it."

"I'm sure."

"What does that mean?"

I huff, feeling frustrated and unsure. "All you had to go on when I was in the tank was the way I looked. You still chose me then. What other reason could you have chosen me for?"

"Nalia, stop this."

"Hm? Tell me." I round on him, drop my towel and watch his gaze drop with it. His nostrils flare. He reaches forward and I'm only a little bit less affected by it than I would have been minutes ago, minutes where I felt totally invincible. His claw scrapes a line directly between my breasts, dragging red across my pale skin, but no cut, no blood. He's very controlled.

He curls his hand into a fist. "It was…a feeling. I don't…I don't know. I just knew that you were mine and that I was yours. Not for shroving. Forever." When he opens it again, he's still holding onto that bolt.

"Why did you keep this?"

He wets his dark grey lips with his pink tongue. "It's… When I first saw you, I wanted to keep something that belonged to you. I promised that, when I…" He takes a deep breath, exhales and folds my fingers around the metal. "I kept it as a promise to myself to tell you the truth. That, when I did, I'd return it to you."

I roll my eyes and turn away from him, taking the bolt and gripping it hard. It's warm. My hand goes instinctively to my heart and I rub it gently with my knuckles. *It's a weak organ. Too weak for this.* "That sounds corny as hell." I drop the bolt in my pocket and watch how his face sinks as the bolt disappears from his sight.

"I don't understand that expression. The translation…"

My heart lurches. The bolt's weighing me down. Or maybe, it's something else. A feeling that, no matter what he's done, I don't care. I should care. I should, but I don't. "Don't worry about it. I just…I need to go practice." I need to *think.*

I dress quickly and head to the exit, a box of mok bir batons and the illegal-to-own-and-operate shield the Oosa gave me shoved into my pocket right next to the bolt.

"Ontte. I'm coming with you."

"I have other people — creatures — I can practice with. And like you said, I have to fight this one on my own."

"Nalia…" he calls, but it's too late. I'm already through the door, the yeeyar glider wrapped around my wrist unfurling to take me to the practice courts where I know I'll find my…friends. Well, my competition.

I find Olanora down at the tables where spectators and participants are crowded together. The gathered all cheer when they see me. I wonder why for about a second until I remember that all of these creatures likely watched me fuck Herannathon in the arena. *Now, they all think I'm a slut, too.* I frown. Not sure what a slut was on Earth or why I think of it with such disdain. I like sex. Is that wrong? I'm not sure. I feel like I should know, but my memories hold no answers.

I huff out a sigh of frustration, pull the sack of batons from my back and thudding them down on the edge of the table. It's not regulation — well, there is no regulation here on the practice tables, but it's still a flimsier than normal thing. I wonder why Olanora is practicing here at this table in particular when there are tables that glow and bounce and fling and are more like the actual tables we'll see in the final.

I open my mouth to ask her as she flies over to me, but she speaks first. "Wow. You have a lot to practice with." She hovers at my right shoulder and she peeks over my head into the bag to see what all I've brought with me.

"Courtesy of my last *fight* in the gladiator tournament."

She laughs. "It looked like a fight worth fighting."

"You saw?" I wrinkle my nose and look up into her gaze, which never quite seems to focus on my face. Her eyes are light grey with small black dots that, if they were more *static,* might remind me of pupils, like mine. But they don't. Because I'm the only human here. Naturally, watching me fuck something would be an attraction. "Everyone saw. It was hot."

My mouth twitches. I can't help it. "That's embarrassing."

"Embarrassing? Why?"

"I..." I don't actually know. My brain is trying to push through to find memories reminding me of why I'm embarrassed, but the fog is too thick to breach. "I don't know," I sigh, feeling suddenly exhausted and frustrated that I'm so exhausted because, all in all, I'm not really mad. Not at Herannathon. Not at any of them for watching. Not even at myself. I just wish I had all the pieces of my thoughts so I could put them together and feel…whole? Yeah, maybe that's it.

"I don't know." I shake my head, laughing slightly. "I had fun."

"I know. Everyone knows. I had fun watching." She laughs and I laugh with her and the strange thing is that her laughter is completely judgement free. Stranger is the fact that I feel like she *should* judge me, but I have no clue why.

She flits to my other side. "Want me to help you practice with those? You earned them."

I smile up at her. "Thanks."

She helps me figure out how a few of the mok bir batons work and it quickly becomes clear that some are more useful than others while some are almost *too* useful. The crowd laughs and titters when the mok bir baton in my hand goes flying hundreds of feet up in the air and tings off of the edge of an Eshmiri glider. It hits the edge of the glider with enough force to tip it and the Eshmiri riding it throws a rock or some other blunt object down at me in retaliation. I lift my arms to block my head, but it never lands.

"Careful there," comes a throaty male voice.

Wincing, unsure if the rock is still en route for me, I hazard a glance up and see Rhogan looming above me wearing a small smirk. He tosses the rock over his shoulder. "Rhogan." My insides tighten up. Every time I see him, I forget just how good-looking he is. It's alarming that he's so good-looking. He could stun with just a glance. "Nice to see you."

"You, too. Though I'll admit, I enjoyed last seeing you even more. That battle you waged in the arena was impressive."

My cheeks burn. I don't answer. His words make me feel a little sticky.

Olanora flutters closer to Rhogan, her voice coming a little breathier as she says, "Don't anger the human. She is embarrassed by the battle."

"Because of who you were rutting?" Rhogan says easily, confusing me.

"What?"

"A Niahhorru pirate. A female like you, I could imagine you'd want better for a male."

Now, I'm frowning outright. "Better? Better how?"

And then he has the audacity to glance down at himself. Olanora laughs a trill little laugh. "A male who knows what he looks like…"

"Isn't what I'm after," I say, cutting him off. "Herannathon is my male, my mate." I meet Rhogan's gaze bluntly. "Any female may want your body, but does any female lay such a claim to you?"

He doesn't answer. I can't even make out his expression. The corner of his mouth twitches and that's it.

"I'm just embarrassed because I don't want to be thought of like that. I don't want people — beings — to think of me as a female who's wanted, never claimed." I shake my head and reach into my bag, pulling out the next mok bir baton. It looks like a plain wooden pipe, hollow in the middle with two notches on either side. "No, I want *him* to think of me as more than that. I don't know. I just — I'm not a — I don't fuck males for tokens or batons or whatever."

I look up at him, feeling awkward, and look away again quickly. He reaches down, green skin surprisingly smooth and cold as it fits over mine. Shivering a little, I let him pull the baton away from me. He presses the sides of the baton in a combination — two pulses up high, three down low, one in the middle — and two side compartments spring open and darts shoot out.

Olanora releases a little squeak as a dart flies past her left ear. She swats Rhogan on the shoulder and he laughs so amiably, I'm forced to forget that he just insulted a guy I kinda sorta like. Maybe more than like. *Definitely more than like...*

I shouldn't. He messed up my head and got me kidnapped. But he...*he also introduced me to my new and wild and wonderful life.* I smile.

"Sorry," he says. There's a certain kindness to his gaze that leads me to believe him. "But this mok bir baton is useless." Rhogan touches my shoulder. His hand is cold. Colder than cold, like ice. I don't mean to, but I wince away from it.

"Good to know." I smile more fully then as he redirects conversation into safer waters, beneath new light. A sleek silver glider whizzes past us overhead and I see a familiar swatch of black hair whooshing in the wind atop it. I wave.

Manila leans over the sturdy railing of her glider — much safer-looking than the decrepit machines the Eshmiri ride, and *definitely* safer than the flat black carpet I ride that has no walls at all — and her glider starts to slow.

"I've been looking for you," she shouts, ignoring the other players that are matched up on either side of the practice table and settling her glider in the very center of its worn reddish-brown surface. She flits an incoming mok bir baton away from her face with her armored arm, and the clink it makes sounds almost violent, like a bullet hitting a shield. She moves fast. I don't doubt Herannathon at all when he says that she would make a fierce fighter in the arena.

As she climbs down onto the top of the table, she points at an Eshmiri in the crowd. "I need to speak with you, as well. Don't go anywhere."

Gibli. She's talking to Gibli. The minute I set my sights on him I grab a mok bir baton from my bag — any baton — and chuck it at his head. I hit him with a yellow and black one right in between his stupid lying eyes. It leaves a powdery pink residue that he immediately starts rubbing at wildly.

"You! I need to have a word with you, you lying cuss."

Gibli, seeing me, waves at me with both hands and laughs wildly, his high-pitched trill nauseating. He points at his forehead and rubs the pink spot where the baton hit him, then points at me feverishly, making gestures I can't interpret as anything besides angry, with both hands.

"Me? No, you! You are the asshole."

"Poop hole?" he shouts back. "I am not a this thing!"

"You lied to me!"

"I did not. I never…"

I grab another mok bir baton and launch it across the table. He squeals and manages to get his own baton up in time to defend himself — a good thing, too, because the purple baton I used *explodes* the minute it comes into contact with his.

He shrieks and many of the other creatures gathered laugh and clap while the air fills with a plume of purple ink. Meanwhile, Olanora tries to get me to back down and Manila tries to approach, but is blocked by Gibli and the other two creatures standing between us — an Oosa and an Oroshi, so that together they appear as little more than a gelatinous, tentacled mass.

Coughing and wiping purple off of her arms, Manila says, "Would you stop that? I have something important to talk to you about."

"Not until I beat him bloody…"

I launch my body at him, fully intending to yank off his ears, and am held back by Rhogan and Olanora, both of whom are laughing. I don't find it funny.

"Next time you try to trick me, Gibli, I'll…I'll crush you! I'll turn you…turn you into a jelly!"

"A jelly?" That seems to stall Manila, who shoves her hands onto her hips. "That's an odd one…"

"Hey!" a voice shouts from above and is followed by the sound of a *very* rickety glider approaching in whirs and clangs and clanks — it sounds like a metal robot choking to death. I look up. No. This isn't a rickety glider. This is an *ancient* glider.

The thing is almost entirely black and red — I'm not sure what color it originally was, but it looks like it's either molded or rusted over completely. The glider is oblong with unevenly stacked slats for a wall and no railing to hold those slats together. There's a hole in the bottom of the glider on one side that I can see a body through. It's *her*. Holy shit.

"Holy shit." I grin. It's the infamous Ashmara.

The cold hand on my left shoulder slips away and I turn to see Rhogan stepping back into the crowd, his tail slashing through the air behind him. I notice the crowd gives him more space than they give me or Olanora, even as they press forward towards the table, as if in anticipation. His gaze is up on the glider, same as everyone's.

Half the crowd is bubbling with excitement as the glider lowers to table-height and a female with similar proportions to mine, but a shock of bright white curls and dark brown skin, steps off onto the table beside Manila.

She's dressed in Eshmiri garb, though her patched together leathers are fitted to her chest, unlike most Eshmiri, who either wear so many rags you can't make out their shapes at all, or who don't wear shirts, only patchy trousers, and go bare-chested.

Meanwhile, the other half of the crowd — including the Oroshi and the Oosa standing to my right — look like they're out for blood. The Oroshi and the Oosa, in particular, are nearly hysterical. The Oosa is beaming a bright and angry yellow from its inner core — at least I think it's angry, I can't be fully sure — while a tall, lanky yellow creature on the other side of the table throws what looks like a dagger up at the female.

He misses. She turns and waves him off, like attempts on her life happen all the time. "Yeeshee, yeeshee, you shroving ingrate. I saved your neck in Quadrant Five, and you know it. You'd never have made it off Xixix without my help. Those warlords would have eaten you alive..." He throws another dagger, this one just as yellow as she is. She ducks and points a finger at him accusingly. "Literally!"

She staggers off of the back of the glider and teeters precariously on her feet as she takes a slow turn around. She looks a little woozy, like she's dizzy or something, before she takes a sharp inhale through her nose and straightens up while both her and Manila's gliders lift back up into the sky, making more room on the table.

"Ashmara," I call up to her now that she's in my clear line of sight. "Thank you."

She looks at me, but only for a second. She doesn't seem to recognize me at all, though I don't know how that's possible. I'm pretty sure she's single-handedly responsible for getting me out of that cell and onto the battlefield and in a position to help Herannathon. I also suspect that she may have been the one to gift me the Andalinian sabre I needed to save Herannathon's life. And that was a pretty epic battle, if I do say so myself.

Hmph. I try not to be annoyed as her gaze darts away from me dismissively and returns to Manila. "You. I need to talk to you."

"Well, I have nothing to say to you. I need to talk to them." She points an elegant orange finger at me and Olanora, then glances over my shoulder. "Centare, get back here, Rhogan. I need to talk to you, too. It's about the final tournament. There have been changes made to the location of the table. There are rumors about Sky assassins in our midst, so we've moved to a more secure location.

"Centare! Don't walk away now, or you won't know where it is. And I've heard that some of you are considering the use of shields. You should know that isn't allowed." She looks at me as she says that, but I just keep a blank expression on my face and my hand away from the mini, palm-sized holo shield in the pocket of my trousers so as not to arouse suspicion. I'm not sure it works as her expression twists and her gaze narrows. Luckily, Rhogan's up to some funny business behind me and distracts her.

"Rhogan!"

"Rhogan?" Ashmara's husky voice booms out a throaty laugh, just as glib as any Eshmiri's though several octaves deeper. "Rhogan, oh Rhogan, is that really you?"

I turn and see a Rhogan I've never seen before. His face…his face looks weird. Frightening. It's…*familiar*. The expression, maybe. I don't know, there's just something familiar about this moment that makes my blood run cold. I reach instinctively for a mok bir baton and find a white one. I don't know how it works, but I can feel energy zinging through it and know that it's dangerous, and I have the odd feeling now that yes, I need to defend myself. Yes. I do.

Ashmara, however, doesn't seem to feel the same. She saunters forward, kicking discarded mok bir batons and other objects strewn across the table out of her way. "Rhogan, heelee, what have you done with your face?"

"I don't know what you're talking about," comes his deep voice from behind me. "I've heard of you, of course, but we've never met."

Ashmara laughs again, more loudly this time. "You're so ugly now." She takes another step forward. I turn in time to see Rhogan take another step back.

Ugly. Is she insane?

Beside me, Olanora's wings flutter more intensely, as if she's outraged on Rhogan's behalf.

"You've got me confused." He smiles at her, regaining some of his charm, but only with one side of his mouth.

"Ohhhh," Ashmara coos. "You're right." She drops down to her haunches right there on the edge of the table, her fingers idly twirling the dart-filled wooden baton I discarded. Her gaze is so focused on him, I feel like I'm intruding on something intensely private. Meanwhile, he's stiff as a board. Still. Like *he's* afraid of her, even though he's twice her size and she looks kinda faded.

She nods, mouth quirking to reveal a flash of bright white teeth. "Yeeshee, you're right. I suppose I should have called you Jerrock."

I would have choked on my own tongue, I would have frozen in time, I would have shouted and bit and champed and screamed...had I the time. But I don't. Because the next moments happen so quickly they all collide directly into one another, smashing together like ships colliding in the silent black depths of the universe.

Manila roars, "Sky assassin! Defenses!" She raises her metallic hand and her glider, now hovering two dozen or so feet above the table, splinters into four separate drones which descend in tandem. A black bolt of pure energy radiates heat as it explodes from one of the drones, heading straight for Rhogan. But...but he grabs Olanora by her left wing and drags her entire body in front of his. The bolt hits her in the stomach.

"No!" I shriek as her wings stop flapping and her body drops at Rhogan's feet. She hits the ground and the Oosa closest to me vibrates wildly, while the Rekkaru floating in the crowd scream. I lunge for Olanora, but Rhogan is already moving, his left arm lifting up.

Black matter moves up and out from his wrist, forming a weapon that looks like a gun. *Like a handgun, a small one.* His fingers, though, don't fit around the handle as they would a human handgun. Instead, he only presses one finger down on top of the long barrel and black pellets explode, heading straight for the Rekkaru flying closer to defend his kinswoman.

My heart drops into my stomach and I reach for the shield in my pocket, but I've only just closed my hand around it when Manila, from nowhere, shouts orders to her drones and her pellets block the path of Rhogan's.

Rhogan turns his wrist to her, but her drones fire on him — all of them, all at once. But he's not hit. He wears some kind of shield that doesn't repel the bullet fire but *absorbs* it. I can feel the heat radiating off of his unblemished green skin as I back up, colliding with the Oosa behind me that genuinely seems to be trying to help me and pull me back. But no one's helping Olanora.

Her black hair is frizzy and wild and splayed across the ground over Rhogan's feet. He steps on her hair while yellow blood bubbles from the middle of her stomach like magma from the mouth of a volcano and rage bubbles up inside my stomach, just as violent as the male himself.

"Fuck you!" I shout at him.

He ignores me and turns his weaponized arm on Manila. She's ready to block his first attack, but she doesn't anticipate the mok bir baton he pulls out of his belt. He launches it at her and, as it spins through the air, the blunt ends form blades that whip out of it, so many that it transforms into a thousand-pointed throwing star.

I withdraw the mok bir baton shield in my pocket and throw it as hard as I can. My timing is perfect. The throwing star hits the shield, ricochets off of it and embeds itself deep into the table. Rhogan fires again with his arm, undeterred, and this time, he's thwarted by Ashmara who doesn't seem to be fazed at all by any of this.

Ashmara simply tosses a black token absently into his path so that the bullet aimed for Manila's forehead hits her orange shoulder instead. Manila staggers back, falls off of the edge of the table, spinning under the velocity of the bullet. My heart catches in my throat and I exhale a tight breath of relief when Gibli lunges forward and catches her.

Rhogan turns his arm to Ashmara and I scream, "No!" I know that there's no chance. My weapons are too far and the crowd is dispersing madly now, creatures running and yelling on all sides. No one is looking towards Ashmara. No one will intervene to save her life.

And yet…she looks at him and smiles. "Jer bear," she whispers, then shakes her head. "Krakaw, Azza."

Rhogan doesn't hesitate. He fires and Ashmara ducks, throwing her hands over her head. But…his arm jerks. It looks like an invisible ally grabbed him by his shooting arm and yanked to the right, just a little bit. Just enough for him to miss. He *misses*.

His shot goes wide, hitting a Rekkaru through the wing and the Rekkaru tumbles to the ground on the other side of the empty table, injured but alive, while Manila shouts up at Ashmara.

"Take it! He's here for me." Her bionic arm unfolds down the center, plates moving in a jigsaw puzzle to reveal a small translucent cube with oscillating colors floating through its center. She tosses it to Ashmara, who doesn't manage to catch it. Like a klutz, it knocks against her nails and falls onto the table.

"Eck," she hisses, bending down like she doesn't have a care in the goddamn world, taking her sweet ass time to retrieve it. She picks it up and Rhogan fires at her again, this time, grazing the outside of her left hand and causing her to drop it.

I turn to look at him and see that he's twitching. Jerking mechanically. His skin is *moving*, crawling like it's being shed, molting like he's a vile and malignant insect. Red shimmers beneath the green. Black, too. And silver metal so bright and sparkly, it looks like a crystalline lake under bright sunshine. I remember that metal. I remember that face, half concealed by it. Fear coats my stomach, making it hard to swallow, but I choke it down and search for a weapon.

Rhogan — Jerrock, the assassin — is faster.

The left and metallic half of his face reminds me of the Sky assassin that Herannathon and I fought before. They must be using the same type of technology. And it's some fucking tech, too. Because his bionic eye shifts, and from it, a small grey droplet pools, looking deceptively like a tear.

He plucks it off of his face with his metallic arm and Manila yells when he tosses it. I reach into my pocket. What weapons do I have left? None. All I've got on me is a single object. A bolt that came off of my stasis tank, the one that started all of this.

I throw it like a skipping stone and the droplet and the bolt meet midair. An explosion sounds and the bolt is eviscerated. I'm lifted off of my feet and sent flying towards the edge of the rocky island.

Darkness.

A ringing in my ears.

A ringing in my skull.

The darkness breaks.

I don't know how much time passes while my thoughts jackknife around in my skull and heat brands my chest. All I know is that I become fully conscious at the pressure of a band around my ankle. My eyes flutter open. Smoke and dust fill my lungs. Everything tastes like burning wood and melting steel. Everything feels oddly like home. *No, it's not so odd, soldier.*

I look up and see Jerrock in his true form, no Rhogan anywhere in sight. He's got Ashmara's body tossed over his shoulder and it looks like she's passed out. He's got Manila tucked under the same arm he's using to drag me while his robotic hand is held out before him. It looks like it's moving, more of that black matter spreading out across his wrist. I don't know what he's doing, but whatever it is, it can't be good and he's working at it diligently as he drags all three of us towards the edge of the rocky red platform. Towards the cliff.

The black matter ticks something in my brain and I look back up just as a rock digs into my spine. A shooting pain splinters through my left shoulder blade and up the back of my neck and I feel...*alive*. Alive.

Olanora.

I crane my neck back, looking through smoke and shadow for a familiar form hidden beneath a pile of debris. The mok bir practice table is gone — completely annihilated — and so is a chunk of red rock that had been beneath it. But Olanora's still there, alive. She has to be.

I carefully will the black around my wrist to unfurl and go to her, and as I idle on the edge of consciousness, I command it to take Olanora to Herannathon in our tent. There's merillian there. She'll live. She has to live. She's my friend. I'm not used to those. *I never was. My sister always accused me of being antisocial. Said that's why I didn't do well in the barracks. But that wasn't true. I liked living with people. They just didn't like living with me. They thought I was worthless, a poor copy of my sister who was without fault and utterly ruthless.*

I groan as another rock stabs into the back of my neck and the base of my skull. My eyes burn and I figure it's a better idea if I close them because Jerrock has reached the edge of the cliff and hasn't stopped walking. He falls…dragging all three of us females with him.

And before fear that I'm going to die after finally finding the bottom of the Below can truly set in, my stomach lurches up into my stomach and I think of a roller coaster ride. *I hate roller coasters.*

Wind punches me in the face. My body jerks and my heart climbs up into my mouth.

I pass out.

18

Herannathon

The tent flaps open and I turn, rote words of explanation and pleas of forgiveness on my tongue, but even though the glider that slips into my tent is familiar, the body riding on top of it is not.

"Olanora." I know of the female and have seen her at the mok bir tables before. I inhale, about to ask her what the shrov she's doing here, but I'm stalled by the scent of fresh blood. "Shrov!" I call the yeeyar forward and rush to the back of my tent. I have a full tub of merillian waiting for me or Nalia should either of us need it, but I don't hesitate to dunk the wounded Rekkaru female inside of it up to the top of her head.

I keep only her nose and mouth elevated out of the substance so she can breathe the air above and I watch as her eyes flutter behind closed lids. She's not going to wake anytime soon. She shouldn't. Her wound lances across her stomach, looking deep. So much of her skin is gone, I can see her vital organs.

"Shh, you're going to be alright," I tell her. "Just calm yourself." I need to get out of here and figure out what the shrov is going on out there…

But as I stand and turn, I hear the little female trying to speak. I turn back, lean in very close to her mouth and hear a faint word, one that changes me irrevocably. *"Ass...assa...assassin..."*

I'm gone, out in the Below, my glider moving faster than it ever has. The Below is in a state of chaos, but it takes me no time at all to uncover the provenance of the carnage. There, atop a platform where there were once mok bir practice tables, are Eshmiri patrollers buzzing about in a panic, attempting to harvest bodies from piles of red rock and wreckage.

As I overhear what the patrollers have to say, it occurs to me that I was wrong before. Gibli wasn't warning me of a Sky assassin, but *assassins.* The female I fought in the tournament wasn't the only one. They can cloak themselves, he'd said, but I hadn't been listening. I hadn't understood. Maybe he hadn't even known. The male my mate was playing mok bir with nearly every shroving solar was the same male who abducted her before.

And now I've let him take her again.

I've failed her too many times now and, even if I recover her, I'll never earn back her forgiveness.

Rage and regret pour through me, adrenaline making the combination a lethal one. Jerrock managed to escape off-world with my female, Ashmara and Manila. The Sky key is with them, so if I don't catch up to his ship — and soon — and they make it back to the Sky planet, they'll be lost. I don't know how I'll track them when they have the only loose key in existence.

I'll have to go assassin hunting, then. And I will. If he takes her back to Sky, it will mean war for the Niahhorru. We will kill every assassin in the galaxy. The bloodshed will be stupendous. And I will rip the one they call Jerrock apart with my own claws. I will cull the yeeyar from his body drop by drop.

I tear back into my tent, grab my communications disruptor and fire it to life. My brother answers on my first herald, his female's voice just alongside his. They're never far apart because he's a cleverer male than I am and never lets her out of his sight.

"What do you need, brother?" he says, while Deena asks, "Everything okay? I thought you wanted to wait for extraction until after the tournaments were over."

"Shrov the tournaments. Jerrock has my female. *Again.* This time, he's taken Ashmara and another female with him."

There is no pause. Rhorkanterannu merely says, "I look forward to killing him."

"But how will we find them?" Deena says, sounding genuinely worried.

I don't know and I'm panicked. But then I hear a rustling that pulls my attention up to the entrance to my tent. Gibli wanders in, unannounced, something quite interesting presented in the center of his palm. I sit up straighter and meet Gibli's gaze. He meets mine and for once, he isn't smiling. His expression is cold. Then I register the small cube that he carries.

Grimacing, I say, "I have a solution."

"Then power up the machine," Rhorkanterannu rumbles. "Let's bring our brother aboard and retrieve his mate."

19

Nalia

Where am I? Where's my tent? Where's Herannathon? I blink my eyes open and frown. I've been kidnapped, that much I know, but this isn't the same ship I was on before…

Big blue cells, a hulking figure standing on the outside of mine. He has four arms and a severe face and I know in my chest, even though I'm not awake — even though I haven't done anything more than register his presence with my unconscious mind — that he's mine.

I'm lying flat on my back on a black table. Everything in here is black, making it hard to see. Soothing for my headache though, which smarts like the lash of a lightning stick.

There's a throbbing in my body and my skin feels hot and tight, like I've been lying out in the sun too long. I try to move my arms and legs and for about a second, I'm successful, making me think that I might just be able to slide off of the table and break free. But then clamps slide up and off of the table's surface — maybe made from the same slick material the table is made of itself — and curve around my forearms and shins, creating impossible-to-break manacles.

Even though they're smooth and cool, my panic kicks up my pulse. I jerk against my restraints as I remember what it felt like on board that Egama ship with Jerrock. He didn't even bother restraining me then. He knew I wasn't a threat. I wasn't. I'd been so panicked, my headaches so severe, I hadn't even tried. My headache is catching now, seeping in through the back of my skull. A sharp, thick fog attempts to sweep through my conscious mind, but I refuse to fall under the spell I was under the first time. No. This time, I'm not that girl. That woman.

This time, I'm a fucking pirate.

I inhale through my nose and exhale audibly through my mouth. *Remember your training. If you're ever captured by the enemy, know that even the worst torture will end. In life or in death, it will end.* Hm. Not the best memory, yet it soothes me somehow. Maybe, it's because of the one who said it. I know her name. I know it…but the headache cuts in and I lose it again.

I bang the back of my skull against the table underneath me and the headache oddly clears, rather than intensifies. I can taste a faraway scent. I don't know what it's called. *Focus.* I open my eyes and scan the ceiling. It's too dark to find seams in the shadows, which seem to move more thickly in places. I have the oddest feeling that I'm being watched.

I test that theory by shouting up, "Hey, you cyborg fuck! You want a piece of me? Come and get it." I don't know why I'm antagonizing the creepy ceiling, or what I'll do if it responds. I just want it to respond because this situation, right here, right now, stuck to the table, is a problem.

I wait an eternity for something to change. It's long enough for my initial confidence to simmer down and for my panic to creep back in. This time, it isn't mine, though. It's on behalf of the other two women.

I don't know how stable Ashmara is, but I do know that there is something that Jerrock wants from her. His detached focus seems to unravel a little bit when he looks at her. And what's more is that he *missed*. I know him. I know him well. Weeks alone with the silent, scary fucker taught me that he isn't a male who makes mistakes. In fact, I've only ever seen him make two.

Once led to him getting caught by the Lemorans and Herannathon and the other pirates.

And the other was just now, when he missed.

Both times Ashmara was the catalyst.

But as for Manila? I shudder, more afraid for her than I am for Ashmara. Manila escaped this place. To be caught and returned to them…I can't imagine that it will end well for her.

By contrast, I have no idea what they want me for or what their plans are or why Jerrock stole me in the first place from that Niahhorru ship. I also don't know if the Niahhorru can find me again. Who has the Sky key? Did Ashmara manage to grab it? Is it still with Manila? Did it get left in Evernor for Herannathon to find? Is Herannathon going to be able to save me? *You stupid bitch, you save yourself…*

The black splits like a curtain to my left and I look over at the sight of another yet unfamiliar half-metallic being moving towards me. He isn't particularly large — not bigger than a Niahhorru, that's for sure — but he also doesn't have eyes at all and I don't like it. Like the female with the braid in the arena, this male has more of that black-grey matter in place of his eyes. It shifts jerkily, autonomously, just like the black walls and ceiling of the ship encasing me. I wonder if it's yeeyar, the same substance my bracelet is made out of. My bracelet… where is it?

Boom.

I remember the explosion and the metallic hand finding my ankle, dragging me to the edge of the cliff. I shudder and open my eyes as a different metallic hand finds my throat.

I look up at the male, unsure if he registers me at all. He has purple skin and no hair. The entire top of his head is metal. Most of his throat is, too, but his chest — what of it I can see underneath his black leather vest — is muscular and purple and covered in thick plates that remind me a bit of Herannathon's.

He looks Voraxian…ish…and Niahhorru…ish…and he has a tail but it's more tentacle than tail and his legs are enormous, thick tree trunks, but they're bent at awkward angles. He looks sturdy and tough and yeah, terrifying, too, but he also looks cobbled together from a whole host of disparate parts. It looks uncomfortable.

"Are you uncomfortable?"

He doesn't look at me or respond. Or if he is looking at me, I can't tell at all. Instead, he pulls out a needle. A large needle. "Oh my. That doesn't look good." He starts to lower it down, past my eyeline. I can't see it when he lowers it beneath the curve of my cheek and moves it around to the back of my head. "I, uhh…I don't think you have to do this. Whatever it is. We can just talk. I'm good at that." Not really. "We can figure out how you got to be such a cyborg dick!"

The pinch at the back of my head, behind my left ear, is what lets me know that I'm fighting a losing battle. Fear controls my limbs for a moment, paralyzing them. I think about what I *saw* in that needle — more black. I think about what Herannathon pulled out of that arena champion's skull when he ripped off the back of her hair — black matter. I think about Jerrock's one greyed out eye, and the ship around me and the glider that's been my most helpful tool these endless days and complicated nights. If he injects that yeeyar into my head, I'm done for. Maybe, I'll become just like him. No eyes, and no consciousness.

I squeeze my sweaty hands into fists and squeeze my eyes shut tight. There's a surge of ice that spears the left side of my head, reminding me of a brain freeze. *Eating a popsicle with my sister out in the sun. We're on our porch. I'm ten, she's thirteen and our parents are somewhere in the barn.* Her name…what was her name?

The cold thickens, becoming sludgy. The male above me frowns and suddenly retreats, pulling the needle back. I can see that it's half empty and I wonder what's wrong as cold continues to move in and lay claim to the heat that had been so present in my brain. I find that, oddly, it seems to soothe the pain in my thoughts. My headache…my headache is nearly gone.

The male grabs my chin and inspects my face — I know he's looking at me this time by the way his frown gets more severe. He shoves me back against the table, clonking my head against the board below. "Ow…"

He moves to my other side and, even though I struggle feebly to get away from him, it doesn't matter. The strength of his arms is a testament to the silver that threads through both of them. It stretches all the way from his center three fingers to his silver armpit.

He pushes my face to the side and the sting of the needle pushes through my panic, and then accelerates it when I feel something cold and chilling and *overwhelming* attack the rest of the warmth that had been, turning everything to ice.

I blink and the darkness of the room encroaches on my vision, blurring it at the sides. I start to breathe harder, panicking. And then that voice cuts in again, harder than the ice and twice as clear as a diamond. *Toughen up, soldier…I love you, Nali…you can survive this. You can survive anything.* I keep my eyes closed and practice a breathing technique I was taught long ago. So long ago. By her.

The ice comes for me and it hurts, but I play dead through the pain. *Yes, that's what the technique is called.* I relax all of my muscles, from the top of my head to the tips of my toes. I don't feel the pain cutting into my skull like an axe and I don't feel the chill there that's making it hard to see, hard to breathe. A corpse doesn't see. A corpse doesn't breathe. A corpse doesn't feel pain. I go numb.

Numb, but conscious. The ice in my mind becomes a storm, spitting needles, cutting left and right and shredding everything in their path. No, not everything. Just the heat. The hot pain, replacing it with a cold one. I don't understand what's happening and struggle to focus. My teeth clench, but I release them immediately. Corpses don't grit their teeth or twiddle their fingers and hands. Corpses just shiver once, maybe twice as the last of the life leaves them.

I shut down.

When I probe the conscious world around me some time later, I feel hands on my arms pulling my wrists free of the cuffs that once bound them.

"She's not absorbing the modified yeeyar. An inferior species, she isn't strong enough. She isn't strong enough to be bred by the horlax, either."

I hear a second voice then, this one more robotic than the first. "That isn't for you to decide. That is for the architects. And from our reports, the humans have adaptable breeding holes. Maybe, with some modifications, she'll be suitable for that purpose."

"Perhaps."

They lift me from the table, one of them carrying my arms, the other my legs even though just one of them could carry me themselves with one arm, the other tied behind their cyborg backs. Meanwhile, I don't move. I actually find that I can't. My head…my head is doing something strange.

It feels like all the pieces of my brain got ripped from their roots, mashed into a ball, shoved into a washing machine and then that machine got turned on, strapped with a rocket and shot into outer space. Cold washes over me and competes with the heat. I can hear words from here and now, but also others that belong to Herannathon and to my family and to the monsters that brought me here.

They were human, those monsters.

And sometimes those monsters were me.

Too overwhelmed to function, I force my conscious mind to retreat again.

I come to minutes later, maybe seconds and when I open my eyes, they open easily. The cool and the heat have come together in my mind and settled and, when I blink, I can see everything so, so clearly. The cutting silhouettes of the Sky assassins dragging me somewhere. The bleak outlines of the shifting ship behind them.

I stare up at the black ceiling, watch the yeeyar it's made of flit back and forth. Everywhere it isn't, colors flare silver and tan and, the longer I stare the more I can *feel* it. I can feel the ship, yes, just like I can feel Herannathon's glider. It pulses like a heartbeat against the walls of my skull, but as this strange, supernatural recognition jerks and slams against and into my thoughts, I realize something else — something quite significant...

My headache is gone.

And I remember *everything.*

I start to smile. And then I start to laugh. Whatever they did to my head messed with it real good. And I do mean *real* good. The cold yeeyar has pacified whatever was broken. My mind feels mended. Mended and *electrified.* I can feel so many things now. The ship around me, yes, but I can also feel *more.*

What...what *is* that?

There are pulses of awareness on the edges of my mind, but two pulses pulse quite close, like thoughts I can't push aside. I laugh a little harder. I'm aware, not just of the ship, but of the other Sky assassins on it and off of it, near and far. *All of them. We're connected through the yeeyar.*

I can't read any of their thoughts or moods or feelings — if there even are any — but I do know where they are. I can feel the pounding pulses of the assassins carrying me. I can feel the movement of the black matter, that malleable alien substance, coursing through my skull just as readily as I can feel it moving through their chests and legs and arms and through the yeeyar Sky keys they carry with them, hidden in places I might be able to find if I just concentrated a little harder. Some of the beings, like the larger of the two assassins dragging me, I can feel more intensely than others. He's almost entirely composed of yeeyar. And I can feel something else, too, something a little frightening.

I can feel the yeeyar moving differently in my head than it does in their bodies. In my head it moves so smoothly, intertwining with what's already there, filling gaps that were, but no longer are. But in them…it moves like it does across the ship, scattering and reforming, lunging and retreating, jolting and jerking, breaking…

It broke them, but I was already broken. *The Sucere Project.* I laugh even harder, thinking back on it all. Thinking how I got here, the different versions of me that I've gone through to get to this one. I think about Herannathon and what he *thinks* he's guilty of — wiping my memory, being responsible for my being here and getting caught, and his vows to keep me safe against anything.

Nah.

He didn't do any of that. I did bad all by myself. I'm the only reason I'm here. And I have every tool in my arsenal to get myself the fuck out.

Because I'm not a damsel in distress.

I'm not a prize to be won, either.

I'm not a gladiator in an arena.

I'm not even a mok bir champion.

I'm a drunk, slutty, degenerate, gambler.

I'm also an ex-special forces soldier dishonorably discharged from a top-secret intra-government project called Sucere, one in which *they* wiped my memory and tinkered with my thoughts. My own sister did it, the bitch that she was. But it's alright, I don't blame her. I did once, right after they put me in the blue tube and shoved me under, but I don't anymore. If she hadn't done what she'd done and if I hadn't been who I was, I'd never have ended up here, exactly who I'm supposed to be.

A shroving pirate.

And I want *my* shroving pirate.

And I'm not going to give up on him, because I know he hasn't given up on me.

Energy fires into my body and I focus. I wake myself up limb by limb until I'm an arrow notched and pointed at its prey, ready for the kill.

The assassins holding me take the next right turn, their footsteps eerily in sync. I see a doorway to the left. It's open and through it, I catch a glimpse of a body tied to a bench. *I know her.*

I yank on my right arm and kick with my left. I drag the male on my arms down, forcing him to stoop. I spin my wrist, unlocking his grip from around my arm. He releases me and his silver hand darts forward to snatch mine back, but I can *feel* him moving before he arrives, almost like an eerie premonition. And I know where to move to block. Our forearms knock together painfully as I do, but it's nothing I can't handle, and I don't hesitate to attack back.

I think of Herannathon and I force my fingers to form a prong, stiffening them together, and then I dart forward, stabbing my hand directly into the purple fucker's eye socket. The grey sinks in deep, and with my jagged and chipped nails, I latch onto the fibers I find there. It's freaky how creepily soft and malleable they are

— like sinking my fist into play dough. Stranger still, the fibers seem to respond to me, folding around my fingers, making it possible for me to yank.

I tear down as hard as I can and watch the yeeyar fibers stretch out of his face until he lurches back, trying to free himself, and the cords finally tear and break. His right hand stabs down, like he's going to impale me through the stomach with his fist, but I crunch up and roll to the side, spinning in his grip so that I'm facing the floor.

He ends up punching me in the side, but I kick back with my leg, hitting the male at my feet — the large, tan-colored fucker — across his rocky face. He reminds me of a species I've seen before — a Lemoran — only his coloring is wrong and his horns aren't grey or white but silver with blue veins running through them.

Electricity sparks between his horns when I kick him again and I jerk when a bolt of what feels like lightning stabs my lower calf, just as painful as the female's braid had been. This time, I fight against waves of crippling heat. I kick him in the face and roll a third time, finally freeing my second arm from Mr. Purple's grip.

I hit the ground and spring up onto the balls of my feet. Both males reach for me at the same time, but I lunge low, grab Mr. Purple's right ankle and pull as hard as I can. In the same instant, I bring my heels up and kick out one of Horny Toad's feet. I use the spring in the floor beneath me to bounce up onto my toes and *run*.

I fly into the open doorway, sealing behind me with nothing more than a passing thought. I hold it closed with the elasticity of my mind, even though I can feel the resistance of the other assassins working together against me to pry it open. I push the pain of the mental strain out of sight and just like that, using seasons of torturous conditioning imposed on me by my sister and even her higher ups, I don't feel it. The door holds.

I go to the table and look down at Ashmara's face. Her eyes are twitching beneath her closed lids and the muscles in her wrists are straining microscopically. I shove her arm. "I know you're awake. You're a lousy actress."

"What's an actress?" She opens an eye, just the one, and frowns. "What's wrong with your eyeballs?"

"What's wrong with my eyeballs?"

"They're all black. Weren't they a color before?"

I ignore her. "Get up. I can't hold them forever."

"Hold who? Also, are you blind now? I'm chained down."

I glance at the manacles wrapped around her arms and legs and throat and waist — they clearly thought more of her than me, because she wears twice as many shackles as I did. "I think I might be able to…" I start, mumbling mostly to myself.

"What are you…" And as the black matter strapping her down peels abruptly back, she shouts, "What in the comets? You're one of them!" She rolls off of the table and into a fighting stance, but she doesn't look good, wavering side-to-side like that. She looks woozy.

"You okay?"

"Get the eck back."

I frown at her, noting that her usually white eyes are colored a very pale yellow-grey-brown. I don't know how to interpret it. "What's wrong with *my* eyes? What's wrong with your eyes?"

She shakes her head and staggers to the left even though the ship's barely moved. I wonder where they've taken us, where we're going, if we're moving at all.

She jerks her chin up though her fists drop half a hair. "You first."

"They tried to jam their yeeyar mind control stuff into my head, but it didn't work. I *think* the yeeyar stuff actually fixed what was wrong with me."

"What was wrong with you?"

The Sucere Project. The Water Wars. My sister. Me. "It's a long fucking story." A huge blast sounds behind us. Fuck. "They're coming in any minute. I think they've given up trying to fight me. They're coming in the hard way. We need to find Manila *now* and get the fuck out of here."

"Fight you? You mean…" Her eyes bug. The colors within them shift, becoming yellower before paling to near white. Her jaw is clenching in micropulses that don't look good. She looks sick. "The yeeyar didn't just fix your brain, did it?"

I shake my head. Another explosion sounds behind me and the yeeyar doors buckle and bend inward. "Centare. It did more."

"It linked you to the Sky bridge." She releases a loud whoop and pumps her fist into the air in such a human gesture that I feel a momentary wave of nostalgia wash over me. It comes once, then it's over. "*You're* an ecking Sky key."

"I don't *think* so. I don't sense anything large enough that could be a planet. But I can feel the other assassins. Maybe just their keys. I'm not sure. In either case, I think I know where Manila is. There are the two numnuts outside the doors, but there's a third key on board the ship and the…I don't know…the *pattern* is different than the others."

"A signature. Yeah. It makes sense hers would be different."

I nod. "But how the fuck do we get out of here?" I grab her arm as the electricity throws off cold air behind us and a hole appears in the yeeyar door. "You look about as useful as a box of hair in a fight."

"Eck you. There's another way out. You can link to the Sky yeeyar system, right?"

I shrug. "Maybe? No fucking clue."

"Of course you can. It's how you're keeping the door closed." She rolls her murky gaze and focuses on the ceiling. "There. We go through the ceiling. I heard a story once about another human doing the same thing on board a Niahhorru pirate ship."

"You must be talking about Deena." I use her shoulder as a crutch and hop up onto the table she'd been mounted to before. I look up at the ceiling and focus my thoughts, which is troubling because the harder I focus on the ceiling, the less concentration I have to focus on the door. Another explosion blasts cool air in through the human head-sized opening they've created. I look up, bite the inside of my cheek and concentrate harder.

"It's working," Ashmara whispers.

I nod up at the black mass peeling apart above me. A huge boom spears through my concentration and I turn to see the Horny Toad slamming his horns into the door. The opening's gone from human head-sized to Egama-head sized and is large enough for at least the purple fucker to get through. "Fuck. Let's go."

I reach down and grab Ashmara's sweaty hand and hoist her up, but the ceiling is still too high. "Push me and I'll lift you."

"You look like you're about to pass the fuck out," I hiss back. "You can't lift… Shit!" The bench beneath us starts to push up as soon as the word *lift* is out of my mouth. We're hurtling towards the ceiling, moving too fast to stop.

"Aughhh!" A roar sounds behind me and Ashmara releases a sharp wail. We push through into a blackness that is supreme and I quickly scramble over the yeeyar ceiling — flooring? — and seal the hole shut beneath us.

"You okay?" My heart is a snare drum in my veins.

"Fine." She sounds like she's in pain. The human in me tells me to assess her injuries and make sure she's really okay. The pirate says fuck that, injuries are only what you make of them. We've got to keep going.

"Good. Let's get the fuck out of here."

"Manila," she croaks and my heart twists just a little bit.

"You know, your whole cold ass bitch act isn't very effective."

She lets out a weak laugh. "What are you talking about? I gotta get that key from her so I can sell it to the Lemorans."

I roll my eyes. "Right."

The sound of our heavy breathing is all I can hear for the next long moments. That, and the sound of Ashmara wheezing behind me as she and I crawl through this strange blackness. It has substance and texture, but no solid form. It simply bends out of my way wherever I push into it, forming loose tunnels of my own making. It's good. Means we can't be easily followed. Unless…

"I can feel the others, but do you think they can feel me?"

"Krakaw, I'm sure they can't," she says half-jokingly.

I snicker, "You're such a bitch."

"So I've been told. Are we getting closer?"

"Almost there."

We crawl forward a little ways more until I can feel that strange, distinctly Sky yet unusually rendered presence. It's so different than all the other assassins and their accompanying keys scattered across the cosmos, a unique presence among them. It reassures me though that it's there. If I can feel it, it means she's alive.

"Here." I point down. "Do you have anything you can use as a weapon?"

"Do you sense any other Sky down there?"

"Not yet, but those other two are moving this way." I can feel one presence that's slight, another that's more woven through with yeeyar, and know that it's Mr. Grape and Horny Toad, respectively.

"Are those two the only ones on board the ship?"

"As far as I can tell, there are only three keys on the ship. Those two and Manila."

"Huh." Ashmara says.

"Are you thinking about Jerrock?"

"Yeah. Wondering where the homicidal fucker went."

"Didn't he shoot you?"

"Yeah."

"You okay?" I say again.

"Fine, actually. I mean, my leg's fucked for now, but he must have put a patch on me. Either that, or the two psychopaths on this ship did."

I frown as I mentally recalibrate and try to form a seam in the floor-ceiling below big enough for the two of us to crawl through. "Isn't that weird. Why did he give you up?"

"He holds my contract. He should have killed me when I was passed out. Instead, the stupid fuck wanted to torture me, I guess. He might have patched my shoulder, but he also took my muuir patch with him."

"What's muuir?"

"The elixir of life. An ecking wild ride. Nirvana." She laughs. "It's good ecking stuff."

I get the sense she's talking drugs, but I don't understand what it is and it's sure as fuck not relevant now that I've got a hole open in the floor and can feel the vibrations of the. Sky assassins approaching faster. "Let's move — the ship's big and they've got distance to cover, but so do we if we're gonna somehow find the escape pods."

I swing my legs over the edge of the hole and drop down onto the floor, which is farther than I thought it would be. I barely manage to keep my feet. Ashmara doesn't manage at all. She collapses in a heap and rolls onto one side, cussing up a storm.

I make a face down at her. I can see her torn and burned skin through a hole in her lower left pantleg, but my attention is jerked up towards a rattling against the wall. "Manila!" Her bionic arm has been removed what looks like brutally. She's leaking green blood all over the floor from the stump that's left.

But the female, tough as she is, still lifts her head. "Nalia."

"Manila," I exhale, relief coursing through me. I don't know her very well, but I still think of her as a friend, somebody who always kinda sorta looked out for human me. In a lot of ways, she reminds me of my sister, Leanna.

Leanna. I start at the appearance of her name in my thoughts. *Yes, her name is Leanna. I wonder where she is now...* Because I know she's not dead. I know it, just like I know Manila isn't, either. She's somewhere in these wild and crazy cosmos.

I cross the room to arrive before Manila and stitches of pain weave down my back as I watch her fight to lift her drooping chin from her chest. She looks at me and smiles. I approach her and carefully shove my shoulder under her full arm before dropping the cuffs anchoring her remaining wrist above her head, too high for her feet to fully touch the ground and forcing her to hang from her shoulder socket like this, for however long we've been here. It must be excruciating.

"You gonna make it?"

"How did you..." She screams as her bodyweight drops fully onto me, her arm not dislocated, but clearly hurting her something fierce. "How did you...do that?"

I explain to her what happened in as few words as I can and, when I'm finished, she tosses her head back and laughs.

"The stupid shroving idiots." Her black hair moves in waves around her cheeks as she and I move towards Ashmara, still sitting hunched over in the center of the floor, breathing hard like she's trying not to throw up.

"The Sky don't make mistakes," Manila says. She looks at me, her glossy black eyes blinking slowly. She looks like she's been drugged with something. I hope it isn't lethal. "But they've still managed to make the mistake everyone else in the cosmos has..."

"What's that?"

She blinks. "To underestimate a human." Coughing from the floor turns her attention towards it. "Shrov, Ashmara, you don't look good."

"Speak for yourself, stumpy." Ashmara cocks her head at Manila's injured arm and I have to acknowledge that she's got a point. I carry Manila over to the bench table in this room, where they evidently chose not to lock her up, and help her sit on top of it.

"We need to get this sealed," I tell her, glancing around, looking for something — anything that might help.

"Here," comes the voice from the floor. I glance down and see Ashmara pulling a knife out of her boot. "Use this. It's a radium knife."

"One of the Voraxian Rakukanna's creations." Manila nods. "It'll do."

"Tell me how it works," I order, taking the knife out of Ashmara's hand and moving to Manila's short arm. I can see bone, but it doesn't disturb me. On the battlefield, fighting in the Water Wars, I saw worse injuries. I just haven't seen soldiers handle them so gracefully.

Manila explains how to turn it on, and when I do, I watch the blade light up, turning from pale blue to teal. "Good?"

"Good," she says.

I glance at her face. "You ready?"

"Centare."

"Excellent. Let's do this." I press the heated blade to the stump of her arm, just above where her elbow should be, and block out the sounds and sensations of pain that emanate from her body. Spittle flies from her lips and she makes a single pained groan before slumping to the side, eyes closed, body clenched. I curse, worried about fucking this up and burning her worse than I need to, but before she can collapse off of the table completely, Ashmara appears at her side.

She holds Manila through the process and in the back of my head, I'm very aware of the two assassins on the other side of the door. I keep it shut, holding it with the tenacity of my mind and wondering why the other two seem to have such a hard time breaking through the newly discovered defenses I've got. Instead, they're going through the hard way again, horns first. It'll give us time, but not a lot.

"Done." Ish. "It'll hold." For now. "Unlike the hold I've got on the door. We need to go now."

"Manila, heelee," Ashmara says against Manila's temple, giving her a small kiss that makes my heart give an uneven thump.

"Don't..." Manila wheezes. "Don't go soft on me now."

"I'm not. I was just gonna ask, do you have any muuir on you?"

Manila starts to laugh, her sharpened teeth flashing, even in the low light. "You're a sick shroving bastard."

"The one and only." Ashmara tries to smile, but it comes off as a grimace. I'm not sure if she meant the request as a joke. "Let's get the key and get the eck out of here."

"Key?" Manila shakes her head, struggling to sit up and needing a lot of help from both Ashmara and me to do it. As we help her down from the table, her knees buckle once, but she manages to pull herself back upright, looking regal in a form-fitting black jumpsuit, even with a mangled left arm.

"Uhh yeeshee, you know, the key I'm definitely going to steal from you before this is all over. Seems like the *least* you can do after not having any muuir and getting me kidnapped with you."

Manila balks, "I didn't ask you to join us at the mok bir tables. That was just you being a nosy little wretch, butting your nose into affairs where it doesn't belong."

"Hey! It's not my fault you couldn't recognize Jerrock the assassin. Did you really think that *Rhogan* was real? He looked totally fake. Like seriously? He looked like a pleasure hologram, not a real flesh and blood male."

"She's got a point," I mutter. "But can we please focus? We need to find the life rafts or the rescue shuttles or whatever the fuck they're called!" I stamp my foot, irritation mounting even though I should be more panicked that we're all about to be murdered.

It's somehow hard to feel panicked when neither of the other two females here betray their concern at all, not even Manila, with her one mutilated arm.

"Ontte. Let's..." Manila says, grimacing as she takes her next step.

"Not without the key!"

"You already got your key, you shroving reaver!" Manila shouts.

"What?" Ashmara and I say at the exact same time, the words overlapping in different tongues as they filter through our translators.

"I don't have my key anymore. I wouldn't have been stupid enough to bring it on the ship. When the explosion hit the mok bir tables, I landed near Gibli and gave the key to him. The Sky assassins only took my arm because it was made to appear as if it still held the key, that's where they put it originally. But the moment you liberated me from their control, I moved the key. I didn't want it inside my body. I've been carrying it in the pocket of my robes for rotations. I even lost it some time ago when I got drunk and fell in a pond. Of course, my drones recovered it..."

Ashmara pauses, then her mouth opens comically large before a huge gust of laughter jerks out of her mouth. The sound is so...strangely guileless — something I know the female incapable of being — it cuts through the darkness like a torch with unending light. "You crazy female!" she shouts. "That's *madness*, even by my standards..."

Meanwhile, I'm not laughing. "Wait. That's not possible. There are *three* Sky signatures on this ship — the two assassins hunting us, and one other. If it's not your key, then what's the third..."

My voice trails off as I follow Manila's gaze. She smirks. "Huh. I saw him leave after he cut off my arm. He's a sneaky bastard, isn't he?"

I don't see what she sees — at first — but when I stare into the shadowy corner of the room, my gaze calibrates to the light in a way that is decidedly inhuman and wholly awesome. The shadows unblur until I can make out a shadowy figure among them. He's so well camouflaged with the darkness, I can't tell which limb he's moving, only that he's moving one. Silver flashes. Red, too. My supernatural gaze sharpens even further and it's only then that I register the weapon in his hand — the same gun-looking thing that he produced from his wrist at the mok bir tables — I gulp.

"Well, fuck."

"Is it Jerry Berry?" Ashmara says, squinting that way.

"It is, indeed, Jerrock the killer," Manila confirms.

"What's he doing?"

I swallow hard. "Pointing a gun at your head — a blaster." He has it trained on Ashmara's face, unwavering, just like his gaze, like every ounce of his concentration. It's like Manila and I aren't even in the room.

"What's he waiting for?" Manila staggers upright and lifts her wounded arm, wincing wildly as she does, like she's forgotten it's no longer there and she intended to use it for something. To fight him? Ha. I hope not.

Meanwhile, Ashmara seems to be harboring the same delusions, because she twists her neck side to side, releasing two large cracks, before lurching forward and planting herself in line with Manila. She wavers wildly as she says, "Don't worry, ladies, I got this." She cracks the knuckles of both her five-fingered hands and waves at the killer in the corner. "Hi, Jer."

"Jesus Christ," I mutter, wondering how the fuck I ended up here with the two most overconfident females in the entire history of not just this galaxy, but all galaxies, about to square off against the most dangerous male in the galaxy, most likely about to be killed by him. What fun.

With a dejected huff, I step up to Manila's other side and lift my fists and the radium knife I've still got clutched in my right palm. "Let's try to do this, I guess." I shake my head. "Alright, Ashmara, you break right when I break left. Manila, you just…" My voice trails off as I look at the wounded female wavering on her feet, and then a limping Ashmara to her right. "Stay here and look intimidating."

"Not a chance," Manila says.

"I told you ladies, I *got* this." And then Ashmara pulls a fistful of what looks like lint from her right breast pocket. "Oh shit. I had a patch with me the whole time?"

"Ashmara, the *bomb*..." Manila grits, but Ashmara's gaze is already unfocused, her concentration lost.

Manila lunges across Ashmara's body and snatches a small green stone from among the lint littering her palm. Ashmara, at the same time, dumps the debris from her pocket onto the floor, keeping only what looks like a translucent bandaid with her. This, she carefully unfolds.

"Oh thank the ecking comets..." She lifts the bandaid to her outer arm only to scream as a bullet — a dark flash of light — tears straight through her hand. A second bullet flashes and disintegrates the bandaid she'd been holding as it floats through the air. "Eck you, Jerrock!" she cries out, dropping to one knee and clutching her hand to her chest, yet looking decidedly more upset about the loss of the bandaid than anything else.

Realizing it really is gone, she looks up, her face contorted in rage and her eyes...her eyes turn a bright and bloody red. "ECK!" She gets up and charges towards him, but a dozen things happen at once that all work together to keep her from her revenge.

The door behind us explodes open and the two assassins enter firing. Ashmara is closest to the door and takes a hit to her side. I lunge, tackling both females to the ground, but not before Manila manages to lob Ashmara's green stone at Jerrock. He fires two shots.

Two shots... Two targets. One expected, one...less so.

But Jerrock doesn't miss.

He hits the stone, even though it's tinier than a human thumbnail, and an explosion shakes the entire room, quite literally *stretching* its yeeyar boundaries.

Heat washes over my back and I cry out as it sears through my clothes. The smell of burning hair — *my burning hair* — fills my lungs. I don't dare open my eyes, but I use the additional sense I've been given to discern that there aren't three Sky keys in the room anymore, but two. And only one of them is moving towards us. The other one — the *different* one — seems to be…fleeing. I don't give a shit about that, but reach down into the pile of limbs beneath me, grab Manila and Ashmara by the arms and yank up.

"Come on!" I charge towards the doorway, which hangs ajar, the yeeyar that once formed it all tattered and fraying like the broken edges of a spiderweb. I almost trip on the body sprawled out over the threshold. It's Horny Toad. And he's dead.

I can see his charred clothing through the haze of smoke that's filled the room and spills out into the hall, but more interesting than that is the black smudge on his forehead and the bulge beneath it, and the pink blood leaking from its pocked center. He's very dead. *By blaster fire. The explosion didn't kill him. A single perfect shot, straight between the eyes. How interesting.*

Because Jerrock doesn't miss.

The remaining assassin lunges towards me through the doorway and I bellow out a battle cry as I drop the bodies I'm dragging and surge forward to meet him. We grapple hand-to-hand, my combat training kicking in and coming back to me. I was always good hand-to-hand. I even managed to beat Leanna almost every time even though she was older and had more badges studding her uniform's left breast. My dad said it was because I was more cunning. My mom said it was because I had more inner rage. I think Mom was right.

But they didn't survive the Water Wars. Leanna and her doctor killed them. She called it their *sacrifice.*

Fucking bitch.

Rage creeps up the backs of my arms and I roar, "Auraaghaaahhh!"

His metal forearm meets mine as we spar. Pain webs out from my wrist to my elbow, but I fight through it, kicking up with my leg and finding his shin. He betrays absolutely no pain, but I don't need him to hurt. I just need him to move a little bit to the right...and he does. I spin and, using the extra space afforded to me, I switch the radium blade on and slash up, scoring a line from his chin to his remaining eye.

He punches me in the stomach hard enough for me to know he's broken a rib or two, but I push through that agony and grab him by the front of his black armor. I drag him against me and when he punches me again, I firm my stomach against the assault and stab him in his empty eye socket. I sink the blade in deep and black and silver sparks fly out to singe my cheeks. There is no blood. Robots don't bleed.

"Arrrrrgggghhh!" I charge, pressing my full weight forward, but the fucker's strong and he's heavy. He fights back, pushing me... Oh fuck. I'm about to lose my footing and if he takes me to the ground, I'll be dust...

And then a weight slams against my back. My stomach lurches up into my throat, unprepared for the attack. Only, it isn't an attack, is it? *It's reinforcements.* A second weight slams against up against the first.

Manila's bloody arm comes around me as she heaves her full weight against my spine. She releases grunts of pain as her feet press into the floor. She buttresses my body, propping it up, and I can hear Ashmara's whooping Eshmiri laugh behind her ringing even louder. I laugh. I *laugh. Fucking Ashmara... Fucking Manila.* We push together until we get the assassin shoved up against a yeeyar wall and we keep pushing but my arms are shaking. He just won't die.

My hand around the hilt of the blade is bloody. It... may be broken. I don't dare release any pressure to check. But, as I watch my white skin, torn and bloodied red, shove against his purple face which sizzles and sparks as he fights back, more colors appear before me. *Hands.* An orange-yellow fist decorated in sharp black claws followed by a dark brown palm with the same pale, chipped nails I have. They move around my shoulders and fit themselves to the back of my own palm so that, when we push against the blade hilt, we push together.

We push as one on the dull end of the blade and we keep pushing the knife into his head until his tongue rolls revoltingly out of his mouth and his nostrils start to make this horrible noise as he tries and fails to take in air. His remaining, functioning yeeyar eye starts to glow a brighter and brighter red. I feel like he's revving up to something and I don't want to find out what...

"Yah!" I free my left hand from the pile of hands and yeeyar and blood and stab it into his soft remaining eye. I rip it out, yeeyar sparks flying, and all at once, the red light shifting across the yeeyar goes out. The male falls to the floor like a curtain dropped. I fall on top of him and Manila and Ashmara fall on top of me. We lie there in a bloody heap, panting and trying not to focus on our injuries. At least, that's what I'm doing. Ashmara, however, seems to be two steps ahead.

"Is his key…still active?" she pants.

I pause, trying to think, and nod. "It's sputtering."

She grabs the knife out of my hand, ripping it out of the dead guy's head to free it. "Where is it?"

"I don't know. I can't see that granularly…"

"His chest. He doesn't have the full arm, so they'd have put it there." Manila, rolling off of the pile to land panting on her back, points to a covered patch of his chest. Ashmara yanks down on the black leather he wears. It's all bionic beneath.

"Brilliant." Ashmara heaves the blade over her head then and stabs straight down, barely giving me time to scramble off of him and not get my left hand impaled in the process.

"Psychopath!" I shout at her, falling onto my ass. The pain in my ribs is screaming at me to lie down, but I'm not convinced we're not gonna die yet.

"Yeeshee, yeeshee," she mutters, pain creeping into her voice as she works on sawing through the flesh of his chest to reach underneath the metal plates. Bright copper blood bubbles up around her blade as she works, the radium knife no longer searing as it cuts. "But if this works…" She grunts, pulling a plate free. "I'll be a *rich* psychopath."

"Incorrigible," Manila hisses, trying to stand. She's in bad shape. We all are. I'm not sure all three of us are going to make it. Manila's situation looks the worst. She's clutching her wounded side with her remaining arm. Her eyelids flutter from the sides as she looks at me. "We need to find the control room."

I nod and struggle up to my feet. It takes me way longer than it should. I look back to help Manila and see her practically clawing her way up one yeeyar wall. I grab her beneath her arm and she twists her head and swallows deeply. "Thanks," she pants.

"Right back at ya." I collapse against the wall and she steps into place beside me, clutching her severed arm between her breasts while I hang onto my ribs.

"You're losing him," I warn Ashmara when I feel the flickering of the only remaining Sky key on board this ship fading out.

She makes a gruff sound and starts hacking more wildly at the poor murderer's corpse, and just before that light goes out, she manages to pry a final piece of black metal free of his chest, sitting where a heart should be.

"Aha!" She wrenches a small black cube out of the male and declares, "It's still luminous." She shakes the small cube, which is about the size of a Rubik's cube back on Earth, only this one is filled with yeeyar and strands of color, gold and silver and blue. "That means it's working, right?" she asks me.

I wait, feeling that the pulse of the Sky key has gotten brighter. "Yeah. Looks like you got it out in time. If the body dies around it, it dies, right? But it can survive on its own?"

"Something like that," Manila answers on a moan. She pushes away from the wall and starts down the corridor. I follow her and, eventually, hear Ashmara's uneven gait behind us. We take corridor after corridor, wandering the endlessly dark hallways until finally, we find a room that's entirely different than all the rest.

I shudder as I look inside a room that's a pale grey instead of black. There's a single stool in front of what looks like a large keyboard, except all the keys are black and shifting. More yeeyar, then. A screen hangs above it, charts I can't read spread across it. There is, in addition, one extra seat to the right, pressed against the wall, that looks out of a huge window. A lap screen is spread across it.

"A two-seater," Manila says, going to the main controls and plunking down in the chair behind them. Her fingers start moving deftly over the yeeyar, which responds to her touch as I remember it responding to Jerrock's when I was on board his ship. I watch her work, completely clueless as to how the fuck this ship works even though I'm a trained pilot.

"Looks like none of the escape pods are missing, but there's an open hatch in the lower level. Must be how Jerrock got out. You're sure he's gone?" She looks over her shoulder at me.

I nod. "Yeah. No other Sky keys on board. The hatch — that dangerous?"

"It was, but I've sealed it now."

I frown. "Why'd he make it so easy? Why'd he leave?"

Manila drops her tone and glances in Ashmara's direction. Ashmara is seated at the portal window banging both fists on the yeeyar screen spread across her lap and muttering curses under her breath. "I want to know why *she's* alive." Manila plugs in what look like coordinates, and I see a small point luminate on the map in front of us and begin moving, though I can't feel the corresponding movement of the ship beneath my feet at all. Silent, this ship, eerily so. Just like Jerrock's was.

"Jerrock's held her contract for rotations. He had her here, unconscious for who knows how long. There wasn't any reason for him not to kill her. She isn't wanted by the Sky as I am. As you are."

"Me?"

Manila nods. "You're human. They've been trying to get hold of a female to breed with their monsters. Your species is known to be fertile."

"Christ."

"Is that an insult where you're from?"

"Yes." I shrug one shoulder. "Sort of. Or a prayer."

Manila smirks. "Well, Nalia, I'd be prepared to use it again. It looks like we've been targeted by a ship and I've got no idea what species is on board."

"I do," I grimace. "And I think we're going to need weapons. Lots and lots of weapons."

"Why?"

"What's going on?" both females say at once.

I stagger over to Ashmara's shoulder and look out on the void of outer space, littered with endless stars. So many stars. And so many of them are *inhabited*. I think momentarily on how wrong we humans were, before shaking my head and focusing again.

"I can't see it, can you?"

"The ship?" Ashmara shakes her head. "I got nothing."

And then Manila's voice behind us, a bleak grimace. "There's only one species with the capability of flying undetected like that. Nalia, do you sense a Sky presence out there?"

"Yes, and it's close."

"Shrov!"

"Eck!"

"Fuck! Is this ship armored?"

"Ontte," Manila says. "Of course."

"Is it armed?"

"Ecking yeeshee!" Ashmara cries out, voice half exaltation, half pained grimace. She holds her left leg stiffly and awkwardly away from her body and clutches at it with her hand. "I know the answer to that, and look — I even figured out how to turn the guns on." She presses down with her full fist on the screen, slamming it, really, like a toddler playing the drums. Still, it's effective. A small light blasts away from us from the upper deck of the ship and I see a flash of color, just a single green spark, when it hits something.

"You're a shoot first, ask questions later kinda female, aren't you?" I mutter.

She snorts, "Is there any better kind?"

I struggle to hold back a grin and tip my chin down at her. "Good. Keep all our guns trained on that ship. Let's open fire."

"Ontte," Manila says. "They're coming closer and they're trying to open a line of communication, likely to try to bargain with us so that they can come on board."

I laugh darkly. "Not gonna happen. Ashmara?"

She bangs on the screen again and more blasts shoot out of our ship in a symphony of colorful explosions against a wall that appears purely black. "Like that?"

"Good work. Is it working?"

Manila sounds a little nervous as she says, "Centare." I look back over my shoulder at her and see that she's wasting forward, clutching the pale edge of the control board before her as if fighting to remain in place.

I go to her and see that her arm is still bleeding. "Fuck. Are you hurt? I mean…more hurt?"

"Shh." Her eyes flutter. "They forced our comms line open. They can hear us," she says.

"They can?"

She nods again. Ashmara continues banging on the board. I clench my jaw and clutch Manila's shoulder, keeping her upright as I speak louder, voice fueled with fire and leveled with threat. "Alright, Sky fuckers. You've got to the count of three before we show you exactly who you're dealing with."

I clear my throat, take a calming breath and stare directly into the screen as if I were staring into Jerrock's eyes…and holding a knife to his throat. "Jerrock, you sick fuck, you made a mistake not killing us before. One…"

There's a pause. I don't plan to give him much more than that.

"Two…"

The sound of shuffling. A hiss. A curse…

"Three…"

<h1 style="text-align:center">20</h1>

Herannathon

"Shrov!" Deena shouts, running around the control room with her hands above her head. I've got my hands working at the controls, attempting to manipulate the yeeyar. For whatever reason, the incoming ship can't hear us. Ironic, that they should be the ones to blow us out of the air now when were instants from leveling the same threat against them.

"*One...*" Nalia's hardened voice says, echoing through the control room.

"Shroving comets, Tev. What's taking you so long to get our comms up?" Deena returns to me and points her finger directly at my nose. "Your female is about to blow us out of the shroving air. That is *your* female, isn't it?"

"*Two...*"

I'm smiling. I can't stop smiling. "It shroving is."

"I have babies on board this ship," Deena mutters, moving away from me to her mate seated at the controls in the center of the ship. He's working on reinforcing our shields while simultaneously bouncing a small hybrid infant on his left knee. The male kitling is giggling wildly.

"*Three...*"

I follow Deena to the primary control seats — four heavy Niahhorru seats facing inward towards one another — grab Nikkowerranorru by his upper hiannru tine and wrench him out of the seat across from Rhorkanterannu just as the first wave of Sky ammunition rocks the ship to the right.

The kit on Rhorkanterannu's knee screeches merrily, his little tines poking through the short cloud-like curls sprouting from the top of his head. His eyes are Niahhorru silver and blink at me up and down, rather than left to right. He's shroving adorable.

I give him a small smile at the same time that Tev shouts, "We have communications!"

"Say something, Herannathon!" Deena hisses at me, looking impossibly tiny in the massive Niahhorru seat bracketing her. I recall the last time she was in such a seat, she almost gave birth in it.

I clear my throat. "Nalia, you can stop firing now."

A pause. And then her voice comes in crisp and clear. "Herannathon? Where's Jerrock? Does he have you? Are you okay? If he's hurt you, I'm gonna rip out his stupid eye…"

"She will," Manila's voice chimes. "She's already done it twice."

"I like this human," Rhorkanterannu rumbles, gathering the kit up to his chest and poking his little nose with his much larger finger.

I meet his gaze knowingly and give him a slight nod. Pride becomes me. "Jerrock isn't on board. We thought we'd find him with you."

"No…centare, he isn't here. He fled. But then why can I sense another Sky key on board your craft?" She sounds suspicious. "Is this really Herannathon?"

Behind her, I can hear Ashmara hissing, *"It's a trap! Don't you remember how Jerrock pretended to be Rhogan? Let's blow their faces off!"*

"This isn't Jerrock!" Deena screeches. "Herannathon!"

"If this is Herannathon," comes Nalia's voice, entirely ignoring Deena's, "I need you to prove it."

I grin and lean forward, bracing both my lower elbows on my knees. "This is Herannathon and I plan to prove it to you readily along with seven of my brothers, all of whom are eager to participate in the shekurr with you that I promised."

Across from me, Deena blinks at me, looking shocked. "She's into that?"

"Hm. I'm not sure it's Herannathon. Herannathon promised me ten other males, not a meager seven."

Laughter blooms across the ship and I can sense my brothers looking at me from all across the control room. They aren't sure if I'm joking. I nod, assuring them, and watch their expressions transform from curiosity to *lust*. Tevbarannos trips and falls over nothing at all and sputters from the floor, "She…she really wants a shekurr?"

"There will be no shekurr unless *I* lead."

"Oh ontte," comes her voice, the sweetest seduction, as hard as stalyx. *"That's Herannathon, alright."*

"Explain the other key," Manila's voice calls, though there is something decidedly *wrong*. She sounds pained. I've never seen the female hurt and my fists clench in concern for all three females and what they may have had to endure. "Explain how you got off of Evernor."

"There are a thousand ways to get off of Evernor," I chastise the female. "As Jerrock proved."

"There aren't," Manila asserts. "Unless it's true? The Niahhorru intra-quadrant transportation machine is real? Is that also how you're cloaking yourselves?"

"There is no such machine," Rhorkanterannu rumbles. "And we have no idea what you mean."

"Fine. Keep your secrets…"

"But what about the key?" Ashmara calls while Manila grumbles unhappily.

"Before I made my departure from Evernor, a friend came to see me."

"It's me, heelee!" Gibli shouts from his seat on the floor in front of the large yeeyar-powered viewpane at the front of the control room. He holds the Sky key in his palm, refusing to ever properly clasp it, as if it frightens him. It means he's a smart male — for a reaver.

"Gibli, is that you?"

Gibli merely laughs. Ashmara does, too. "Don't you dare let any of those shroving pirates take that key from you."

He growls at the nearest Niahhorru who moves towards him on an entirely unrelated task. Rhorkanterannu shakes his head. Deena merely laughs. "Well, what are you waiting for? Come aboard, friends."

Ashmara says, "We were waiting for an invitation."

My nerves are strung taut as we manage to dock the Sky ship to ours. It's built to neither dock, nor be boarded, so we have to jerry rig a solution by bringing the entire ship into the loading bay. Luckily, we brought the full strength of the mothership to hunt down the assassins, so our craft is large enough to take theirs fully inside the hangar.

We all move to the loading bay and the energy and tension is palpable as the Sky ship finally unseals itself and the three females walk out. Centare, they don't walk out...they *crawl.*

"Shroving comets!" Deena shouts.

"Quintenanrret!" Rhorkanterannu roars at the same time. "Take the females to the healing bay."

I rush to Nalia, shocked to see the state she's in — shocked and furious — but nothing shocks me more than the color of her eyes. They were brown before — they still are — but not all the time.

"What the *shrov* did they do to you?" I lock my arms around her and try to pick her up, but she moans.

"Don't...my ribs. The purple fucker broke my ribs..."

"Shrov..."

"I don't think he meant your ribs, Nalia," Deena says, appearing at my side. "What's up with your eyes? Those don't look human. Were they like this before?"

"Centare," I hiss.

"They fixed her," Ashmara shouts from her position reclined on a stretcher, Gibli at her side holding her hand with one of his while still holding the Sky key aloft in his other.

She's bleeding red blood everywhere from a severe-looking wound in her side. By my tally, my female was beaten, Ashmara was shot at least twice, and Manila's arm was severed. Yet...Ashmara said *they.*

"They?" I say.

Nalia nods, accepting a stretcher that's brought for her. She sighs out a breath as I help lower her onto its grey tantu leather surface. "There were three of them."

"You killed *three* Sky assassins?" Rhorkanterannu says, moving with the cluster of pirates and stretchers as we all accompany the females to the healing bay. The victors.

"Two," Manila calls. "Nalia is responsible for both almost single-handedly."

"Hah. Funny joke, stumpy," Ashmara calls.

"You're a real bitch, you know that?" Nalia says, laughing, like she's known these females for lifetimes, rather than a few solars.

She's such a different female. Spattered in blood and gore...blood in so many different shades and colors yet...very little of it appears to be her own. "I love you, Nalia," I blurt, looking down into her face, watching her eyes crinkle as she smiles back at me. "I know I don't deserve your love in return, after what I've done..."

"You've done nothing. My brain was broken already by *humans*. I was a soldier, supposed to be in this top-secret mission called Sucere. I was a soldier back home but it...ooph!" She grunts as we round the corner and Tevbarannos takes it too sharply, causing one edge of the cot to dip.

I slap the back of his head and Nalia laughs, "It's... it's a long story. But they wiped my memories, and when the Sky assassins tried to reprogram my brain with their yeeyar, they fixed the glitch. I remember everything — who I was, where I come from, all my fighting skills." She grins. "And I remember seeing you when I was still in the tank. And I know why you took me. I know it here." She touches the center of her chest. "I didn't know you then, but I was connected to you beyond reason. And now that I know you, I love you beyond measure." She exhales. "Must be Xiveri, I guess..."

I smirk down at her and touch some of the marks on her cheek, stains and burns and blood. Her hair looks like a bonfire, half blackened and unevenly cut. Shrov, she's stunning. "Pirates don't do Xiveri. How'd you learn of it?"

"I'm a human soldier and a Niahhorru pirate and a mok bir champion…I hear things."

"You didn't win that tournament!" Gibli shouts ahead of us.

Behind us, Manila groans, "I vote she did."

I ignore them, keeping my gaze pinned to her face as my brothers carry my mate through the healing bay doors.

As I load her carefully onto a flat bed that I cover with a heavy fur to block the space in the middle where a Niahhorru's tines should go, another voice shouts from the next bed over. Ashmara's. "You forgot one."

"One what?"

"One title."

"And what's that?" Nalia says with another pained grunt.

"Sky huntress." She laughs. "If you think they wanted her before, just wait to see how many contracts appear on her head now. You'll have the entire Sky fleet after you once they figure out that she's linked up to their yeeyar."

"Good," I whisper, leaning down to Nalia's lips, refusing to be rattled by this newfound knowledge or her newfound gift. "Let them come."

I kiss her deeply, sliding my tongue against hers and tasting her life and her essence and knowing that no matter how many times she's caught and captured, I will always follow. Because she's right. There is something more that binds us. Perhaps it is Xiveri. Perhaps it is this thing called love. Perhaps, it is only madness.

She shakes her head, pulling back and leaving just a breath of space between us, one I plan to swallow whole. "Centare. I don't want to wait for them to come to us. You heard Ashmara. I'm a Sky huntress, I know where they are. And now that we have a Sky key and can actually find the architects who think they're safe somewhere on their moving planet while they steal and imprison and torture other creatures, I want to go *hunt*."

"Mmm...bloodthirsty female," I growl, my cock tightening in my leathers at the thought of watching her slaughter Sky assassins with her own two human fists. Weak — is that what I once thought her? Soft? Ha. Not a shroving chance.

"As soon as you're off this table, we'll hunt the Sky to extinction, just for shroving sport."

"Mmm," she muses, blinking at me seductively while black swirls through the colored part of her eye, as if her pupil in the middle is now the eye of a storm. "You're forgetting one thing though, Herannathon..."

"You know that key belongs to me and Gibli, right?" Ashmara mumbles, sounding like she's in immeasurable pain as Quintenanrret begins working on repairing the bloody gash above her hip.

Nalia's lips quirk, but she otherwise keeps her gaze focused on mine. "We'll go hunting, but you promised me a shekurr first."

21

The Shekurr

I'm sitting on the edge of a high, light grey table, nerves rattling up and down my arms. I don't think I was even this nervous when I squared off against three Sky assassins in this Quadrant of the galaxy, or plunged headlong into war in the ancient galaxy I came from.

I'm alone for now. The room is light grey and all soft edges, completely different from most of the other dark, yeeyar-powered rooms on Niahhorru ships. But we're not on a Niahhorru ship. We're in a tower on Kor — a *pleasure* tower — one that's heavily guarded around the base and spire so that inside, Niahhorru pirates and Niahhorru females can couple with relaxed and wanton abandon in various rooms, each holding a separate shekurr.

Herannathon is outside now in the receiving room talking to the other males we mutually agreed would participate. He's outlining the rules.

The males will take turns.

Herannathon will determine their order.

There will be no scratching or biting.

Any male to fall into rut will be removed.

Any male who does anything I don't like will be removed.

Any male who does anything Herannathon doesn't like will be removed, less a hiannru tine or two…

I wet my lips, eager, as my thighs clench on the table. I'm already wet, dripping onto the smooth table below. Anticipation grips my toes, making them curl. I cling to the edge of the table, my gaze *fixed* on the light grey door. I'm so fixated on it, I jump when it finally opens and Herannathon steps through.

He's wearing a fucking loincloth. A loincloth. Jesus Christ, I'm going to combust. His gaze rakes over the light red robe I'm wearing and my nipples stiffen and peak under his inspection. He growls, "Are you sure you're ready for this?"

I nod, nervous. "I'm sure."

He rumbles low and deep in his chest, louder this time as he steps right up to me and spreads my knees with his two lower hands while his two upper hands grip either side of my jaw and tip my chin up. He claims my lips with his own. His upper hands are warm and smooth while his lower hands feel hot and rough as they work up my inner thighs, kneading and massaging until he reaches their juncture.

He peels back the edges of my robe and slides his thumbs over my lower lips. He didn't just retract his claws, but clipped them for this — just in case. All the males did.

I moan as his thick thumbs spear my wetness while his tongue slides in and out of my mouth. I whimper, sounding every bit the damsel in distress that I now know I'm not. I break the kiss by biting his lower hip hard.

"Don't tease me."

He rears back with a smirk and kisses the tip of my nose. He pulls his thumbs from my heat and lifts them up between us. He sucks one clean and places the other to my lower lip. "Suck," he breathes.

I bend forward and take his thumb into my mouth, the scent and taste of my own tangy arousal making me even hotter. His cock is lengthening behind his loincloth and I reach for it, but he blocks my hand. "Centare. I want to watch my brothers ruin you before I finish you off."

Oh my god. My heart is hammering. "I'm a soldier, a pirate, and a gambler who doesn't lose."

"Oh, but darling, you will not win in this." He strokes his wet thumb across my cheek before returning to the door and pressing his palm to the reader beside it. I watch, transfixed, as the door glides silently open and allows ten Niahhorru males entry, their hungry, lascivious gazes pinned to me. And they're all wearing loincloths. *For fuck's sake.*

I whimper at the sight of them and two of the males trip and stumble, one falling into the shoulder of another, who shoves his brother upright. Their cocks are all in varying stages of hardness, pushing their loincloths into tents.

The atmosphere in the pleasure tower is calibrated to allow the males to be able to keep their cocks out without needing a synthetic. So much eye candy and all of it's hidden from me. It makes me whimper with a need so ferocious, the table under my ass is already slick. The doors glide closed and Herannathon returns to me, looking devilish, rakish and very much like he's up to something.

He slides his arms around my body and I loop my hands around his neck, letting him move and maneuver me however he likes. He's in charge here. I'm just the willing recipient of pleasure.

He pulls me from the table and turns me around so that I'm standing barefoot on the floor, my back to his chest. His lower hands come around my waist. He unknots the robe. His upper hands pull my hair — shorter now than it was before my Sky battle — back over my shoulder so that when he finally fans the robe open and drops it, I'm totally exposed.

The males stir, becoming restless. I can see one male holding another back and another pair whispering to two others. I don't recognize most of the males. There are only three that I do. Herannathon calls one of them forward.

"Tevbarannos," Herannathon says. "Come."

I smile up at the male who stumbles towards me and watch the grey of his eyes swirl madly as he gapes. "Me?"

"Nalia wanted you to be her first in the shekurr."

Tevbarannos balks. He is the youngest male here and has never been with a female before. "I…I'm *honored.*"

"And I'm horny," I moan, reaching for his loincloth. I slip my fingers underneath the waistband and tug him forward. I lean in when he still doesn't react except to hold his four hands to the sides, like he has no clue what to do with them. It's sweet. It's not going to get me where I need to go though, and I'm grateful for Herannathon behind me, his warm presence a torturous tease of what I know he's capable of. All those sinful wonders…

"Touch her, Tevbarannos," Herannathon says.

I lick a line up the center of Tev's chest, his skin salty and sweet under my tongue, and feel his entire body shudder. Hands come around my hips, four from the back, four more from the front. They stack on top of one another and I have no idea who's touching me where, only that I want it. I want *more*.

"Kiss him," Herannathon commands, to me this time, his breath hot in my ear.

I look up and into Tevbarannos's enormous eyes. His pink tongue is pressed against his lower lip. He looks utterly lost. I slide one hand over the rough plates of his chest and pull at his neck. He bends down low, lower still, low enough for me to be able to press my open mouth to his. He grunts wildly, staggering closer. His hands start moving frantically, petting me everywhere he can. He seems afraid to touch me below the waist and I find that delightfully endearing. He even seems wary to cup my tits.

I whimper as I continue to peck at his mouth. Herannathon barks, "Tevbarannos, touch her *everywhere*. She needs you. Can't you hear her beg?"

Herannathon reaches around me to drag one of Tev's hands over my right breast and then my left. Tev doesn't hesitate to squeeze me roughly. I moan.

"There..." A light kiss on the back of my neck before Herannathon steps away from me, leaving a chill where his warmth just was. "That's a good girl. Moan for him." I do. I do loudly, wanting to obey his every command.

While I kiss Tev and he continues to pet my breasts and shoulders and hips, Herannathon calls to the other males. "She needs to be primed before her tight channel will accept any of us. Who would like to tongue her sex?"

There's a rough chorus of shouts that only lasts a second. A second after that I feel a hot, hulking presence at my back before it drops low...and then hands come against my ass cheeks and spread them apart, and a face buries itself in my ass and pussy. A tongue darts into my body and I hinge at the hips, body instinctively bending to give the male — whoever it is — better access.

I cry out and Tev catches me. I hold onto him and moan while Herannathon commands him to kiss my neck. Tev does what he's told, sucking on my skin every place he can. His lips are rough — way rougher than a human man's — and definitely rough enough to leave a trail of hickies from earlobe to collarbone with how urgently he's moving. I toss my head back and close my eyes and the male underneath me spreads my legs even wider.

"Wrentennaret, prime her rear hole. It will be difficult to take her here, so we need this area wet. You, join Wrentennaret on your knees and wet her front."

I literally black out when the third male joins the first two and a tongue enters my asshole at the same time that two fingers plunge into my pussy and a mouth swarms over my clit. "Holy shit..."

I'm ignored as Herannathon continues speaking to the other males. It makes me feel *filthy*, little more than a vessel. "Ontte. Suck on her nub, that swollen swatch of skin." The male does what Herannathon tells him and I start to shiver immediately. "Watch her now. She'll unravel in five...four...three..."

I don't make it to two, but scream into Tev's mouth. He captures all of my cries on his tongue, while below, my legs give out. I don't move anywhere. Hands hold me up. So many fucking hands... It's too much.

Overwhelming. And so far this is only three of eleven males.

"Tevbarannos. Enough. It's time. Lift her up and enter her now."

Twelve hands. I know that rationally there are only twelve touching me now, but it feels like there are so many more. They lift me up and I hold onto Tev's shoulders, trying to focus as I come down from the stars. I loop my legs around his hips and suddenly two other males are standing there, holding my calves and thighs. I'm completely surrounded. One of the males ducks his head between Tev and I and licks the tip of my nipple. My left leg spasms and Herannathon eggs the male on, encouraging him to suckle my breasts harder.

"I want to see red abrasions on her speckled white skin when this is over, evidence that she's been ravaged."

I gasp as the male starts sucking even harder and loop my arm over his back, careful to keep my wrist in between his tines so I don't cut myself on accident. Meanwhile, Tev at my front is fumbling a little bit, so I reach between us and slide my hand down his smooth length. He's fully exposed, and when I touch the soft skin of his smooth, round erection, he gasps and moans, choking as he tries to do both simultaneously.

"Nalia…" he says, sounding shocked. I tug him forward by the cock and line him up with my entrance.

"Fuck me, Tev," I whisper, glancing to the right. I meet Herannathon's gaze. He's staring at me, his half-naked brothers an overtly sexual image behind him. He's got one arm folded across his chest while another touches his mouth and the two hands below clench and unclench. He looks like he's barely holding himself back.

"Fuck her, Tevbarannos. Impale her roughly."

The head of Tev's cock breaches my swollen, tender, *hurting* labia and pushes past my lips. "Are you…sure?" he asks me hesitantly.

I nod. "Please…" I beg.

He jacks his hips up in one abrupt thrust and I cry out, "Yesss."

Tevbarannos looks like he's going to collapse. His skein is fluttering wildly over his eyes. One of his brothers comes up against his back. "Fuck her, Tevbarannos," Herannathon says. His voice is deeper, changed. I look over at him and the glaze of pure lust coating his shimmering eyes is enough to cause my inner walls to clench.

"Shrov," Tev curses. He starts to pump in and out of me. He shakes his head, expression twisting as if he's being tortured. "I can't…much longer…" He pumps inside of me, movements frantic and jerky, but it doesn't matter. His length feels incredible. Huge and hard and smooth and, thanks to Herannathon priming me for this, capable of entering me all the way up to the hardened plates at the root.

"Nalia!" he cries out, body tensing and releasing in a gush. I can *hear* it, the sound of him squirting seed inside of me and, when I look down, I can see thick grey cream gushing out around the base of his cock and soaking my red bush.

Tevbarannos collapses forward onto me. His lips find my lips and he kisses me so sweetly I smile. "Thank you for this honor," he says and I can see all of his plates flapping up from his chest as he releases heat. I know that if he were a human man, he'd be sweating profusely.

"The honor is mine," I whisper back.

He smiles and steps away, cock sluicing out of me in a gush of fluid. The male who'd been at my right leg takes his place. His cock is already dripping with cum. I can feel seed covering me in a number of places, including my back. I can feel something else happening behind me as well. There's shifting all around me as I'm passed between waiting hands. Tevbarannos moves back and Herannathon sends two more males forward. One of them reaches between my legs and uses cum — Tev's or someone else's or maybe his own — and starts massaging my back hole.

In front of me, the male bends down and kisses me while I struggle to keep my head upright. I'm panting hard, sweating all over. "I am honored."

I grin at him, finding this small ceremony of kissing very touching from big, tough, bloodhungry pirates. "Thank you," I say, voice scratchy and hoarse.

"Wait," Herannathon barks. All of the males freeze at once. "Water."

A male standing against the wall comes forward with a small silver packet in his hand. He cups the back of my head and lifts the packet to my lips and cool, hydrating water pours down my throat. I finish it off and blink up at him gratefully. "Thank you."

"Resume."

The male at my front shows none of Tev's hesitation. He thrusts forward brutally, entering me swiftly and wonderfully. He commands the male on my left leg, "Touch her button. I want to feel her detonate."

The male reaches down and I glance in his direction to see his cock out, his loincloth gone. He gathers up the cum weeping from the head of his own cock and brings it to my clit. At the same time, I reach down and start jacking him off.

We mutually jack each other off while the male inside of me continues to pump in long, even strokes. I feel myself climbing slowly and steadily as I build from the previous orgasm. But what I don't expect is for one of the males behind me to shove one long, blunt finger into my ass hole.

I gasp and jerk and the male on my left tit bites down and it's over. I'm done. I release a wild wail as I come, clamping down hard on the cock inside of me. The male curses a thousand times in his own tongue and I can feel him fighting desperately against his own release, but he fails. He comes crashing down with me and one of his brothers has to stop him from taking the whole pile of males and me to the ground.

"Shrov…shroving comets," he gasps, knees buckling as he staggers back. "I've never…" He looks at me as if stunned and I can only nod along limply as he leans forward and nips at my mouth with his sharp teeth. "I'm honored," he says before stepping away from me.

Another male moves to take his place, but Herannathon stops him. "Corvenarennu. Lie on the table. It's time she shows us what she can do with her mouth." Groans of lust chime through the males as another male moves forward from the wall. I can see Tev and the other one who came collapsed into net seats that hang suspended from the ceiling. They're both panting hard. They're both touching themselves. Christ… All of the males are that aren't actively touching me are touching themselves. And the cum…There's grey glistening *everywhere*. I want to fucking roll in it.

My lust kicks up even higher than it had been as the males move me to the table and lower it slightly. One of the males removes the covering that had been on the table before and I see a long opening running up and down the center. He lies down into it, his tines fitting in the empty grooves. His four arms open wide to catch me as I'm turned around and lowered to all fours. I crawl on top of him. My arms are shaky and I'm grateful for the support he provides as he lines himself up with my core.

He lifts up and kisses me deeply, more savagely than the last two males had. "I'm honored," he says, breaking the kiss, but only for a moment.

I like kissing this one and lean in and kiss him some more while his cock fits inside my body and I start to bounce up and down on top of him. Meanwhile, there are hands on my ass, peeling apart my ass cheeks, rubbing more lubrication onto and into me. Three fingers enter me this time and I bellow out a moan.

"Her mouth. Now," Herannathon growls.

Mouths break away from mine and a cock springs in front of my eyes. I look up at the male there, eager to obey Herannathon and ready to take him with my tongue. Before I can, he leans down and kisses me softly. "I'm honored."

I nod, stunned mute as sensation rides over me, debilitatingly. I've never felt like this. Never. I think back to the men I had sex with on Earth and how they used to call me whore because I liked sex. I liked it a lot. And that was back then, back before I knew what it could be to have and to want and to lust and to take and to be taken without judgement. No, not even that. To be *honored* for it. It makes me want to laugh to think that, even for a moment, I regretted being shipped off of

Earth. It makes me want to laugh to think that I used to like sex when I *never* in a thousand years could have imagined anything feeling this good.

And what feels even better?

Looking up as the male feeds his cock into my mouth, I meet Herannathon's gaze. He stands further back, apart from the crowd, overseeing it all. I *love* watching him struggle not to touch himself even though his loincloth isn't doing much of anything to cover his length, but instead is held up from his body and flutters like a goddamn flagpole. I want him. I want him *badly* and not just because I love him with my whole heart, but because I trust him with my whole soul.

I'm still holding his gaze as the two males finish inside me — one in my pussy, the other in my mouth. The one in my mouth pulls out and sprays cum all over my face. A rag is produced from somewhere and someone and wipes cum off of my eyes. Lips kiss me quickly, two sets in quick succession before another cock is in my mouth and I'm sitting upright while the new male under me bounces me up and down.

So many sets of hands on my body and the males — they don't give a fuck about getting in each other's way or crossing swords. The male with his cock in my mouth is standing over the male with his dick in my pussy. There's another cock rubbing at my right breast from the side while my left hand jerks another male off simultaneously.

The male in my mouth cums and my jaw starts to hurt. I'm too full of that salty sweetness and, when the next male comes for my lips, I shake my head.

"She's ready, Ewanrennaron. Take her rear entrance."

I'm lifted up into arms, cum and sweat-soaked. A heavy hand turns my face to the side so that the hard lips of the male at my back can kiss me feverishly. He doesn't stop. The male holds me upright while another male moves between my thighs.

The one at my front teases my clit with the flat head of his cock until I can't do anything else but fall the fuck apart, and as my orgasm subsides, I feel something much, much larger prod at my ass, which is still clenching and unclenching in reckless spasms.

"Oh god…" I moan as his cock slowly, slowly enters me from the back. Though Herannathon and I have done this before, it doesn't seem to get any easier as he fits the first few inches inside.

"Shrov, she's tight," the male behind me hisses. "How should I proceed?"

"Lay her down," Herannathon commands.

The table is lifted and I'm laid down on top of it, hinged at the waist, legs dangling over the side. Someone picks up my wrist and fits my hand to a cock. I start to pump. Someone else does the same thing to my other hand.

I pump feverishly, arm muscles working as the male bends over me, spreads my cheeks and slides his cock between them. "Relax," he commands, whispering in my ear.

I do my best and soon, he's sliding in and out of me easily. "Oh my stars," I groan, the slick on my hands getting thicker and thicker. He starts pumping harder and harder into my ass, feeling like he's fit a foot into me at least. My pussy spasms, feeling envious of my ass, wanting to be filled. The male shouts wildly and that sound alone is enough to tip me over the edge.

I come and he curses and pain floods my lower half as he gets bigger and I clamp down. Cum spurts into my ass. I can feel it everywhere in me, on me, dripping down my thighs. He's panting hard and I can feel his plates lifting and scraping against my back as he bends over me and drops a kiss to my cheek.

"I...I will not ever forget this. Thank you," he tells me.

I nod and grin. "Thank you," I croak.

Herannathon calls another water break and asks me how I'm doing. "Ready," I tell him. It's a lie, but I've got too much adrenaline to stop.

He laughs, silver eyes glittering. He looks like a mad scientist. "So my brothers haven't broken you yet?"

"Not a chance," I pant, sitting up on the edge of the table and drinking from the silver water packet Herannathon feeds me.

The males all chuckle.

Herannathon picks the final two males who haven't come inside me yet and calls them forward. "Then let us break our huntress fully. I want one of you in either hole."

I nearly squeal in delight as the first male holds me up and enters my primed asshole. Settled, he starts to move slowly in and out of me, the cum coating my insides making it easier for him to thrust. After he starts to work up a good rhythm, the remaining male comes to me from the front. Both kiss me and tell me their sweet, calming words, and soon both are seated deep in me.

"By shrov..." I gasp. The fullness. "The fullness." The fullness...

They work in a rhythm, moving carefully while other males help hold me up, touch my breasts, rub my clit, kiss my mouth. Two males kiss me at once. Jesus fuck. Their tongues swirl around mine. They're kissing each other as much as they are me. I try to keep up and fail, too overstimulated by what's happening below my waist. I can't...I can't hold on...hang on...Herannathon's right.

They're going to break me.

I orgasm harder than I ever have. Harder than hard. I detonate in a chaos of stars, biting one male on accident and scratching another on the cheek. Chuckles and curses and groans sound around me as cum fills both of my holes simultaneously.

They pull out and Herannathon says words that are damning. "You aren't finished yet, huntress. Now, it's time for three." He calls three more males and I'm lowered back to the table, one male under me, one male standing up behind me, one male slapping his cock against my cheek. I take him in my mouth as the two other males enter me simultaneously.

This goes on for two more rounds. Two more sets of males before I'm ready...it's time. I've come three more times. Maybe four. I can't...it's too much. I'm covered in grey so thick I could wear it like a coat. My hair drips cum down my spine.

The males pull out and kiss me and I drop forward onto the table, alone, while all ten males who've just been inside of me — spent inside of me, ravaged me so wonderfully — stand back and either collapse into nets, looking as ravaged as I feel, or stand, hands on their cocks, and continue pumping away madly like they're balancing on the verge of rut.

I close my eyes, prepared to pass out, but a hand knocks my left knee and rolls me fully onto my back. I look up and see Herannathon undoing the ties at the edge of his loincloth. "Now, it's my turn."

He covers me with his body, kneeling on the edge of the platform. He strokes a hand down the center of my body, gathering cum as he goes. He brings it to my lips, a tease of what he did with his thumb earlier, and I lick it clean, desperately, a slave to him now, a slave to this.

"How did my brothers treat you, huntress?"

"Fuck, Herannathon… I fucking love you." I palm his cheek and lean up and kiss him with every breath I have left.

He kisses me back hard up until the point that I can no longer hold myself up and collapse back. He shoves me against the table and runs his hand up and down the length of his cock. "I need to see how well my brothers broke you in. I'll work your every hole, to sample how well they did. If they didn't do a good enough job ruining you, I'll call one or two of them back."

I shiver in fear and excitement, unable to decide which is the dominant emotion. My lips sputter, "Oh god, ontte… Take me, Herannathon."

"On your knees. Mouth open."

It takes me an eternity to prop myself up on shaky arms and legs. I manage to get upright and open my mouth. I stick out my tongue and look up at him and he grimaces, like he's trying to keep cool and keep himself under control, but his cock betrays him. He's dripping all over me, and his cock is nearly *vibrating.*

"You poor baby," I whisper. "You're hurting, aren't you?" I lick a line up the underside of his erection.

His hand darts into my hair, fisting it. "Easy," he warns.

I tease him again.

He doesn't like that.

He cups my jaw and enters me all the way to the back of my throat. He fucks me hard, he fucks me mercilessly. I don't back down though, but keep sucking. "Rhegaran. I want her to come," he barks.

A second later, a male slides upside down under my body and madly starts to lick my cunt. I moan around Herannathon's dick and Herannathon curses above me. I tremble violently and I don't make it long. I spiral out of control, entering another realm, and am only distantly aware as Herannathon does the same, holding me up by the throat in order to use my body to empty himself.

"*Fawwkkk,*" he curses above me, making me smile as he lowers me back down to elbows and shins. The male who'd been at my pussy leaves and Herannathon takes his place.

His plates are rising and falling in flaps and his chest rises and falls in waves with each of his labored breaths. "Let's see how loose my brothers rutted you…"

He moves behind me and jerks my hips high off of the table, leaving my forehead planted there — welded there in globules of slick. He holds my ass in his hands, pulling it against him as he enters my tight — well, my *once* tight — puckered hole. Now, it's gaping open and ready to receive him.

"Shrov, my brothers…they did well," he says as he pumps his hips madly, thrusting wildly. I have no strength left. None whatsoever. It takes two of his brothers coming forward to help hold me firmly in place. Herannathon reaches around my body to touch my aching, sensitive clit. He rubs it so lightly — I can't stand more than that — until I gush all over him and release a keening scream to the table underneath me.

Herannathon bursts inside of me and doesn't stop there. He's still coming as he moves from my ass to my pussy, sliding inside and rutting me hard before sliding back into my ass again. "I don't know which of your holes I...love more..." He grunts, sounding mad, both angry and insane. With his skein lifted, I can see that his eyes have darkened from silver to grey to charcoal, and when I look up at him over my shoulder I can see my own reflection in them. *I look fucking wonderful.*

"I love you," I mouth up at him.

His expression twists and shudders. He opens his mouth, as if to respond, but releases a moan and explodes inside my core, finishing me off fully just like he promised. "Aughhhh...Nalia..."

He collapses on top of my body and his brothers back away, releasing me with reverent touches and pats and soothing strokes.

"By the stars, Nalia," Herannathon says, moaning into my throat. "I love you."

He licks a line up it to my ear before working his way across my jaw and finally reaching my mouth. He kisses me, though I taste like all his brothers' cum, sucking on my tongue while his hips microthrust against my belly. He holds his weight off of me as much as he can, keeping himself half propped up on his forearms on the table while his legs shake with the effort of keeping himself upright and standing on the floor below. I don't mind. I don't care if I'm crushed under a love like this.

"Are you broken yet?" His whisper tickles my throat.

"Ontte..." I'm barely conscious, but I can feel a smile irrevocably stain my lips. "Are you?"

"Centare." He heaves out a breath. "I'm honored."

I wrap my hands around his head and toy with one of his sharp spikes. "I'm so glad you opened my tank, because I'm where I was always meant to be — what, I was always meant to be."

He chuckles and nuzzles between my tits, kissing each of them before lifting himself up fully on four shaking arms. "Covered in the pleasure of eleven males?"

I laugh to the ceiling while the other pirates within earshot chuckle around us. "Centare."

"Then what?"

I close my eyes and sigh while feelings of pure radiance skitter through my limbs. Might be Xiveri, or maybe it's just the yeeyar. Either way, I feel it. I feel absolutely and irrevocably...

"Free."

I hope you enjoyed Nalia and Herannathon's story!
Reviews, even the one-liners, are very much appreciated
on Amazon!

You can also sign up to my mailing list at
www.booksbyelizabeth.com/contact.

Follow me at:
Instagram: @estephensauthor
TikTok: @elizabethstephensauthor

Then, continue the journey in Taken to Sky.

Until the next time,
love unapologetically

Elizabeth

Taken to Sky

Xiveri Mates Book 9 (Ashmara and Jerrock)

Most creatures in these cosmos know Jerrock as Sky's most sadistic and effective bounty hunter. To Ashmara, he's her ever present threat. To be free of him, she might just need to free him and become a bounty hunter herself.

Available in ebook and hardcover on Amazon and in paperback anywhere online books are sold

1

Prologue – Ashmara

Due to spoilers included in chapter 1, this preview begins with chapter 2…

2

Jerrock

"More."

The architect before me responds, not in gestures or in words, but in sensations. All of them reflect pain. It's good, but it's not enough to erase my failure.

As the burning fades from my limbs and my stalyx-infused bones settle, I say, "More."

They repeat the process.

"More."

The architect and I continue this excruciating loop until my vision begins to fade in my remaining biological eye — a nuissance. I would have it removed, but its organic quality has come in handy in disguising myself. Some can see through the matter displacement shield and those that can always look first to the eyes. *She always looks first into my eyes. No matter how skillfully I shield my appearance, she always sees me.*

"More." My voice comes out scratched, charged, like a roar. The architect is unconcerned by the change in my tone, likely interpreting it as pain — or rather, misinterpreting it. It is not pain. Pain is inconsequential. It is rage. Rage is a dangerous emotion. Rage causes

mistakes. I am fortunate only that the architects know nothing of those that I have made.

As ionic pulses flare through my body, causing the sinuous muscle to sieze and my thoughts to scatter just as rapidly as the yeeyar that contains them, the architect flits to the door. Its hand, if you can call it that, disappears into the black yeeyar wall, registering something in the yeeyar controls I cannot sense as the next charged wave pulls through me. I lose vision in my biological eye entirely.

The architect releases me and I slump forward against my chest restraint. The door before the architect opens and they disappear through it soundlessly. The only sounds to be heard at all are my breath and the wind as it crashes against the outside of the tower. It is so constant, it sounds like waves.

I focus on the sound until the pain fades enough for me to be able to move my arms. I use my stalyx and yeeyar-reinforced arm to release the chest restraint. I stand, irritated at how quickly the sensations of pain fade. Pain is the only thing that feels grounding and, for too long now, I've been unstable.

But the architects created an assassin with endlessly terrible abilities, even some that they themselves perhaps do not know. Because even though we speak with our thoughts, there are thoughts that I have managed to keep from them. *Hesitation. Failure. Treason.* They do not know, the architects. They cannot. If they knew of my treason, I would be decommissioned.

I should decomission myself. I *would*, except for the fact that I continue to hold one outstanding contract. All of the others I have completed and I have declined to take on any others. Not until this is finished. I refuse to allow her to live. She *cannot* live. She is too powerful. There is something about her. I don't understand it. She is my greatest failing, my only failing, and I do. not. fail. I am Sky's most feared assassin. I am their greatest creation, a gift from the Architects to Death itself and still…

She lives.

I killed an assassin for her. The hesitation in my next step brings me to the door, but not through it. I think about what I am up against, this…pathetic excuse for an opponent that has become my greatest enemy yet. My nemesis. The only one I've ever had as every other to challenge me has fallen like wave. It is inevitable. And yet…I'm not certain of my abilities to kill this one. So, I have safeguards in place. Safeguards that will ensure, should she defeat me and somehow manage to introduce me to Death before I can introduce her, that there will not be an assassin who does not know of it. I will send the full force of the Sky for her.

I take a deep, fortifying breath before willing the door to open.

A brutal wind crashes against my body and may have taken a lesser being from the platform into its grip. I remain standing through it, white hair whipping around my face as I look out over the other Sky towers, rising up into the pale purple sky. The black towers look like the jagged shards of screa cliffs against such brightness. It hurts my biological eye.

As I watch, sweeping gales of orange wind climb through the purple and wrap around the tallest towers' tips. I am not on one of the tallest towers now. Those are reserved for the experiments. As I was, once.

Now, I am perfect.

Almost.

My ship sits on the edge of the platform. There are no railings, only black yeeyar shifting beneath my feet. Below, all the way at the bottom, are the slums of Sky where wretches native to this planet scavenge for the few resources that are left.

So far below, I cannot even see them from here, but my hearing is excellent. I can just make out the sounds of screaming and lesser beings succumbing to pain. They attempt to rebel, these creatures, upon occassion. But they are no match for the architects and their assassins. I do not understand it, their will to defy Death. Death is king. You either exist on his right hand, as I do, or you bend the knee to him. There is nothing else.

But her. She bends to nothing. Only that isn't true, is it? She bends to muuir. And I cannot even manage to catch her when she's addicted to the vile, mind-addling substance.

The thought of muuir makes me restless. *Angry.* No. I don't...know. I don't understand. I should think favorably of muuir. It is the only thing that slows her down. She has to make many stops at ports in the Grey Zone to acquire more of the illicit drug. I wonder which of them she has chosen now.

On board my ship, I power on the locator, fingers moving deftly over the yeeyar panel before me even though the fingers on my red hand — a testament to Drakesh biology — are stiff. I flex them and watch the screen turn and twist, grey yeeyar mixing with reds and yellows and blues.

To anyone else, it would appear as if yeeyar was simply moving in random patterns, rising up and falling from the control panel. But in my yeeyar eye, I see everything, the full span of the Quadrants and, among them, a single beacon that's illuminated, even though it shouldn't be.

My arms lurch and I grab hold of the edges of the table. Something isn't right. Her shields are down. The Eshmiri are known for their shield technology. She would not be so careless. Perhaps, under the influence of muuir she might be, but members of her crew wouldn't. They are Eshmiri and none of them are as careless as she is. No one in the cosmos is so careless.

So why is her tracking beacon on and why are her shields off?

I take a closer look at where she is and my toes curl in my boots. She's on the Tiringdam pleasure planet. My ship separates from the platform under directions I did not consciously give. My subconscious mind is active and it should not be. It should not even exist. Yet…

The ship takes off regardless and I do not redirect it.

3

Jerrock

Her screeching, slurred voice does not bother me. It does not bother me at all. "And when the ship…docks… at the port of pianzaaaaa…all of the sinners sayyyy…."

"Grab the hibi! Hide your tokens! You're here in Tiringdam where legs and bars are always open!" The crowd's shouted-sung response doesn't bother me. It doesn't bother me at all.

I have Ashmara the Eshmiri's ankle trapped in my red hand. In my red hand. I should be holding her with my stalyx hand, but I'm not. I should be…but I'm not.

Her skin is warm — I'd go so far as to call it hot — against my rough palm. Her skin isn't soft, either, but her leg hairs prickle my hand. While not necessarily soft, she's still smooth. Tender. Easy to tear through. I recall how easily my blaster fire had torn through her hand when she'd reached for the muuir on board the Sky ship where I'd detained her. Where she should have met Death, but didn't, because I failed him and offered him up another in her place. Not this lunar, though.

She was easy enough to find on the pleasure planet. In fact, she was singing loudly as I approached her, too. She'd been reclined on a floating divan, drinking amidst a disorderly cluster of species all equally as intoxicated as she was — and still is. She's got a muuir patch behind her ear and her eyes are a hazy yellow-grey-brown that, in Voraxian ridges, would reflect illness, only her eyes fill with spots of other colors, mostly blues and purples. Pleasure. Satisfaction.

She's on drugs.

My fingers twitch around her ankle and she kicks her other leg into the air as she begins a second refrain of the same song. She's been singing it over and over again, changing the words subtly every time, as if unable to remember them. Her body drags on the filthy ground behind us, her white hair catching sticky substances and becoming stained by them.

"…can't be found on the map, but once you find it, it's a trap…"

"The pleasures of pianzaaaaaa…" comes the chorus, shouted by beings who line the walkway.

Water thrashes below the synthetic platforms, an endless maze of waterfalls whose gravity causes water to rush up the stones near the center of the island before crashing back down the outer island. Nothing lives within the water. Nothing exists of this place besides the water, except for the platform that we walk along now.

No one cares that I am here, an assassin in their midst. Not even Ashmara seems to care, even though she's in my grip. She never does. It's as if she knows something I do not. It's as if she trusts me. Perhaps, she is friends with Death.

The thoughts ravage my mind and I focus on the sounds of the water falling below so as not to kill everyone on this platform when their collective singing picks back up. A Voraxian pair hails their horns at

Ashmara as I drag her past and she laughs wildly, deep and from her belly. Her eyes dance with blue-green mirth as she stretches her fingers towards the Voraxian female. She hands Ashmara her cup and Ashmara drinks from it — tries to drink from it — but ends up spilling most of the liquid on her face, neck and chest.

"Whoo!" She tosses her cup aside. It hits a Rekkaru in the wings and they turn and toss a mok biz token down at her. It's aimed fairly accurately at her face. I twitch, watching the token sail through the air in slow motion. My hand. My perfect hand. My perfect hand behaves imperfectly. It launches a small dart without my telling it to — no, with me telling it expressly not to — and collides with the token, dissolving it midair.

Ashmara doesn't seem to notice. She laughs and shouts up at the Rekkaru, "Is that the best you got, heelee?" She uses a term of endearment that makes the Rekkaru smile.

"You look like you have your hands full, reaver," the Rekkaru replies, flashing an uncertain gaze to me.

She laughs. "What are you talking about? I'm having the time of my life." She laughs as I drag her all the way through the pianza pleasure port, down the ramp leading to the lower pleasure rooms where mostly aquatic creatures are serviced, across the rickety wooden bridge that leads to the docks, all the way to the largest hangar where ships remain parked in no discernable order. Chaos is the only constant outside of the known Quadrants. Chaos is what I have come to expect. But right now, as I look around, I do not expect this.

My ship is not where I left it. With my yeeyar eye, I search for its signature, finding hints of it where I left it in between two gold ships from Quadrant One. I go to the spot, dragging Ashmara with me. I can scent the presence of several other species, Eshmiri most strongly. I glance over my shoulder at Ashmara, lying on the ground, ignoring me entirely in favor of whatever high has dragged her down.

What has she done?

The urge to ask her is strong, though I don't know why. She isn't coherent enough to give me a reply and I have no intention of torturing information out of her. I have only one intent. To decommission her. In private.

I follow the scent trail the Eshmiri left to the edge of the platform. The flimsy wooden barrier has been broken. I step up to the edge and look down into waters that shine an irridescent white and a cutting blue. There, scattered across yellow rocks, are traces of yeeyar, but traces only. The water rushes too hard and too fast to identify any other larger pieces of what was once my ship.

I turn and follow the Eshmiri scent trail to the center of the hangar, and then right. I continue to follow it easily — it's been laid on thick — until I reach what I know to be Ashmara's ship. The putrid thing is larger than many of the others crowded beside it, though it looks thirty rotations older than any other ship here. Rusted metal, the thing emits steam from a right exhaust valve. The fact that it even has such valves is deplorable. It smells like oil. Ancient oil. And it's leaking. Did her Eshmiri horde think to discard my ship and take to the skies? Did their ship break before they could? Or is that what they wanted me to believe?

I glance back at Ashmara and see that she's looking at me. My entire chest ripples — stalyx and all — beneath the slick black synthetic leather that covers it.

She smiles. Her teeth are white. The bottom row of her teeth are crooked, the front two right teeth slightly overlapping.

She's wearing Eshmiri rags and, because of how I've been dragging her, they've lifted to show her stomach. Her skin is a dark brown color whose closest comparison can be made to the skin tone of a Rekkaru or a Lemoran. The color pulls at something in my subconscious, but I cannot access it and that, more than anything makes her dangerous. I have corrupted the yeeyar to be able to keep information from the architects, yet I have the feeling that there is something inside of me, even deeper than that corrupted yeeyar that shields itself even from me.

"I will kill you this solar," I tell her.

The sound of my voice is odd. I have not spoken to anyone in this form in rotations. With the architects, I communicate solely through the yeeyar that binds us. Otherwise, my matter displacement shields allow me to speak in other tones more resembling the creatures whose likenesses I wear in order to deceive. The sound of my voice now is…no. It does not bother me. Neither does her response.

"Did you like my singing?" She blinks slowly and tries to prop herself up on her elbows. I yank her forward and she slumps back, boneless. She is barely living. How has it been so hard to kill one already so close to Death?

The ramp of her ship has been lifted shut, but I go to the metal block guarding the control panel and quickly flick it free. I extend my stalyx wrist towards the black and copper-colored cables and a series of needles slip free of my arm. I stab them into the center of the control box and allow the yeeyar to work. It takes less than the span of a heartbeat to break into her ship. Her heartbeat, not mine. Her heart beats so slowly. An effect of the drugs? Or does she truly not have any fear of me or Death?

As the metal monstrosity screams its way open, I find my lips slightly tense in an unfamiliar frown. Steam wafts from the darkness and smells of sweat and spoiled food as I make my way on board, dragging Ashmara behind me. I leave the door open as I glance around, the scent of Eshmiri thick yet the sight of Eshmiri distinctly absent.

I kick aside odd objects and metal boxes, bins full of discarded equipment and weapons that look like they haven't worked in eons, as I make my way to the control room. It sits at the front of the ship in front of a large and murky bay portal window in a defunct style. Most modern ships take after the Niahhorru and Lemoran styles, where controls are located in the center of the control room and windows can either be found everywhere or nowhere.

Yet, this is not a modern ship. Six seats occupy the control room. They were organized once — I can see it in the scorched and charred markings on the floor where the control seats were once placed, but they've been moved. Now, they sit scattered in what looks like random order, four facing forward, one facing right, another facing left. One is tilted at an angle. Another is missing its left arm.

I stand in the center of the cluster and drop Ashmara's leg. She doesn't bother to move, but lays there with her white teeth shining up at me and her white eyes swirling with indecicive emotion that causes me a small measure of distraction. In the color wheel, I catch a flash of tan, a color which I know to Voraxians means pain. But I haven't touched her yet...

I open my mouth. She parts her lips. "Azza," she whispers and my mind fires with confusion, my subconscious rising like the tides of the waters far below before crashing down with just as much violence. What is this word? Why does she call me by it? Wait — what did she just say?

"Azza!" She shouts this word again, but this time she shouts it as if it were a fist where before, she spoke it as a caress. The latter was more painful.

A latch opens in the floor and an Eshmiri reaver pops his head through it and stabs me in my biological leg through my leathers. He stabs with a needle, which is perhaps the only reason the tool penetrates given that the leathers are Sky threaded through with ion iron ionyx'ix. I point my stalyx arm at the creature but Ashmara, in a feat of swiftness that I had not thought possible with how intoxicated she seems, rolls her body on top of his and I fire. I hit her in the side. Not in the spine, where I'd been aiming. Not in the spine...

A panel opens in the wall before me and I fire into it, but it's empty. Several other panels open, each with the same intent to distract me and causing me to consider that perhaps these reavers are not so foolish, after all. Because they succeed. And when the panel opens above my head, I do not expect the Eshmiri to fall out of it on top of me and stab me in the side of the neck with another needle.

Ashmara rolls onto her back, pulls what appears to be a crude whistle from beneath her tunic and begins to blow air into it feverishly. The high pitched sound has no effect on my ears, but I could nearly smile with the cleverness of this technology. I have seen it, but it is crude and there are more effective ways for a creature of my skill level to disable or to kill.

These creatures are not of my skill level however, and the device inserted into my neck is connected to the other inserted into my leg and, when she whistles, charged vibrations run between them that immobilize most of the stalyx in my body. I lunge for her on my Drakesh leg and, as my sight shorts in my yeeyar eye, I grab her throat with my red arm.

I lift her from the ground and it is effortful in ways I do not like, now that my stalyx limbs have been weakened, but I fight through the agony of the devices at work and I squeeze Ashmara's skinny neck until the sound of her whistle cuts off. My muscles ease.

"Azza," Ashmara whispers. She reaches out and touches my jaw. Her fingers… My thoughts… And then I feel a second prick in the side of my neck and I see the rush of excitement reflected in her eyes and I know…

I drop her. She lands in a crouch, her eyes never leaving mine.

I know…

I fall against one of the command chairs as the yeeyar in my mind fights for control and that swell of subconscious surges up.

I don't break the line of her gaze, but watch her rise to stand and I know…

As the drunk, drug addicted Eshmiri reaver hybrid slinks towards me with a look of concern in her eyes… I know that I have lost.

---

*Continue reading on Amazon in ebook or hardcover
or in paperback anywhere online books are sold*

All Books by Elizabeth

Berserker Kings - Enemies to lovers. With magic.
Dark City Omega, Book 1 (Echo and Adam)
more to come!

Population - Battles and Heroes that Bite.
Lord of Population, Book 1 (Abel and Kane)
Monster in the Oasis, Book 2 (Diego and Pia)
Immortal with Scars, Book 3 (Lahve and Candy)
more to come!

Twisted Fates - Mafia. Brotherhood. Murder.
The Hunting Town, Book 1 (Knox and Mer, Dixon and Sara)
The Hunted Rise, Book 2 (Aiden and Alina, Gavriil and Ify)
The Hunt, Book 3 (Anatoly and Candy, Charlie and Molly)

Xiveri Mates - Aliens. Heat. New Worlds.
Taken to Voraxia, Book 1 (Miari and Raku)
Taken to Nobu, Book 2 (Kiki and Va'Raku)
Exiled from Nobu, Book 2.5, a Novella (Lisbel and Jaxal)
Taken to Sasor, Book 3 (Mian and Neheyuu) *standalone
Taken to Heimo, Book 4 (Svera and Krisxox)
Taken to Kor, Book 5 (Deena and Rhork)
Taken to Lemora, Book 6 (Essmira and Raingar)
Taken by the Pikosa Warlord, Book 7 (Halima and Ero)
*standalone
Taken to Evernor, Book 8 (Nalia and Herannathon)
Taken to Sky, Book 9 (Ashmara and Jerrock)
Taken to Revatu, Book 10, A Novella (Latanya and Grizz)
*standalone

Collections

Xiveri Mates - Aliens. Heat. New Worlds.
Collection 1: Books 1-3 + Exiled from Nobu
More to come!

Audiobooks

Xiveri Mates - Aliens. Heat. New Worlds.
Taken to Voraxia, Book 1 (Miari and Raku)
Taken to Nobu, Book 2 (Kiki and Va'Raku)
Taken to Sasor, Book 3 (Mian and Neheyuu) *standalone
More to come!

French Language

Passion Xiveri : Unis Pour La Vie – Des extraterrestres. De la sensualité. De nouveaux mondes.
Capturée par le Roi de Voraxia, tome 1 (Miari et Raku)
Convoitée par le Seigneur de guerre de Nobu, tome 2 (Kiki et Va'Raku)
Kidnappée par le Métamorphe de Sasor, tome 3 (Mian et Neheyuu) *l'intrigue se situe hors du Quadrant 4
D'autres livres seront bientôt publiés !